BLOOD WISP

SARINA LANGER

All books by this author

Relics of Ar'Zac trilogy
Rise of the Sparrows
Wardens of Archos
Blood of the Dragon
Shadow in Ar'Sanciond (#0.5)
The Relics of Ar'Zac Box Set

Darkened Light duology
Darkened Light
Brightened Shadows

Blood Wisp
Blood Wisp
Blood Song
Blood Vow

Chaos of Esta Anderson
A Dream of Death and Magic

Find out more about Sarina's books at
sarinalanger.com

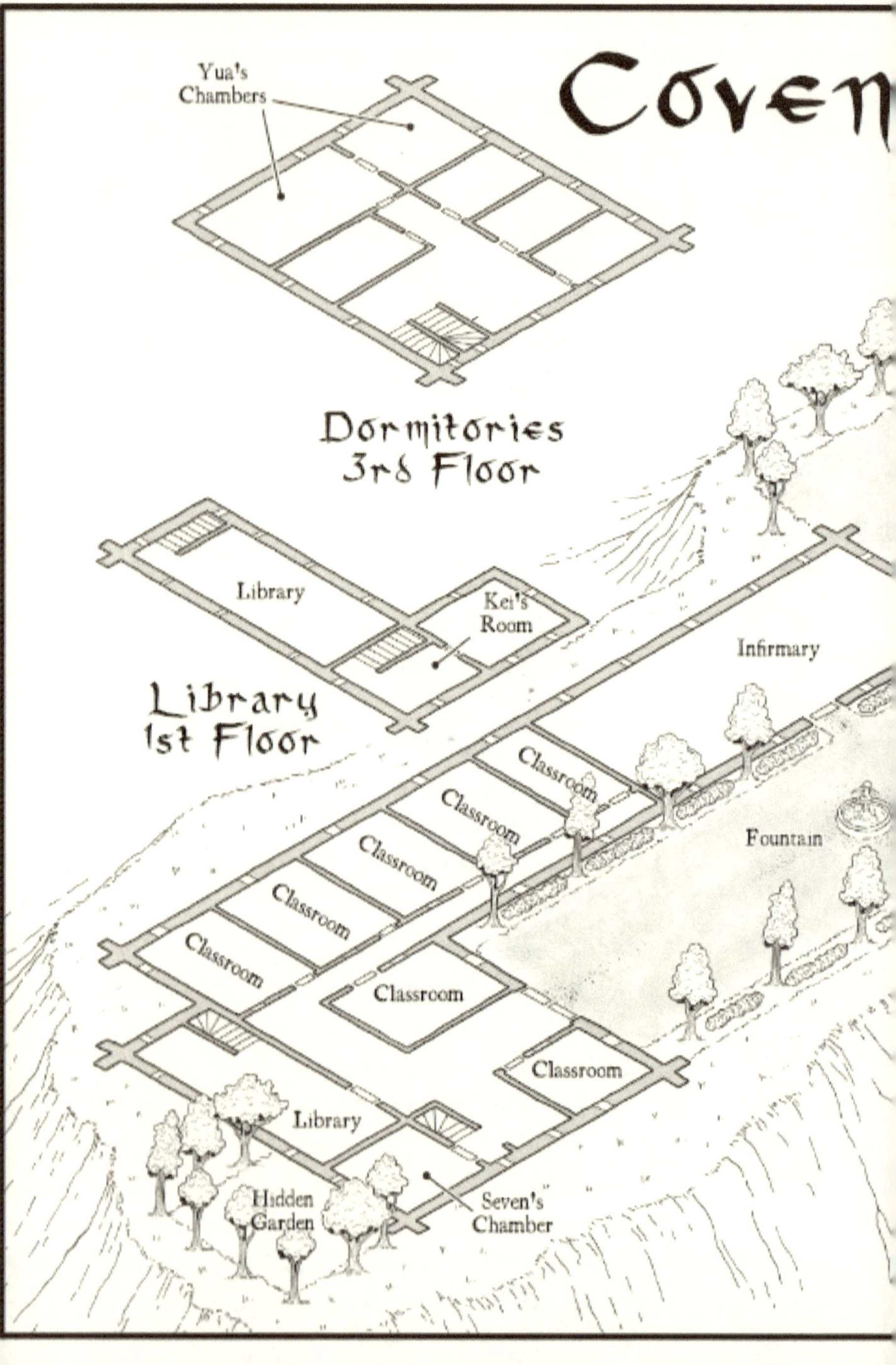

Yua's Chambers
Dormitories 3rd Floor
Library
Kei's Room
Library 1st Floor
Classroom
Classroom
Classroom
Classroom
Classroom
Classroom
Classroom
Library
Hidden Garden
Seven's Chamber
Infirmary
Fountain
Coven

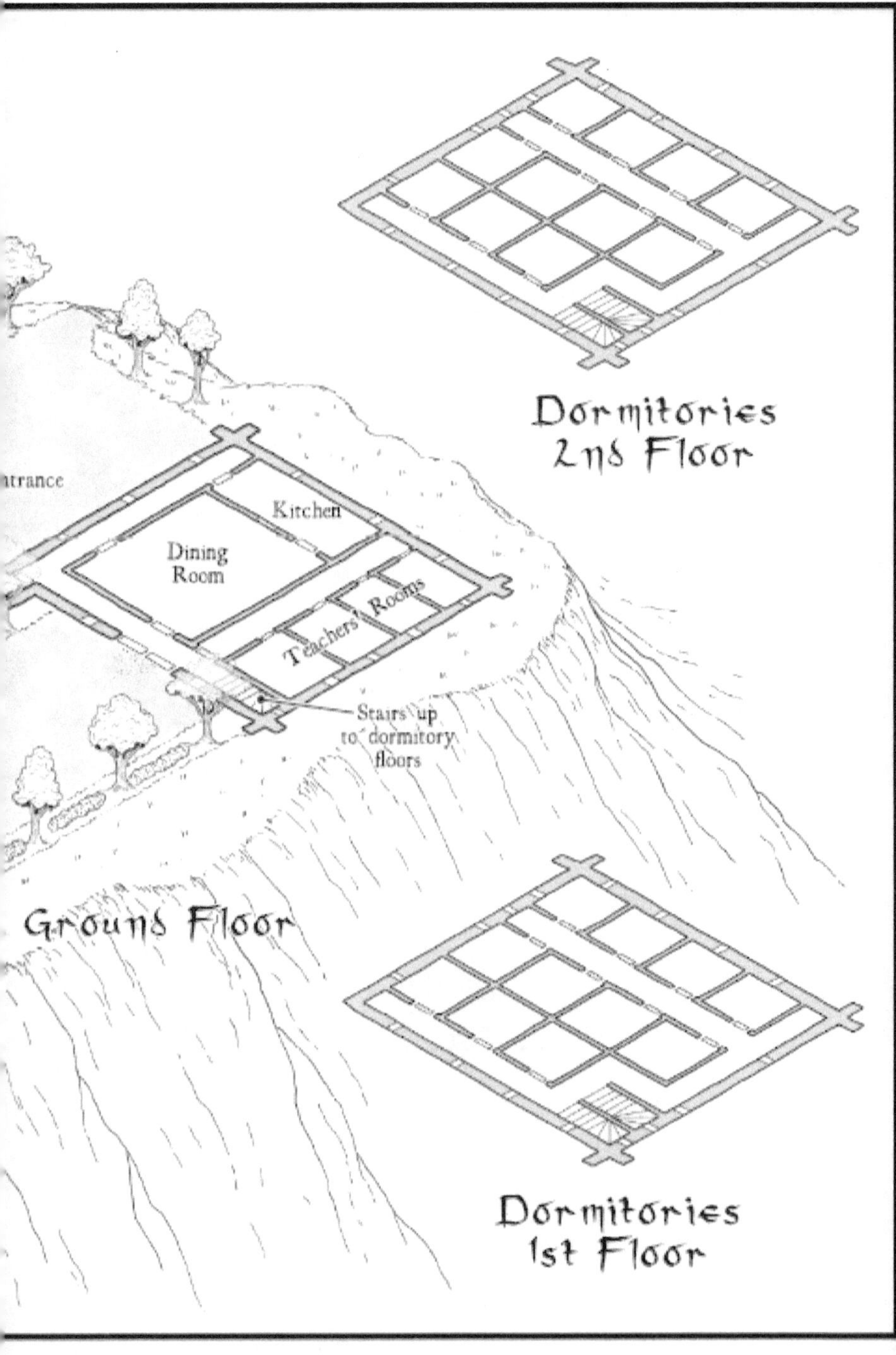

Dormitories
2nd Floor
Entrance
Kitchen
Dining Room
Teachers' Rooms
Stairs up to dormitory floors
Ground Floor
Dormitories
1st Floor

Content Warning

Please be aware that Blood Wisp contains scenes of violence,
blood, and intrusive thoughts.

For all you lost witches and shadow workers.

Chapter One

Ohira Yua stared out of her window and wondered what it was like to be free. She imagined flower meadows as far as she could see, oceans as blue as summer, and sometimes—when she felt optimistic—she dreamed of a place where no one feared her, made fun of her, or shunned her…

But if such a place existed, she'd never see it, so she got lost in her daydreams until someone interrupted her again. Usually, these were her attendants—young women who thought they were braver than the rumours, who made sure Yua got up in the morning, reminded her to bathe, and brought her two meals a day to keep her from starving. They pretended that she didn't bother them, but Yua saw their glances at her sleeves, knew they waited for a glimpse the next time the fabric rode up her skin just a sliver. She had steeled herself to it over the years, but she still inwardly flinched every time she followed their eyes. Her current attendant, a novice named Himari, was better at hiding her fear than others, but Yua knew it was there. It always was.

You should give her something to fear. Justify her worry.

She blinked at the moon and marvelled at the pink light of dawn mixed in with the silver moonlight gently blanketing Maishi Hou. She was still alone, and she would make the most of it. Himari wasn't here yet to make sure Yua was up and ready for her day of nothing—no, not nothing. Her day of being *good*. Non-threatening.

Ever since Ohira Kei, the Mist Women's leader, had brought Yua here, she hadn't done one mildly dangerous thing, but thirteen years wasn't long enough to quell the rumours.

And the rumours surrounding Yua were louder than screams.

Since there was no sign of Himari, Yua moved her sleeve up and glared at her marks like one look could make them go away. If the rumours were true, she could do that and much more, but the only thing that was special about her was that she was unremarkable. All other Midokans were born with the gift. It was their birthright, and as far as anyone knew, the gift had never skipped a generation. In Midoka, not having the gift made her as useless as nothing else could have done. The marks, which traced her veins in black, were only there to doom Yua to a life of whispered cruelties and no possibilities.

The stories about Yua killing her family and their friends didn't help, either.

If the rumours were true, only she had survived that night, and Kei found her amongst the bloody corpses. The Mist Women and novices knew the story, saw her black veins easily enough, and whispered of darker things in her blood.

A knock came at her door. Yua asked the visitor into her room out of habit. In her memories, the smell of copper, of *blood*, overpowered everything, and she had caused it… *if* the stories were true. Had those corpses been her parents? What about the others? Great Dragon O-Yu forbid someone tell her the truth, or at least parts of it.

Yua traced the black veins from her wrist to the crook of her elbow. Maybe they were her punishment for that night. The growing sunshine fell on her arm and cast shadows over her skin. Over the lines. Such ugly things. If only she had grown up without the damning lines, she might have blended in like everyone else. They were the reason she wore long sleeves. The moment someone saw her veins, the whispering started, dropped dishes clattered and broke, and people gasped like the marks alone could curse them. Yua was their only victim.

The door fell shut, and Yua snapped out of her daydreams. Himari stood by the door, wide eyes fixated on Yua's arm. Not even a *good morning*.

They were always brave until they saw.

'I've been up for an hour or so,' Yua said, desperate to dissolve the tension the shut door had trapped in the room with her. She and Himari had been all right until now. They were far from friends, but Yua didn't want to lose what little they had.

Himari gulped and nodded, but she didn't take her eyes off the marks. Yua pulled the sleeves down farther, gripped the hems in her fists, and Himari blinked as if Yua had broken the spell. The thought left a foul aftertaste in Yua's mouth. If she had that much magic, she might have done more at this coven than sit and dream of better lives. She might have been a novice Mist Woman like the others.

'Did you sleep well?' Yua asked. She hated small talk, but this silence was worse. She had endured it too many times already.

Himari nodded, but still stared at Yua's covered wrist. Yua's heart sank. It was over—again.

She touched the fabric over her wrist. 'Honestly, they're just veins. I can show you there's nothing—'

Himari stepped back on stiff legs.

Yua swallowed her sigh. She wore the same plain shirts and trousers the other novices wore, but no one ever looked at her sleeves like they were just that.

'We can eat earlier,' Yua said. 'I've been up for a while.'

She'd go to the kitchen herself—if she stayed inside the coven, she could go wherever she wanted with few exceptions—but she'd long since grown frustrated with the stares and the whispers. *Here comes the Blood Wisp*, they'd say. *Don't make a wrong move or stare at her or she'll kill you like she killed her parents.* It grew old fast, and Yua had given up on moving through the coven for her own sake. If she needed or wanted anything, her attendants got it for her. Most of the time, that meant food and books from the library.

She couldn't attend any of the lessons—O-Yu forbid she learned something useful—but that didn't mean she didn't want to learn. When she had first arrived at the coven, Kei had her take some basic lessons to control her gift. When it became obvious that whatever slept in her was not only dangerous but uncontrollable, Kei and the Seven had stopped trying to teach her and had taken her off every list. Even so, Yua had devoured the theory of magic.

The only lessons she could have attended didn't involve the gift, but she couldn't participate in those lessons either—they didn't want her more dangerous, even if no one had said as much—and sword theory was useless without a teacher or a weapon.

Still, it beat boredom.

But Yua's favourite lessons included fictional stories of brave people exploring the world. It didn't matter if it wasn't her own world—she lived through them, regardless. She'd never leave the coven, but through novels, she experienced unknown places and daring adventures. It was almost as good as the real thing, she told herself. Perhaps one day she'd believe it.

Himari straightened. 'What would you like from the kitchen?'

Yua shrugged. 'I don't mind. Surprise me?'

Himari nodded and left.

It didn't seem right to tell her what to do after Yua had already scared her. Maybe choosing would give Himari some sense of control back. Maybe everything would go back to the way it had been when she returned.

Something dark inside her smiled. *You know it won't. They are too afraid of us. You should just kill her and be done with it. Drink her blood so we can use it.*

Yua gritted her teeth. Whatever lay beneath the tainted veins, it was vicious, and it was loudest on the days when she hated herself more than usual.

Himari wouldn't come back, but Yua hoped otherwise anyway. Until this morning, Himari hadn't caught one glimpse of her marks, but she would have known they were there. Seeing them couldn't have shocked her that much. Besides, Yua hadn't *done* anything. Maybe she'd reason through it on the way to the kitchen.

But seeing her black veins always made them more real, like saying out loud that someone you loved was dead and not coming home. An admission to herself. Until a few moments ago, Himari had pretended the black veins weren't real, maybe even convinced herself that Yua was too nice to fit the rumours. That delusion was destroyed now.

Yua didn't *want* to hide what she was. But it made things easier.

You shouldn't have to hide. We could be glorious.

A shiver ran down her spine. If Kei knew Yua thought like that, she'd be left to starve in this room. It wasn't like she did it on purpose—the thoughts popped into her head out of nowhere, and whether they belonged to her or someone else, the thoughts were there. Since they came from inside her, that made them hers.

Yua grabbed her current book from her bedside table to distract herself—not fiction this time, but the true story of a Mist Woman who had served all over the world and had seen all kinds of wonders. Yua sat on her windowsill and dreamed of what it'd be like to travel, to be free, to be a Mist Woman… and dared to forget her reality.

Chapter Two

Himari came back, and she brought breakfast—an assortment of cheeses and meats with crusty white bread—but things had changed between her and Yua.

Before, they had talked about everyday things Yua would never have, like the family Himari would return to one day and what she studied at the coven. Himari had one brother. Her mother was sick, and her father had died many years ago. She specialised in healing magic at the coven so she could help her mother and prevent her brother from developing the same illness. All things considered, Yua was grateful Himari had been this open with her.

But now, Himari didn't say one word.

Yua forced a smile. 'Thank you for bringing breakfast. This cheese is my favourite.'

Once upon a time, another attendant had told Yua it came from Rifarne, far across the Zestian Sea. Food was an easy way to experience other cultures, so Yua treasured what little she got. She suspected the attendants just grabbed the first things they saw in the kitchens so they could return to her, lest they make her angry and murderous. She had a feeling there was more variety—the coven's novices came from all over the world—but she couldn't confirm it without venturing into the kitchens herself. It wasn't worth the stares and whispers. But she was curious. Would the coven limit their selection to teach the novices modesty, or would they cater to as many tastes as possible to keep the novices happy instead of homesick?

'I don't think we've ever talked about cheeses,' Yua said. 'What's your favourite?'

O-Yu damn her if she didn't at least try, hard as it was to be nice when Himari trembled just from being in the same room as her.

Himari stopped chewing for a moment. She nodded to the Rifarnee cheese Yua had picked up. 'This one, my lady.'

The same one Yua had singled out? Yua sighed—she didn't believe it. Worse, gone was the casual familiarity they'd had. Gone was her name. She was just someone to serve now.

Let her serve you then. Take her blood. You have every right.

'Are you only saying that because it's my favourite?' asked Yua.

It was slight, but Himari flinched. Yua knew she shouldn't have accused her, but the words had come out before she thought it through. And Yua really wondered. Was this just an attempt to pacify her? Had there been others since Himari had become her attendant that Yua had missed? Maybe they'd had no connection, not even a semblance of one. Maybe Yua had imagined it all…

Again.

She was tired of this story, but she didn't know how to rewrite it.

Himari balled her hands into fists and stared at the floor. 'N-no, my lady.'

'You know, if I wanted to hurt you, I wouldn't do it over something as trivial as differing dairy preferences.'

Yes! Tear her open!

Yua already regretted her words before she'd finished speaking. Himari flinched harder. Yua shouldn't have said that. She shouldn't have said any of it. The right thing to do would have been to dismiss Himari, allow her to wait outside the door until Yua needed something. The mature thing would have been to get things herself, but then she'd have to face the gossiping novices, and it would have robbed Himari of the few chores she was supposed to fulfil; although, Yua couldn't imagine serving her was more exciting than her studies. Kei had mentioned that it was good practice for all the patients who would need Himari's full attention in the future, but Yua wasn't stupid. Mist Women didn't serve as carers. Mist Women served at courts and influenced the fate of countries.

Yua hated pretending everything was fine. She hated pretending that she was all right with everyone treating her like the most dangerous criminal in all Midoka because of some rumours and black veins. It was all just stories shrouded in shadows and fog. No one could prove she had done those terrible things. It didn't look good, but that wasn't proof. Her attendants reacted based on prejudice; Yua didn't care if it made her sound like a whiny child, but it wasn't fair.

'How long have you been my attendant now?' Yua asked.

'Two weeks, my lady.'

'It's Yua. In those two weeks, did we not get along?'

Himari nodded.

'I thought so, too. Have I done anything to worry you in those two weeks?'

Himari shook her head.

Yua rolled up both sleeves and lay her arms on the table. 'These marks haven't appeared this morning. They've been there all along and since before we met. Nothing has changed.'

Himari glanced at Yua's veins with trembling lips and nodded. 'I just… I hadn't…'

'What does it matter that you didn't see them sooner? They were already there. That you've seen them now doesn't change anything.'

You're trying too hard. Can't you smell her fear? You've lost her.

Yua was pushing her too hard, but she was desperate to understand. She hoped that something would snap, and Himari would see reason.

But Himari bowed. 'I'm sorry I've offended you, my lady.'

'It's Yua—use my name. Or are you afraid it'll twist your tongue and make you swallow it?'

Why do that when we could have so much more fun?

She regretted that more than anything else, but there was no taking it back now. And besides, she meant it.

'N-no, my l—*Yua.*'

Himari was shaking and still bowed. Yua shouldn't have gone so far.

'I'm sorry.' Yua wanted to take Himari's hands, pretend for one more second that they could have been friends in another life, but she knew Himari would move away if she did. 'It's just… This is exhausting. Being me is exhausting. I haven't done anything.'

Himari sat up a little and nodded. 'I know.'

She didn't mean it—Yua could tell from her tone. Like she was done with all this, just as Yua was. The only difference was that Himari was free to leave.

Yua sighed again and willed strength into herself when she inhaled. 'Thanks again for breakfast. When you've returned the plates to the kitchen, could you pick up a new book for me? I don't mind which one, just something fictional.'

It would give them both space to calm down. If Himari came back, Yua needed to do better. Yua didn't deserve their prejudice, but her attendants didn't deserve her anger. They were here to help, and they did it all while being scared and studying to become Mist Women. It was braver than Yua had ever managed.

Chapter Three

Himari took a long time to return. Yua gave up on waiting and accepted that another attendant had left. After how Yua had talked to her, she wasn't sure she would have acted any differently, but that didn't lessen the disappointment. It made it worse.

Yua opened her window and climbed onto her roof. All Midoka—or at least it felt that way—spread before her. Green forests. The ever-purple royal empress trees of the coven, kept in bloom with the gift. Rivers that sparkled emerald from the lush greenery. Mountains covered in expansive woods. Towns and lakes Yua would never see any closer. The other novices would eventually graduate, become full-fledged Mist Women, and see the world, while Yua had to stay content with this small view. Few people got to see the country from this high up; she loved what she saw, but she wanted more. She wanted to experience it, not just daydream about it.

Yua had considered running away, but even if she could somehow get down from the roof without breaking her neck, the Seven would track her down. Kei was their leader and their most powerful, but the Seven had earned their prominent positions, too. Every one of them would have found her no matter where she went. The real novices could simply walk out and visit the city below, but Yua doubted the same freedom applied to her.

A meow to her right made Yua admit it could be worse. If nothing else, she had Newai, a ginger cat who shared this roof with her. He had joined her about two years ago and had kept coming back. Newai had been shy at first but had warmed to her when Yua had stretched out her hand to let him investigate her scent on his terms. Most people around the coven referred to him as an *it*, but to Yua, he was better than any person. He was her only genuine friend, even if he knew nothing about her other than that she scratched his head and petted his fur. She loved him more than he could ever know, but she hoped he felt her gratitude and adoration on some feline level. Years ago, she had read that cats slow-blinked at one another to say *I love you*. She did the same with Newai, and whenever he did the same with her, she liked to think they understood each other.

Newai meowed again, and Yua held out her hand. He strode forwards on soft paws and rubbed his head into her palm. She stroked his head, gently scratched his chin, felt his purr in his lungs, and thanked O-Yu that she had him in her life. Although, if the Great Dragon really cared about her, she doubted she'd be trapped here with her marked veins and her reputation.

'You're the best,' Yua said.

Newai huffed.

'Yua?' someone called.

Newai bolted and threw himself off the roof at the nearest branches.

Yua sighed and stuck her head back into her room. 'Yes?'

One of the kitchen aids—Ichiro, she thought his name was—stood in her doorway with two mugs and a tea pot.

'I've brought you tea,' he said.

Yua paused. They hadn't exchanged many words, but those they had were friendly. He didn't seem as scared of her as everyone else, and she liked him for that alone. He seemed younger and as reserved as she. Yua remembered nothing about her family, but it was easy to think of him as a little brother—a little *estranged* brother, since they didn't make it a point to spend time together. He looked a little awkward standing by her door with the tea tray, like he wasn't sure if he should be there or whether it'd be best to just go.

Yua climbed back into her room. 'Himari already brought me food.'

She felt just as lost with him bringing her tea as he looked waiting for her reaction. He looked unsure, but she still didn't think he looked scared. It felt more like two cats carefully pacing around each other on the way to different places.

Ichiro nodded behind him. 'I just saw her near the kitchens. She looked...' He cleared his throat. 'I thought you could use something calming, so I brought you chamomile tea.' He raised the tray a little, like she might not believe him without it.

Her heart fell when he couldn't bring himself to finish his description of Himari, but it warmed again because he had brought her tea without anyone making him. She didn't remember the last time someone had brought her anything just to be nice. Did he know how much she liked tea, or were they simply similar like that?

Yua sat at her table. 'Thank you.' She bit her lip. 'Did Kei ask you to do this?'

He placed a mug of calming chamomile in front of her and stood aside. His eyes were curious, not scared.

'No one sent me to keep an eye on you, if that's what you're worried about.'

'Then why…' As much as she wanted to believe he was just being nice, that wasn't normally how it went. 'Sit.'

His hovering made her nervous. Even her attendants had always sat with her.

Ichiro sat and nodded at the tea. 'Do you mind if I have some? It's not time for my break yet, but since I'm here… You won't tell the head chef, will you?' His brows knitted together as if he'd made a mistake confessing as much.

She shook her head, too perplexed to speak, and he poured himself a cup. He had to have some reason for all this, but he gave nothing away. His uncertain stance, the worry on his face at the mention of the head chef… Yua couldn't figure it out. Whatever he wanted, she hoped he'd be more obvious when he asked for it.

Ichiro sipped his tea. 'I've seen you around the coven a few times. I've heard what the novices say about you, and you must have heard some of it too. If the rumours were true, I figured you'd have killed all of us by now, but you stay in your room and bear it.' He set the cup down. 'You seem perfectly human to me, and all humans need friends.'

She balled her hands in her lap to stop them from shaking, but it didn't stop her vision from blurring. 'You don't know me. You wouldn't sit here if you'd seen my marks.'

'So show me, my lady.'

She hesitated. Was this too good to be true, or was she just so used to being treated like a monster that any act of decency raised suspicions?

She bit her lip but didn't touch her sleeves. 'Just Yua, please. No titles.'

Ichiro nodded. 'Show me, Yua.'

She gulped as she rolled up one sleeve. Ichiro stared at her black veins for a moment longer than she was comfortable with, and she hurried to cover them up again.

'I grew up in the bad part of town,' he said. 'I've seen some disgusting things.'

Her heart sank. She stared at her tea so she wouldn't have to watch him leave.

'I saw a man once with tattoos all over his arms of headless puppies and— I know nothing else about him, but I knew enough then to run the other way. Your marks are just lines tracing the veins everyone has. I can't see anything dangerous about them.'

Her eyes filled with tears. Ichiro refilled her mug.

'I should get back to work or the head cook will have my hide,' he said. 'If you'd like, I could bring you tea every day around this time.'

She wanted to accept, but…

'Himari already does that,' Yua said. Assuming she was coming back, but even if she wasn't, her next attendant would pick up where she'd left off.

Ichiro shrugged. 'I'm sure she won't mind a break. She already does everything else for you, right? I'm not looking to replace her.'

Slowly, Yua nodded. 'Thank you.'

He left, and Yua sat with her shaking fists in her lap until her tea was cold.

The following morning, Yua leaned against her window and stared into the distance when a knock came on her door. She suspected it wasn't her attendant. Himari hadn't returned last night to bring her dinner or the book she'd asked for, so she had resigned herself to Himari leaving. Kei would want to talk to her about that… and the next unfortunate soul who would inevitably hate her. Yua had hoped she'd have a little longer before she was introduced, but O-Yu forbid the cycle didn't immediately continue.

Yua braced herself. 'Come in.'

It meant something that Kei didn't simply enter, but she had long since given up on trying to understand her. It was likely more the worry that Yua was naked than the decent thing to do.

Kei entered. The disappointed shadow on her face said it all.

Yua pretended not to care and turned back to the world outside her window. 'Himari left, didn't she?'

They never talked just to talk, as mother and daughter. Kei had offered Yua to stop by her office for a chat anytime, but it wasn't the same and Yua didn't really know how. It simply wasn't the relationship they had, and wishing it were different wouldn't dissolve the awkward formality between them. Kei had been the leader of their coven long before she adopted Yua, so she was more prison warden than mother.

From the corner of her eye, she saw Kei nod and sit at the table. Yua dug her nails into her palms—Kei rarely made herself at home in Yua's chambers. She still looked out of place with fancy emerald-and-gold fabric wrapped around her like armour, but the look on her face—like she wasn't sure how to say what she wanted—set her apart just as easily. The myths told of the Great Dragon O-Yu, whose emerald scales had fallen on Midoka and blessed their country with green life; the Head Mist Woman and the empress were supposed to incorporate the colours into their wardrobe as representatives of the deity who had given Midoka life. Usually, Kei looked every bit as fearsome. Today, her confidence wavered.

When Kei didn't speak, Yua turned to look at her. 'Have I done something else wrong?'

She didn't mean to sound so harsh, but it was impossible to keep the pain out of her voice. Kei's distance was one more cut after a long line of gutting punches. If Kei couldn't be warm for once, Yua didn't want her in the room. She didn't need a lecture, she needed…

She needed a *hug*. But she wouldn't tell Kei that.

Kei shifted as if she wanted to get up and walk towards her, but she stopped herself. Even her adoptive mother didn't want to be near her.

With a slow, measured voice, Kei said, 'I worry about you.'

'You worry about the coven's reputation,' Yua said.

The words tasted bitter on her tongue, but the thought had crossed her mind before. Theirs was the head coven in Maishi Hou. If all Mist Women were nobility amongst the common people, then Kei was their queen and the Seven their ruling elite. Only Midoka's empress stood above them. All Mist Women and their covens were important and given almost complete freedom, but when they reported to anyone, they came here. There wasn't another coven like it in the world. Even the smallest coven had nearly complete rein in their research and work, as long as it didn't endanger their status. Kei and the Seven couldn't have anyone slather filth onto their name, not even Kei's adopted daughter.

'I worry I haven't done right by you,' Kei said. 'This life… It must have been hard for you.'

Tears burned Yua's eyes. 'You've just noticed that now? I've lived here for thirteen years, and you've *just* noticed that *now?*'

Yua hated how severe she sounded, but she'd never been good at conflict, especially when that conflict involved talking to Kei. Too many raw emotions were involved, and Kei hadn't taught her how to voice them.

She crossed her arms and leaned against the wall. If she could have disappeared in the shadows between its bricks, she would have done. She wouldn't go to her knees and cry, though. Not while Kei was here.

Something behind Kei's eyes changed. Whatever her moment of regret had been, it was gone when their eyes met again.

'Any partnership requires co-operation from both sides to work,' Kei said. 'We know it's difficult for you, but they struggle too. Still, they face their fears to attend to you. And what do you do? You throw a tantrum whenever one shows a shred of fear—a fear you feed.'

Yua pushed herself away from the wall. 'That's not fair! You don't know what it's like to—'

Kei flew to her feet. 'Spare me the outburst. You are no longer a child, but a young woman. It's beneath you to throw a fit when things don't go your way. Do you think you're the only person in the world who's unhappy with her life? Had you been born in Tramura, they would have killed you that night without another thought about your age. In Rifarne, no one would have taken you in; you would have died a slow death on the streets. In Krymistis, they would have used you as an assassin.'

Yua glared at her. 'So, I should be grateful to be a prisoner who's hated over some rumours? At least I'm alive to suffer through it, right?'

Kei's arm snapped back like she was about to slap Yua, but she caught herself. Her angry eyes fell, and her shoulders sagged.

'Yes. At least you can do something with your life. At least you can make friends. Your life may be sheltered, but at least you're not in constant danger.'

'*Friends?*' Yua scoffed. 'Is that what you call the attendants? Well then, have you arranged my next play date?'

Kei stepped away like Yua had hit her, and Yua fell back against the wall. It steadied her and stopped her shaking legs from crumbling.

'Yua—'

'Just go already. Don't you have work to do? You normally do.'

Yua focussed on nothing in particular outside her window. She didn't react when Kei stepped closer. Kei didn't touch her, but warmth radiated from her. At least some part of her was capable of it.

'If you want them to accept you and love you, you first need to accept and love yourself, *chiha* I want happiness for you. It hurts me to see you defeat yourself at every turn.'

Her eyes burnt fiercer, but Yua swallowed it. Kei rarely called her *daughter*. It always affected her.

Yua wanted to say something, to turn around and hug Kei even if Kei wouldn't hug her back, but then she'd have lost the argument. She refused to admit defeat. She was too angry to admit that Kei made some good points, and she'd never back down. Her feelings were valid—her *pain* was valid—no matter how Kei tried to spin it.

Kei sighed and stepped away. 'Please think about what I said. You know where to find me.'

Kei was always in her office, where she had meetings and helped shape the future of their country. There was nowhere they could talk that felt reassuring. It was always business with her adoptive mother.

After a few more seconds of heavy silence that stretched the abyss between them ever farther, Kei left her alone and closed the door.

And Yua felt lonelier than ever.

Chapter Five

The young woman looked Krymistian. Bronze skin. Golden hair. So much confidence in her step Yua hated her already.

You should teach them all a lesson this time, the darkness inside her whispered. *Rip her throat open and drink her blood as soon as Kei turns her back. Only that will break this cycle.*

Yua tried to ignore it as she watched the Krymistian from behind her curtains, but it was hard. This woman would learn to hate and fear Yua like Yua would always hate and fear her darkness. The whispers were wrong—she feared this cycle would only end when Yua died of old age.

Because Yua and her Shadow were one, and if she gave in to its temptations for one second, someone would die.

Kei walked her new attendant across the front garden, pointing out their carefully trimmed hedges, the sweet royal empress blossoms, and the small fountain that represented the way magic flowed in and out of all things. The Krymistian wouldn't stay, but Kei still hoped, because she knew better than to expect a miracle. They both did.

Yua moved away from her window and sat on her bed. Not long now until they were introduced, until they wrote another chapter in the same book, telling the same story as always. Yua loathed the repetition, but there was nothing she could do to change it. *Yua, this is your new attendant. New attendant, this is Yua.*

Yes, the Yua you've heard so much about. The Blood Wisp. That's her. You're hers now. Skip forwards a month, often less, and the new attendant had felt enough fear or hatred to last five lifetimes. Just like Himari.

So, let's write the end, her darkness whispered. *You and me together. Let me show you what we can be.*

The knock came at her door, and Yua stood. She did her best to smooth her plain novice's shirt and look like a normal person. She even tried to hide her black veins so the Krymistian wouldn't get a shock the moment she entered Yua's room.

Another knock—Kei was impatient today. Then again, Yua suspected she had better things to do than play tour guide or mother.

'Come in.'

Ichiro stepped into her room, balancing a tea pot and two cups on a tray. He nudged the door shut behind him with his foot and bowed as deep as the tray allowed. Yua blushed. She hadn't allowed herself to believe that he might come back.

'I thought you might appreciate a cup of relaxing chamomile.' He nudged one of her four chairs—four just to tease her, she expected, since she didn't get visitors—out of the way and placed the tray on her table.

Was this what it was like to have friends?

Yua dared a smile. 'Thank you. I didn't think I'd—' She cleared her throat. 'Thank you.'

Ichiro returned the smile. 'How are you feeling?'

Yua felt a little shy talking to him. Since boys couldn't study at their coven—all Mist Women were female, without exceptions—she had no experience talking to men… even if Ichiro was more like a little brother than a grown man. That's how it had always been, although Yua didn't know why. That didn't stop them, however, from hiring male staff. Yua had once asked why and had been told that it was good for men to see first-hand why people feared Mist Women. No one tortured or mistreated the staff, but you only walked into lessons to assist with menial tasks so many times before the magic on display spoke for itself.

'I feel…' She was nervous about the Krymistian. She didn't want to see another attendant's fear and know it was because of her. 'I'm unsure. All other attendants have studied here or were from elsewhere in Midoka. What are Krymistians like?'

She pictured deserts as far as she could see and buildings the same colour as the sand. She had read that Krymistians used their gifts alongside their weapons. In her mind, they were fierce warriors. Her heart missed a beat. What did that say about the Krymistian about to enter her life?

Ichiro poured a cup of tea, and Yua gratefully accepted. He was right, she could do with the relaxing chamomile.

'I don't know,' he said. 'I've never left Midoka. I heard they are skilled warriors, but that's about all I know.'

Yua nodded. Everyone knew that. But she wouldn't complain—not when Ichiro had brought her tea to help her nerves and talked to her like a friend might. The Krymistian would follow Himari as soon as she could—Yua wasn't naïve enough to pretend otherwise—but Yua wouldn't ruin a potential friendship with Ichiro, too.

'This one might be different,' Ichiro said.

Yua grimaced and hid behind another sip. 'She won't be.'

'Think about it—everyone in Midoka has heard about you, but Krymistians have their own stories. She might not know anything about you, and even if she does, she might not care.'

Yua shook her head. 'I find that hard to imagine.'

He shrugged. 'Maybe a little Krymistian warmth is just what you've been missing.'

She wanted him to be right, but it was never that simple. If he was right and she'd never heard of Yua before, it would only make the first impression more shocking.

'I give her two weeks before she breaks,' Yua said.

Ichiro checked her cup and refilled it. 'You don't want that.'

It was her turn to shrug. 'Doesn't matter what I want.'

Ichiro poured the rest of the tea for himself and placed the pot back on the tray. 'She might surprise you. Keep an open mind?'

Yua snorted but didn't argue. She valued his opinion and this normal, relaxed chat more than he could ever know, but he was wrong.

Ichiro stood. 'I'll bring you another tea later. Maybe I can meet her.'

Yua glanced up at him and felt her heart lighten a little. This was nice. Despite herself, she prayed it would last.

'If she hasn't run for the Krymistian border,' she said.

Ichiro grinned, bowed, and opened the door…

Just in time for Kei to freeze mid-knock.

Kei smiled, looking every bit like a surprised parent who hadn't realised their child had friends after all. 'I didn't know Yua had company.'

Her heart hammered in her chest now Kei was here with the Krymistian right behind her. The door hid her new attendant, but Yua had done this often enough to know she was there. She couldn't get what Ichiro had said out of her head—maybe one day, she'd meet someone who wasn't afraid of the girl she was in the stories. Maybe, just maybe, this was it.

Ichiro gave her a look as if to remind her on his way out, and Kei stepped inside.

'I would like you to meet Aza Karalis.' Kei waved the woman into the room. 'She will be your attendant from today.'

Yua wasn't sure if it was Aza's sun-kissed skin or the sparkle in her eyes, but the room seemed brighter with her in it. Like Aza had brought a piece of the Krymistian warmth with her. Usually, new attendants had this unsure air about them, as if they knew they were walking into a trap, but they did it anyway. Aza walked in like she belonged here.

Don't choke on her confidence. Choke her *with it.*

Yua smirked. 'Welcome to my prison.'

Aza raised an eyebrow, and her smile faltered a little. She didn't look any less friendly though. If anything, she looked curious.

Like you're an animal that behaves differently to how she expected. Let's show her our teeth.

'I'm sure you'll get along well,' Kei smiled. 'Once you've got to know each other a little, why don't you show Aza the coven? It's her first time here.'

'Of course,' Yua said. 'I've done this before.'

She hadn't; she just wanted to get Kei's polite friendliness out of her room before she choked on that instead. Since her usual attendants were novices, they had known the coven better than Yua, but Aza would know even fewer corners than Yua if she really had never been here.

Aza inclined her head in greeting and smiled. Yua didn't miss the daggers on her hips or the golden glint in her brown eyes. Aza wasn't an attendant; she was a bodyguard—but whose? Hers or the novices'? Yua's stomach knotted. Kei had given up on trying to do things for Yua's benefit, although she'd no doubt spin it that way. Aza was here to protect the novices, simple as that. Not that Yua had ever done anything to warrant that, but she supposed Ohira Kei, esteemed leader of all Mist Women and confidant of the empress, couldn't take any risks or show weakness. Still, it hurt.

'Then I can leave you to it.' Kei turned to Aza. 'Talk to me if there are any issues.'

Kei wanted to discourage attendants from just running off one night, never to return, but this time it felt personal. Like Yua might hurt Aza or threaten with worse. Yua had never hurt anyone besides that time she was five, and Kei still held it over Yua's head like the curse Yua knew it was.

Why not become the monster they already think you are?

'Thank you, *kyastra*,' Aza said. 'I'll be fine.'

Yua grimaced. They always said that, minus the words she didn't understand. Aza had insulted Kei with the worst Krymistian slur she could think of for all Yua knew; although, Aza's smile made her think it wasn't anything offensive. Maybe she'd ask another time, if she felt close enough to Aza to ask and if Aza stayed long enough at all.

Kei closed the door behind her when she left. It amazed Yua there was this much trust between them.

'It's nice to meet you.' Her accent was thick and warm like the sun, her smile soft like sand dunes. In another life, Yua might have liked her. In this life, she dreaded the day Aza's voice would shake and her features twist with fear.

Yua nodded but couldn't bring herself to return the sentiment. The more removed she was now, the less it would hurt later.

Chapter Six

Yua leaned against her windowsill and watched Aza as she inspected the room and learned its corners. She didn't look much older than Yua, but looks meant nothing—living amongst Mist Women who preferred to look young no matter their age had taught Yua that. But Aza didn't look intimidated either. That was a first.

Yua frowned when Aza looked into the bathroom. 'I don't know what you're looking for, but I doubt you'll find it in there.'

'Just getting a feel for the space.' Aza ran her hand over the wall next to the door like it was a false panel or something equally exciting. Like Yua wouldn't have found anything like that by now. Like it wouldn't have made her sentence more interesting, at least for a little while.

'How did Kei find you?' Yua asked. 'Usually, she doesn't look farther than Maishi Hou.'

It surprised her Kei still found anyone so close to the coven at all. Plenty of attendants had fled the building in tears, sometimes even the capital, unable to handle the weight of the rumours. Word must have spread beyond the archipelago by now. Anyone leaving Midoka could have spread disturbing stories about the Blood Wisp. She had wondered if she'd become a test of courage—whoever could bear her presence the longest won extra dessert privileges or something like that.

Aza closed the bathroom door. She turned to Yua with one palm still on the door. 'My reputation preceded me. I guess we have that in common.'

Unsure what to do while Aza searched her room for traps or an ambush or whatever it was she was looking for, Yua sat on her bed. Normally, her attendants just stood in the corner and made as little eye contact as possible. No one had ever bothered to get *a feel for the space* before. Aza was really planning on staying.

'I doubt our reputations are anything alike.' Still, Yua wanted to know more. This was the most casual conversation she'd ever had with an attendant. 'What's yours?'

Aza sat next to her and shrugged. 'I'm a Sand Blade. Didn't Ohira tell you?'

Yua grew a little paler under her already fair complexion. She shook her head. Aza wasn't a bodyguard—she was a trained assassin, and not just any assassin, either. One of Krymistis' infamous finest. Just in case Yua tried anything bloody.

And Aza had *shrugged*, like it meant nothing to her.

Yua bit back her response that Kei never told her anything. 'And who is Kei paying you to protect?' She nodded towards her door. 'Me or them?' She couldn't help the hurt in her voice, even though she hated herself for the weakness. This wasn't at all how first meetings usually went. Hiring an assassin to keep an eye on her was too much. Yua no longer cared if Aza ran as fast as her feet could carry her. Why couldn't Kei just ground her like normal parents? Yua already spent her whole life locked up anyway… but she wasn't a normal young woman, and she certainly wasn't a normal Midokan, so her punishment had to be harsher too.

She didn't know how to behave around Aza. She'd read books about Sand Blades, fictional as well as factual. If any of them were true, Aza could kill her as effortlessly as breathing, and Yua wouldn't even notice she was dying unless Aza killed her slowly with poison or cut her limbs off one by one. Sand Blades were capable of either. Or maybe Aza would simply stab her and be done with it. Maybe she had searched the room for the quickest escape route.

Aza studied her face like she was trying to make sense of Yua. 'I'm not here to protect anyone. Ohira hopes I won't scare at the first display of magic and run back to the desert.'

Yua struggled to relate the casual young woman before her to the stories she'd read. She didn't look dangerous except for the daggers on her hips, but Yua didn't trust it. Aza had probably learned how to blend in and appear non-threatening.

Yua stood. 'You'll be disappointed then. Kei must have told you I have no talent for the gift.'

She walked over to the window. Aza followed and stood next to her.

Yua frowned. 'Did she tell you to do that? Follow me around just in case I trip and accidentally release some dark magic they can't control?'

Aza looked genuinely taken aback and took a few steps away from her. 'No. I'm sorry. I thought if we're going to work together I should—'

Lies. Kill her before she kills you.

'I'm not a child,' Yua snapped. 'I can look after myself, with or without the gift.'

Aza grinned. 'I don't doubt it. You don't look like someone who'd just lie down and die.'

Yua straightened. Was that a threat or was she reading too much into it?

'I'm not.'

The words were hollow, but Aza didn't know that. Yua didn't know what she'd do if anyone attacked her. Without the gift, she was as good as pointless in Midoka. Even their trees glowed with magic at night, while Yua couldn't summon the smallest flame. A newborn was more dangerous than her. From the moment Kei had brought her to the coven, she'd left Yua out of every class. Their coven didn't offer many choices besides magic, but Yua would have liked to learn how to use a dagger or maybe a bow. She couldn't go into the sparring room, where some novices kicked and punched at each other to let off steam or to show off what they were doing before they came to the coven. No Mist Woman had to know how to use weapons or hand-to-hand techniques since their gift was their greatest asset, but some liked the exercise. Most novices were above anything that made them sweat or ruin their looks though. Mist Women strived to always look flawless. Ruffled hair and flushed cheeks wouldn't do. The few novices who used the room in their first year quickly moved on to other things.

And still Yua couldn't go inside.

Aza nodded to Yua's arms. 'May I ask?'

'You mean Kei hasn't filled you in already?'

Aza shook her head. 'She told me you had black veins all over your body, but I think she hoped you'd tell me the rest. You know, so we can get to know each other.'

Yua sighed and leaned against her windowsill. Aza *had* asked, and honesty now would get it over with.

'I really can't tell you much more than that,' Yua said. 'I've had them for as long as I can remember. My memories start when I was five, so it's possible I was born with them. That's about it.'

Aza scooted a bit closer, eyes bright with genuine curiosity. Yua liked her a little more for it. It also put her on edge. How did she know Aza's curiosity was real? No one had ever been curious before. What if Aza was just trying to figure out her weaknesses?

'Really?' Aza asked. 'All you know is that you have them?'

Yua nodded, hackles raised. 'Why are you so interested? Are you another specialist Kei hired to figure me out?'

Aza leaned back and stared at her like Yua was the unreasonable one here. 'What? No! I told you I'm a Sand Blade, born and trained.' Aza leaned in more again, like they were already the best of friends sharing a juicy secret. Yua liked her a little less for that. 'Did she really hire specialists to… what, examine you?'

Yua shivered. For the first three years at this coven, her life had been nothing but. She barely remembered anything else from her first year. After that, the wave of specialists had slowed down, but it wasn't until she had been at the coven for nearly three years that Kei and the Seven had given up and accepted that no one knew what was wrong with her. Some had come from as far away as Vistria in the Northern Reaches. All had tried to figure out what was wrong with her, how close she was to shattering. What might break her. Like she was a disease that needed curing or cracks on a vase they could fix if only they applied enough mending magic. Even then, Kei had been secretive—the specialists had been told that Yua's veins had turned black, but no one had whispered a word about the night that had changed everything. Yua remembered Kei telling her not to mention it. If any of them asked, she didn't know how they had appeared… which was true. Yua had overheard one of the Seven 'talk' to one specialist. She had used magic to make sure they didn't remember anything potentially dangerous. A knot had twisted in her gut that day, and she had done her best to forget it. She wasn't dangerous—any specialist could have told them that—but all she knew was that they hadn't found a cure.

Yua stared into the distance. 'We don't know what these markings are, why I have them or how I got them. They didn't stretch or distort when I got older; they grew with me like any other part of my body.'

'But you don't like them.' It wasn't a question. Aza thought she had Yua figured out, and it made her skin crawl. Who was she to just walk in here from another country and make assumptions? Yua wanted to be angry or at least defensive, but no one had ever looked at her marks the way Aza did. Without fear. Without apprehension. Even the specialists hadn't touched or looked at them when they could avoid it.

Yua swallowed. 'They haven't exactly made my life easier.'

'I think they're beautiful.'

Yua blinked and turned to Aza. She had never been sure what to call them besides every variation of *problematic*. They were a constant reminder that something was wrong with her. Of all the things she might have called them, *beautiful* wasn't among them.

'You really don't know the story?' Yua asked.

She was still suspicious of Aza's motives, but it was nice to talk without Aza being scared or running away. If Yua really thought about it, she wasn't sure what a Krymistian might see in the marks that no one else had over the years. If there was one thing Yua was sure of, it was that magic had traced her veins black, and there were no greater experts on the gift than Mist Women. There was nothing a Sand Blade, especially one as young as Aza, could have seen in them that a coven full of experts and the Seven hadn't. Maybe she really was just here as Yua's bodyguard.

Yua relaxed a little, if not much. That Kei thought she needed a bodyguard at all didn't sit well with her.

Aza smiled. 'I guess the rumours didn't reach Krymistis.' She winked. 'We were too busy creating our own nightmares.' Aza sounded like she was joking, but Yua couldn't get the stories she'd read about Sand Blades out of her head. Torturers without mercy. Killers without equal.

And now, one was in her bedroom making small talk.

Yua wanted to tell Aza and get it over with, but despite the rumours that had come out of Krymistis, she didn't want Aza to leave either. The stories about Yua weren't true. Maybe the stories about Sand Blades exaggerated too. Maybe, if she told Aza and Aza didn't fear her for it...

You're too old to be so naïve.

But perhaps it was possible.

She'll leave you. She'll kill you for being you, and then she'll disappear like everyone else.

Yua looked back outside. She wasn't used to telling her story, and the outside, even if she didn't focus on anything, was nicer than the unavoidable shock and disgust in Aza's eyes. Yua didn't want to see it. Not again. She wanted her eyes to wander like her feet couldn't.

'Kei found me when I was five. It was night—sometime past midnight so it was dark. She probably smelled me before she saw me. The whole neighbourhood must have been able to.'

Aza chuckled. 'Smell you? Hadn't you bathed in a week?'

Yua's smile didn't even reach the tip of her nose.

'I stood in the middle of ten, fifteen bodies—it was hard to count the remains. All these corpses, all that blood, and I looked like I'd bathed in it.'

Aza raised an eyebrow. '*That*'s your first memory? *Kelsos*, Yua, how did you not go insane?'

Yua focussed on the fountain outside, but she imagined fear entering Aza's eyes right about now.

'I was the only one alive. I killed all these people, and I don't remember their names or why I did it. All I remember is that too-sweet undertone of—' She couldn't say *blood*. She couldn't make it sound like she'd done more than bathe in it. Tears stung her eyes when the memory hit her—she could taste it on her tongue, felt the saliva pool around it.

Aza is right there. No one will think anything of it if she disappears on her first day.

Yua glanced at Aza's neck. Her Shadow was right, it really was right there. Soft. Vulnerable. The vein pulsing just under her skin. How many attendants had left within a day or two? They had known what they had agreed to, whereas Aza hadn't heard the rumours before. No one would question it if Yua told them it had proved too much.

'Anyone could have done that if that's all you remember,' Aza said. 'What makes you think it was you?'

Yua blinked to get rid of the memory, but it never went far.

'Why would the murderer have let me live? I know it was me. I can feel it. When I close my eyes, I can almost—'

The screams. The scent. That taste.

You loved my nature that night. Don't deny us for their sakes.

'So, Kei found you in the middle of all *that* and thought what you really needed was a home?'

Yua nodded. 'She tried to keep how she found me quiet, but the rumours spread quickly. I was a sliver of a child and covered in blood. They call me *Blood Wisp*.' Yua grimaced. 'I suppose they could have called me worse.'

She hated the pity in Aza's eyes almost more than she would have hated her fear. Like Yua had been wrong all these years and just didn't understand how lucky she really was.

'Ohira saw something in you,' Aza said. 'She wouldn't have brought you here otherwise.'

Yua huffed. 'She saw danger. I'm something to be studied, not someone who studies with the others. Something dark lives inside me, and they've suppressed it ever since. I don't even know what I can do because everyone's too scared to find out. Given what I did that night, it's better this way.'

Yua bit her tongue. She hadn't meant to say all that.

Yes. Surrender to me. Let me take control.

For a moment, Aza was silent. Yua braced herself. Any second now she'd say she couldn't do it and leave forever, and then *Aza* would be another name Yua oughtn't have learnt.

Instead, Aza looked at her like she'd never seen anyone like Yua. Not like she wanted to study her, but like she didn't quite believe her eyes. Yua didn't know what to make of it.

'And you tell me you don't have the gift.'

Yua tensed. 'I don't. I have a curse.'

From the corner of her eye, she saw Aza slowly shake her head. 'Whatever you have, it's yours and it's unique.'

Yua dared. She looked into Aza's eyes and found no fear.

'You're not scared of me?'

Aza grinned. 'I've been here for about an hour now, and the scariest thing you've done is stand too close to the window. You're alive because Ohira saw something in you. Is it so odd to think that I see more than whatever stories the kids tell these days?'

Yua wanted to believe it, so much, but she knew better. She wasn't special. Not in any way that mattered in Midoka. Aza was wrong on another count, too: Yua wasn't alive because Kei had seen some untapped potential. She was alive because Kei wouldn't kill a child. That's all there was to it.

All Yua had wanted for years was for someone to see past the rumours. Aza seemed to see past it now, and Yua wasn't convinced she liked it or believed it. She was a thing from nightmares and cautionary tales, the darkness parents threatened their children with if they didn't behave. She didn't want Aza to be afraid of her, but wouldn't a bit of fear have been normal? Yua wanted to open up to her, but what if Aza was a good liar and just another specialist after all? What if she was scared under her tough exterior?

Yua glanced at Aza. Her exterior wasn't tough, it was kind smiles and warm sunshine. Not at all what Yua had expected from a Sand Blade… but then again, maybe she had been unfair in her assessment. After all, she had judged Aza based on rumours. They were both just stories to each other.

Aza raised an eyebrow when Yua kept staring at her. 'Should I do a spin?'

Yua sighed. If she expected the world to give her a chance, she could do the same for Aza.

'Kei said to show you the coven.'

Aza still sat next to her on the bed. Fearless. Curious. Genuine. A rare thing… like a Midokan without the gift.

'Don't you have other things to do than play tour guide?' Aza asked.

Yua grimaced. 'Not at all. Do you want to see it?'

Aza grinned. 'Yes, please.'

'Then let me show you all the classes I'm not allowed to take.'

Yua stepped into the corridor outside her room. Aza followed with a skip in her step like she'd never seen the gift at work before.

'Don't they have magic in Krymistis?' Yua asked. 'You weave it into your weapons and armour, don't you?'

'Yes, but you use the pure form—no weapons necessary. Back home, no one shows us how to fling fireballs at people; we're taught how to order enchanted tools and clothes. Completely different.'

Yua had never thought about it. Krymistian visitors were rare, and she wasn't introduced to the few who did visit.

'Then I'm sorry to disappoint you, but no one has shown me how to fling fireballs at anyone either.' She nodded to Aza's daggers, one on each hip. 'Are they enchanted?'

Aza drew one and twirled it between her fingers. 'Just this one. It's enchanted with a basic fire spell. It burns anyone and anything I cut. The other I sharpen every night so that it cuts through everything.'

Krymistian writing was engraved on the enchanted blade.

'What does it say?' Yua asked.

A sad smile entered Aza's lips, like she was lost in a bitter-sweet memory. 'Desma.'

'You named your weapon *Desma*? Aren't things like that called… I don't know, War Ender or something equally dramatic?'

Aza laughed. 'Desma is my sister. She's very competitive and loyal like the fiercest hound. I chose the fire enchantment to match her.' Aza stroked over the name with her thumb and sheathed the weapon. 'I haven't seen her in years. She went to Grozma across the sea in Tramura a few years ago, and I've been working different undercover jobs until Ohira found me. Last I heard, she isn't even in Tramura anymore.' Aza shrugged with a wistful look in her eyes. 'But who knows?'

'How do you know she's alright?'

Aza's knuckles whitened around the hilt. 'Because she's the best Sand Blade there is, and because she's my sister. I just know.'

Yua didn't understand but nodded. It would have been nice to have a sister. Someone who loved her and understood her no matter what the world threw at her. Someone who didn't call her Blood Wisp behind her back. For all she knew, she'd had a sister but killed her that night with those other people. There was no point dwelling on it. Talking to Aza was the most effortless conversation she'd had in… ever. Maybe this was what it felt like to have a real friend, but a part of her was still suspicious. It was too easy. Her heart raced faster the longer they talked, but it was probably because she anticipated the stares and whispers once they reached the lower floors.

'How come you haven't contacted her or she you if it's been this long?' Maybe she was making assumptions, but by the way Aza had gripped the dagger's hilt, Yua thought she really cared about her sister. It seemed odd to her that Aza missed her so much yet did nothing to talk to her.

'I guess you don't know what undercover work is.' Yua blushed, but Aza smiled. No malice intended. 'I wasn't allowed to talk to anyone who wasn't involved. I reported back to my boss, but that was it. I know she's okay. I don't need a letter to prove it.'

Yua didn't believe it but didn't press her. 'Through here.' She opened a door and led Aza outside.

It was a hot day—the last heatwave of the season, she suspected—but Aza spread her arms wide and soaked up the sun. Large purple empress trees lined the path on both sides. Behind her were the dorms. Ahead of her, the school curved around to almost connect with them. The garden itself was a long, elaborate path more than anything. It dropped off to their left, revealing a view over Midoka that Yua would have loved if she could have found a quiet moment. No visible fence separated them from the drop. Instead, a magical shield had been put in place to stop anyone from taking one step too many. The fountain was the calming centre piece. Even though it was hot for late autumn, a cooling breeze caressed her skin and made the warmth comfortable.

'How does the heat compare to Krymistis?'

Aza laughed. 'You haven't known heat until you've run laps through the desert because you lost a bet to your sister.'

Yua raised an eyebrow. 'Wouldn't you die of dehydration before you completed one lap?'

'Only if you're stupid enough to circle the entire desert. I only ran around my town. Lots of people nearby in case I was an idiot after all.' Aza smiled. 'I like this garden. It's very peaceful.'

Yua nodded. Years ago, when Kei had first adopted her, she'd come here every day. It hadn't taken long before the stares of the novices had got to her. It was more peaceful to stay in her room.

'We've just left the dorms. My room is on the top floor. The teachers' rooms, kitchen, and dining room are on the ground floor. Most novices stay on the first floor, but the novices close to graduation stay on the second floor, one below me.'

'But Ohira told me to find her in the school building if you tried to kill me.'

From Aza, it didn't sound like an insult. Yua was surprised to feel her lips curl.

'The Seven and Kei are an exception. Kei is the Mist Woman in charge of the coven—all the covens, actually. Her office is in the school building and her chambers are adjacent to it. She prefers to be near the teaching.'

Aza's forehead wrinkled. 'I was told to call her Ohira at all times. Isn't Kei her surname?'

'No.' Yua had forgotten that other countries named the first name before the surname. 'In Midoka, the family name stands first. It's tradition and an easier way to identify someone. Your first name doesn't tell a stranger much, but your surname might be recognisable. It's also a sign of respect. First names need to be earned.'

'So, you use her first name because she's your mother and you've earned the right by default?'

Yua nodded.

'Should I call you Ohira then?'

'O-Yu, no. I'd kick you out myself. It's Yua if you don't mind.'

She was relieved when Aza laughed. Other attendants had been intimidated at the request.

'Got it, Yua.'

Her heart missed a beat. It felt nice to hear her name so casually.

'You called Kei something earlier.' It seemed like a good moment to ask since Aza had asked her a question about Midokan tradition. Knowledge for knowledge. 'Ka… what was it?'

'Kyastra?' Aza asked. Yua nodded. 'It means *ma'am*. I wasn't sure what to call her besides her name, but I thought it fit.'

Yua repeated it to herself so she'd remember it later. She liked the way it rolled off her tongue, though it didn't sound as warm as it did coming from Aza. Maybe she could learn more Krymistian from her. It wasn't quite as good as visiting the country herself, but it was more than she'd had a day ago.

'Shall we, kyastra?' It sounded clumsy from her lips, and Yua blushed. But Aza had used her name when Yua had asked her to, and she wanted to return the gesture. Aza grinned, and her blush deepened. She'd never thought she'd feel so awkward speaking another language to someone who grew up with it. Aza had to be judging her pronunciation. Yua didn't mind it too much, though—it was a nice change to the usual judgement.

Yua cleared her throat. 'Kei officially adopted me a week after she took me in. She believed I was traumatised from all the death I caused and wanted me to have a mother.'

Aza smiled. 'That explains the way she talked about you. She really cares about you.'

Yua focussed on the gently trickling fountain. Her heart was still racing from speaking one Krymistian word; she hoped the fountain would do its job and calm her mind.

Yua stared at the water's surface where the falling water made gentle ripples and tried to even her breathing. 'She has an odd way of showing it.'

Four novices took a wide berth around her but watched her like she was about to set them on fire or tear them apart.

Aza frowned. 'Are they all like that?'

'I'm used to it.'

'But—'

Yua didn't want to talk about it. There was no point.

'The garden was created to be relaxing and have a soothing effect on the novices passing through. Its purpose is to clear their minds before lessons and help them wind down when they're returning to their rooms.' She glanced towards the cliff edge and Midoka beyond it. 'We're high up to remind the novices that they have a responsibility towards the rest of the world, but I think it just makes them more arrogant. Nothing strokes the ego like literally being above everyone else.'

It was a steep walk up the thousand steps. Most novices rarely left the coven, but the ones who did made the climb with pride. They weren't just any school, after all—they were the head coven of Midoka's most respected gifted. Mist Women were employed all over the world and enjoyed more liberties than anyone else—partly due to the respect they received, but mostly because no one could stop a Mist Woman who wanted to leave. Studying here was an honour. Yua wondered what that was like.

She opened the door to the school building and led Aza inside. All coven buildings were in the same traditional Midokan style—white walls with green, wooden accents, and pale-purple slate roofs. Light wooden floors. When she looked down into Maishi Hou, she could tell that architecture had moved on, but Mist Women were nothing if not traditional… as much as women who didn't take orders from anyone could be. Groups of novices walked from one class to another. They stared at Yua like they were scared she'd kill them with a glance. Yua glared right back. If she had that kind of magic, she wouldn't be here. At the very least she'd attend classes.

Yua crossed her arms and looked at the closed doors, behind which novices were learning all the useful things Yua would never be able to do.

'What are Krymistian schools like?'

Aza shrugged. 'Sand Blades don't attend the regular schools. We learn on the job.'

'But you were just a child,' Yua said. 'They must have taught you some skills before they sent you out to…' She wasn't sure how to phrase that they would have sent children to kill people. Yua shivered. She had killed her family by accident, but Aza had been taught how to kill people from roughly the same age. Maybe they weren't that different in that regard. Was that why

Kei had hired her? Yua scoffed at herself. Having killed people from the age of five wasn't a healthy thing to bond over.

Then again, she had no one else who might understand. Maybe she really could be open with Aza.

'They told us to be quick and not be seen.' Aza winked at her. 'I'm very good at both.'

Yua nodded, unsure what to say. She had the feeling that, if Aza weren't good at both, she wouldn't be alive to show off about it.

Yua smiled to hide how awkward she felt about having brought up something so personal, but it didn't make her feel any better. 'I suppose this coven isn't a regular school either. I don't know what they teach in the rest of Midoka, but here, they teach what you probably expect from a Mist Woman coven: uses of the gift, history, politics, things like that. The library has some books about Mist magic, but actual practice is forbidden.'

It was brief, but Yua noticed that Aza's breath stocked. She paled under her bronze complexion. 'You mean there are novices here who study the forbidden side of the gift?'

'I might have oversold it,' Yua said. 'You can study what little theory we have on how the Dark One works, what kind of demons there are, and what the Dark One will do to you if you dare enter the Mists, but those books aren't lying around where any novice can pick them up. They're deep in the archives, and only the Seven have access to them. I don't think anyone specialises in that field, but it's not like I asked around. The Mists have nothing to do with us, and as I said, it's not easy to get to the books, so I don't think the novices see the point in studying what they can't use. The Mists are like another country that's best left alone and that's near impossible to enter, only more...' She looked to Aza for the right words, but Aza shrugged. '... more infernally ethereal.'

Aza raised an eyebrow. 'You know a lot for someone who doesn't study here.'

'You can learn a lot through observation.' She gritted her teeth. 'Mind you, it's hard to blend in when you're me, so I don't know any details.'

'You mentioned the Seven. Who are they?'

Yua shivered. 'Experts in their field. Kei leads the Mist Women, but the Seven make a lot of the decisions. Kei only steps in when she doesn't agree with them, which never happens.' Yua had never been called before them, and she was grateful for that. Even without the gift, she felt the power emanating from them just by being near them. 'Rumour has it they are merciless.'

Aza nudged her with a wink. 'Rumour has it you're a terrifying monster.'

'The Seven are in charge for a reason. They're the most powerful Mist Women in the world, and even the weakest ones are feared.'

But maybe Aza had a point. Yua had seen some of them in passing, but that was it. One of them, a Rifarnee called Willow, ran the infirmary and taught the novices who wanted to become healers. How bad could someone like that be?

'Aren't they known in Krymistis?'

The Seven held so much power in Midoka that Yua hadn't considered that other countries might not know as much about them. Mist Women served all over the world, after all. One advised the Krymistian ruler, Lady Nerine.

'We know a little,' Aza said. 'We sometimes joke that they're the real rulers of Midoka, that the empress is just there for tradition and holds no real power, but that's all things that happen in another country. We don't know *that* much about it.'

Yua supposed it made sense—she didn't know much about who held what powers in Krymistis either.

'What kind of things do they specialise in?' Aza asked.

Yua shrugged. 'All the most important Mist Woman duties, like history and politics. There's a healer, and…' A shiver ran down her spine. 'One of them specialises in the Mists, but she doesn't teach.'

Aza gave her a look. 'And she can get to those forbidden books?'

Yua had never dwelled on it, but now Aza mentioned it… 'I suppose she can, but as I said, they're the most powerful people in the world. None of them would be so stupid as to open a door into the Mists just to see what happens.'

Yua couldn't imagine why anyone would want to risk it. She had read enough history books to know it was a terrible idea that always ended in disaster.

'I hope you're right.' Aza nodded towards the closed doors. 'Forbidden disaster magic aside, you're really not allowed to study any of it?'

Yua shrugged again, but her heart felt heavy all the same. 'Why would I? I'll never serve at court somewhere.' She was fine with that too. They wouldn't have treated her any different somewhere else.

'But even so, you could learn basic self-defence skills. There isn't a child in Krymistis who doesn't know how to defend herself.'

Yua gave her a mocking smile. 'I don't know if you've looked around since you arrived, but Mist Women and self-defence? They'd get all sweaty. Most consider it beneath them. We don't even have a teacher for things like that.'

'But Kei said you have a sparring room or something like that. She told me I could use it.'

'And you're the first person who would really appreciate it.' She sighed. 'Even if we had a teacher, I wouldn't have been allowed to learn. They think me dangerous enough as it is.'

Aza looked her up and down. Yua blushed.

'I could teach you if you want.'

Yua's heart skipped a beat. 'I don't… I wouldn't know what to do.'

Aza smiled. 'That's why it's called teaching.'

Her heart warmed. Thirteen years in this coven, and this was the first time someone had offered to teach her something new. Now she had the chance, it felt like a strangely big decision. Like she was doing something forbidden.

'I'll think about it.'

'Take your time,' Aza said. 'It's sad that you're not allowed to study your gift. In Krymistis, we nurture skills, we don't suppress them.'

Yua frowned. 'It's not a skill. It's a—'

'A curse more than anything. You said. But how do you know? What if it's something wonderful?'

Yes, what if? Surrender to me and we'll be magnificent.

Yua's stomach twisted. She wouldn't entertain that thought.

'I could kill everyone,' she said. 'It's not worth the risk.'

Two novices' heads shot around to her, and they hurried off in the other direction.

Yua sighed. 'I should show you where Kei's office is.'

Aza stepped in front of her. 'Have you never thought about it?'

She had, but she was prisoner enough as it was. If she voiced just one of these thoughts aloud, Kei would never let her leave her room again.

'It doesn't matter. Let's—'

'It does matter,' Aza said. 'Control makes all the difference. You might get bruised and break something on the way, but those are necessary lessons. Do you think I did *this*'—she twirled her daggers between two fingers—'when I was five? I nearly lost a finger the first time. You can still see the scar. But now look at me.'

Yua glanced at Aza's hand. 'They didn't heal the cut?'

Aza shrugged. 'Sand Blades wear their scars like trophies.' She held up her hand and struck out her finger so Yua saw the barely visible white line starting at the joint bone and disappearing in Aza's palm. 'It hurt—a lot, actually—but I learned from it, and I did better next time. This is proof of how far I've come.'

Yua looked away. 'I'd do more than hurt someone. Even our Seven wouldn't be able to heal the wound I'd cause.'

'But what if—'

Yes! What if!

Yua couldn't stand it. 'It doesn't matter how you do things in Krymistis. This is Midoka. We don't feed our shadows.'

She stepped around Aza and walked ahead.

But the thought was there now, and she couldn't shake it.

Chapter Seven

When they returned from the library, Ichiro was waiting for them outside Yua's door. His eyes flicked from Yua to Aza and back again as they approached, like he was trying to figure out Aza or how they were getting along.

'Were you expecting visitors?' Aza asked as soon as they turned the corner from the stairs onto the corridor.

Yua shook her head. 'It's alright. He's…' Could she call him a friend? She wasn't entirely sure where they stood. She felt like it took more than one tea together, even if he'd had the best intentions out of anyone who'd talked to her here.

Aza raised her eyebrows but didn't comment on her hesitation.

'He works in the kitchen,' Yua said. 'He brought me tea before you arrived.'

Aza eyed him. 'I don't see any tea now.'

Yua swallowed. Did Aza think he was a threat? Her hands didn't hover near her daggers yet, so Yua didn't think Ichiro was in any immediate danger. Then again, how fast could a Sand Blade reach her weapons when they were on her hips?

Ichiro cleared his throat when they reached him. 'Aza?'

She and Yua nodded.

'Kei has asked me to prepare a room for you.' He held out a key. 'It's yours while you're staying here. I'm afraid it's nothing fancy but let us know if you're missing anything.'

Aza eyed the room and took the key. 'I'll have to thank her when I see her. I don't always get a room.'

'Where did you think you'd stay?' Yua asked. 'My room?'

Aza glanced at her and shrugged. 'Why not? It would make sense since I'm supposed to work closely with you.'

Yua frowned. 'Not that closely.'

She was glad Kei had assigned Aza her own room; although, she did agree with Aza. It would have made sense for Kei to always keep them together. She breathed an internal sigh of relief—Kei couldn't be worried about Yua's safety after all if she didn't insist on Aza sharing her room. Or maybe she counted on Aza reaching her fast enough if it came to that? Yua didn't want to dwell on it. She thanked O-Yu that Kei left her at least her chambers to herself and pushed further worries from her mind.

You don't need her protection. You have me.

She ignored that too.

Ichiro shuffled his feet and looked between them. 'I'll bring you tea tomorrow. I'll, er, be in the kitchen if you need anything.'

Yua nodded. 'Thank you.'

He gave Aza another glance but hurried down the corridor until he was out of sight.

'That was weird,' Aza said.

Yua raised an eyebrow. She agreed, but she was used to this life. If Aza, who had only just got here, thought it was strange, she'd be in for an experience. Although, it had been odd—like

Ichiro had sized up the new attendant while Aza had tried to figure him out. She wondered what they made of each other.

'How so?' Yua asked. She opened her door and entered with Aza right behind her.

Aza went to sit cross-legged on Yua's bed. 'Are you two…'

Yua blushed. 'No, he's just a…' She still didn't know what to call him. The way he'd sized up Aza felt like he was trying to look out for Yua, which was nice if unexpected, but she didn't know what it meant. Was this what friends did? She bit her lip, hating that she didn't know. 'Well, not a friend, but he's nice to me.'

'Does the kitchen staff often prepare rooms?'

Yua shrugged. 'It's possible Kei just ran into him at the right time and tasked him with it. We don't have servants in the traditional sense. No one tidies up after us. Mist Women are expected to clean up their own messes—not that many leave much of a mess.'

Aza scoffed. 'Not the ones I've seen in Krymistis. They behave like they own everything.'

'I wouldn't know,' Yua said. 'I've never left the coven.'

She didn't mean to sound so bitter. At this point, she worried that it was a reflex, like her hands flying up to protect her face when someone threw something at her. Which had only happened once, years ago. She didn't know what had happened to the novice.

Aza turned her head to look at her. 'You've really never been out?'

Yua shook her head. She'd been in the courtyard between the coven's buildings, but she hadn't been outside in any way that mattered.

Aza rolled onto her side. 'I can tell you about Krymistis some time if you'd like? I haven't exactly travelled the world, but I've been to more places than that.'

Yua swallowed. She hated that her eyes burned from the small kindness. 'Thank you.'

Aza rolled onto her back again and stretched her arms out behind her. 'Between you staying here and the novices tidying up after themselves, they teach so much responsibility and yet they won't teach you how to work with your gift?'

Yua shivered. She had the uncomfortable feeling that Aza wouldn't let it go until someone got hurt, and then where would that leave Yua? Things weren't great now, and all people had to go on were rumours. If she hurt somebody… The Seat of Seven were strict. They would punish her. Severely.

Yua had once read the saying 'an eye for an eye' in a book about Rifarnee history. She hadn't understood what it meant until now. She shuddered.

'No,' she said. 'That would be irresponsible.'

'But—'

'It's better this way. Please drop it?'

Aza sighed, but Yua doubted she'd give up so easily. 'Alright. Sorry. I didn't mean to make you uncomfortable.'

Yua snorted. It was more likely that she'd make Aza uncomfortable before the night was over. Was there a limit to how many attendants Kei would force on her? Maybe a Sand Blade was her final warning. She dreaded to think where Kei might go from there. Exile, if she was lucky.

Aza sat up and patted the duvet next to her. 'Sit with me? I still feel like I barely know you.'

Yua froze. Her heart dropped. In her mind, she saw a pretty picture of two friends sitting on one bed, talking and laughing for so long they had exhausted regrets in the morning. Aza fit that picture with her warm smile. Yua couldn't see herself in it.

Aza winked. 'Promise I won't bite unless you ask me to.'

Yua did as Aza asked. It felt… every bit as awkward as Ichiro had been only moments ago. No, worse. Much worse. Like Yua was visiting Aza for the first time, not the other way around. She caught herself looking around her room, noticing everything from a different angle for the first time, and reminded herself that this was still her space. Aza was the guest here.

Aza laughed. Yua flinched a little, but the sound wasn't malicious, just… surprised, and as warm as her smile.

'I've never seen anyone so uncomfortable just sitting down before. Sorry. You can sit or stand wherever you want.' Aza shrugged with one shoulder and an apologetic smile. 'Just thought this would be friendlier.'

Yua balled her hands into sweaty fists.

'No, it's alright. I just wasn't expecting it.'

She'd feel too pathetic admitting that no one had ever asked her to sit next to them before.

Aza lay back again. 'It's different for me too. Usually, I'm given a name to protect or kill and that's it. I don't usually get this close to the contract unless the client specified it.'

That didn't help her relax.

'What's it like, being a Sand Blade?'

She hadn't wanted to judge Aza on rumours alone—she knew how unfair it was—but Aza had just said herself that she killed people. How could Kei trust her with Yua's life?

I told you, she's here to kill you. Kill her before she makes her move.

Aza watched her as she spoke. 'Me and Desma did it together. They've trained us since we were children.'

Yua sat back a little. 'You've had a weapon since you were a child?' Aza had said something like that, but Yua had been too distracted by how easily Aza had twirled her dagger through her fingers to pick out that detail.

Aza drew her dagger and twirled it through her fingers again. 'Sure, but all Krymistian children do. They're just not usually sharpened until we're adults. The point is, you and I have both had weapons since we were little, right? I've had this dagger and you've had your g—*curse.*' Aza held up her free hand in apology.

Then, she threw the dagger at Yua.

She jumped back with a gasp, right against the bed frame. The blade landed on the duvet where Yua's ankle had been seconds before.

'What are you doing!'

'Pick it up,' Aza said.

'Why would I—'

'Just do it. I'm trying to show you something.'

Yua glared at Aza but picked up the dagger like the hilt alone could hurt her.

'Have you ever held a weapon before?' Aza asked.

Yua frowned. 'I think it's obvious that I haven't.'

'Would you say we're roughly the same age?'

'I'm eighteen.'

'Ah, so close,' Aza said. 'I'm twenty-one.'

Yua tried to hand the dagger back, but Aza didn't take it.

'You saw how I ran it between my fingers?' Aza asked. Yua nodded. 'Try doing that.'

Yua let out a nervous laugh. 'Absolutely not. I have no idea how you did that. I'd cut myself.'

Aza nodded like her point was made. 'We both have our own individual weapons. We're almost the same age, and we've had them for almost the same lengths of time. In your hands, this dagger is barely more than a paperweight. You could guess at where to cut someone to kill, but you'd also need some measure of luck unless you went for an obvious spot, like the throat.'

The weapon felt heavier than it was in her hand. Yua placed it next to Aza.

'All that proves,' Yua said, 'is that I can do more with your dagger than you can do with my curse.'

Aza nodded. 'That's one thing, I suppose, but it also proves that practice makes perfect.'

Yua's stomach twisted harder.

'Krymistians are naturally good with a blade,' Aza said, 'but Midokans are naturally good with magic. Think of what you could do today had you practiced every day since you got yours. You've seen my scar earlier. I told you how it happened. But you've also seen some of what I can do now, and I promise you, I can do so much more with this.' She picked up her dagger, gave it another twirl, and sheathed it. 'Just think what—'

Yua stood. 'You said you'd let it go.'

'And I will, I promise! I just want you to see yourself and your gift like I see you.' Aza stood. 'What do you see when you look at me?'

Yua stepped back. 'An annoying woman who won't take no for an answer.'

Aza grinned. 'Earlier, then. When you first saw me. When you first found out I'm a Sand Blade.'

Yua refused to play Aza's game. When she didn't reply, Aza came closer. Yua didn't move—she had backed away enough in her own room. If anyone left, it would be Aza.

'Did you think me a killer when you found out? Did I look confident to you? Dangerous?'

Yua nodded, if only to get to the point faster.

'And do you still think this of me now?'

She nodded again.

Aza sighed. 'Then I've given you the wrong impression. I can be dangerous, especially with these daggers though I don't need them to kill, but that's not all there is to me. I cut myself when I first held my sharpened dagger. Many Krymistians do, but we're still known as the best warriors in the world. We're not scared to make mistakes.'

'Mistakes?' Yua huffed. 'When I received this curse, I killed everyone I knew, including my parents. That's not a mistake, Aza.'

'Your gift is more dangerous, true, but—'

'Stop calling it a gift!'

Aza sighed and sat back down. 'Do you want to know what I see when I look at you?'

'No.'

'I see a lonely young woman who's too scared of herself to embrace who she really is.'

Yua was beginning to see why Kei had hired Aza, but it wouldn't work. This wasn't a matter of loving herself enough, it was a matter of not killing anyone else. The gap was too large.

Yua clenched her teeth. They felt too big for her mouth, and she hoped Ichiro would bring her something to eat with that tea he promised—she wanted to bite something, tear something apart and—

She sank her nails into her palms to steady herself.

You're no fun.

'What would you know of loneliness?' Yua hissed.

Aza's eyes darkened. 'Desma and I were as close as you can be. I want to believe that I'd know if… if something had happened, but maybe I don't. She's good at what she does. We both are.' Aza's eyes wandered far away. 'She wouldn't take this long unless something went wrong.'

Yua swallowed. 'I'm sorry. I didn't—'

'I named my dagger after her because I know she's alive and because I feel closer to her, if only for a moment, when I call it by her name. No one else means anything to me. Not like she did.'

So, Aza did understand loneliness, but it didn't change anything. Yua's curse was still just that, and she couldn't risk teasing it. Her darkness was too loud as it was, like a shadow that hung over her all the time.

'I'm sorry about your sister,' Yua said. 'But it's not the same thing.'

Aza's gaze was on a long-ago memory. 'Maybe you're right.' She blinked and looked at Yua. 'I won't mention it again. Dinner?'

'What?'

'It's late and we haven't eaten yet. I remember where the kitchen is. Want something to eat?'

Yua nodded. She was too mad to speak—too mad at herself for reminding Aza about her sister and too mad at Aza for being so persistent.

'I'll be right back,' Aza said and left the room.

But Yua knew better. She had crossed a line tonight, and like every other attendant before her, Aza wouldn't come back. A small part of her regretted it…

Because an equally small part of her—the one she was scared to admit to herself—wondered if Aza was right about practice and perfection.

Chapter Eight

Yua was lying on her bed when her door opened and Aza stumbled in with two trays of food, one in her hand and the other balancing on her forearm while Aza pushed open the door with her other hand. Everything looked one second from clattering to the floor, but Aza's hand flew back to the second tray before anything slipped.

'You came back.' Yua was too surprised to jump up and help.

Aza shoved the door shut with her foot. 'Of course I did. I said I'm hungry, didn't I? I don't promise food and then don't deliver, Yua, that's just rude.'

Aza placed the trays on the table. She had got two servings of the same things: steaming beans, carrots, and peas, meatloaf—a delicacy from Rifarne—hot gravy, and mashed as well as roasted potatoes. Aza had even included slices of chocolate cake. Yua had never seen so much food in her little room. Previous attendants had made sure she didn't starve, but they had rarely treated her to this much… and themselves even more rarely. Most of them had eaten in their own time, away from her. It felt like a feast, and she didn't deserve it.

Yua took a deep breath in to steady her hammering heart. She sat opposite Aza, who hadn't started without her.

'I'm sorry,' Yua said. 'I appreciate all this, I really do.' She swallowed. 'I appreciate that you came back.'

'I'm sorry too,' Aza said. 'I'm sorry that you've come to expect less, and I'm sorry I pushed you. It's your power, so this is your decision. I still think it's a shame to not explore it, but it's your choice. I swear I'll let it go now.'

Yua nodded and chewed on her vegetables.

'This is a lot of food.' She felt hungry enough to eat it all, but she feared her body would refuse before she emptied half of her plate.

Aza drowned her potatoes in gravy. 'It's our first dinner together, *and* my first dinner in Maishi Hou. That deserves a celebratory meal, wouldn't you say?'

Yua nodded and silently chastised herself for her smile. Sure, they were celebrating right now, but how long would it last? *Could* it last, or was she getting her hopes up only to have them destroyed one week later? She did wonder if Aza was right. Yua had killed so many as a child, but she *had* been a child. She was terrified of the vast amount of power in her veins, but what if…

'I've been thinking,' Yua said before she lost her nerve. The thought alone felt like treason. 'There's a darkness inside me, and I'm scared of what it'll do if I let it out or as much as promise it freedom. But…' Her fists scrunched her trousers. 'What if there's potential for something good? It's just a power, right? Like magic? That's not evil. People can use it for evil, but I wouldn't, at least not intentionally. I'm not a bad person, Aza. I'm not—'

Aza shuffled around the table and took Yua's fists into her warm hands.

'Hey, it's alright. Breathe.'

Yua complied. She hadn't realised how much she was shaking until she felt Aza's steady palms on her clenched knuckles.

'I don't want to be scared.' Her eyes burnt. 'But if it goes wrong, it goes *wrong*. Do you understand?'

Aza nodded. 'We don't have to start with anything big, just some theory.'

'There isn't any. I'm the only one with this power, remember?'

Aza grinned. 'Leave it to me—I'm good at finding things that don't want to be found; although, I admit, people leave an easier trail to follow, but someone must have seen something that night.'

It hadn't occurred to Yua. All she remembered was the bodies and the overwhelmingly strong smell of blood on her skin, in her hair, on her clothes. She didn't remember what had surrounded them. She wasn't even sure if it had happened inside or outside. Had she seen a sky that night, or a ceiling? The blood had been everywhere—that was all she knew for certain.

'Even if someone did,' Yua said, 'we can't leave this coven to ask around. And even if we could, no one would talk about it.'

Aza winked. 'I have my ways.'

Yua frowned. 'No torture.' Or whatever it was Sand Blades did to get answers.

'Tor- Yua! I'd never—' Aza stared at her meatloaf in thought. 'I just meant some threats, but torture would—'

'No.'

Aza chuckled, and Yua let out a nervous giggle. She thought Aza was joking, but Sand Blades didn't kill their targets with kindness. It was hard to imagine Aza as a cold killer.

'I appreciate it,' Yua said, 'more than you can imagine, but it's pointless. It's too long ago, and people are too scared. We'll have to—'

She stopped herself before she could say something she might regret. They were rushing into dangerous territory, and she was afraid she wouldn't be able to stop if she fell into a run.

Aza raised her eyebrows. 'Yes? Go on.'

'We'll just…' Her heart beat so fast she feared it would rip out of her chest and land on Aza's plate. 'We'll have to cope on our own.'

Aza grinned. 'That's the spirit.'

Very deep down, Yua was at least half as excited as Aza. Part of that was genuine curiosity at what she might do with just a little control. Aza had started something in her, and Yua couldn't ignore it now she had allowed herself to feel it. Another part of her feared the death and suffering she would cause if it went wrong.

And yet another, much darker part of her had the same thought and grinned.

Chapter Nine

Lying on her bed with her eyes closed, Yua felt the shadow inside her veins. Right there, just beneath the fine layers of her skin. It sang to her. Made promises of power. *Was* power. But what kind, exactly, she didn't know, only that it was different and wrong and even Kei feared it. Kei hadn't said it out loud, but Yua knew her well enough. Kei was fearless, but she had that look in her eyes whenever Yua had brought it up, so she'd stopped.

The more she focussed on it, the louder it whispered without words. It used feelings, her own heartbeats, and memories. All those people, bodies broken. The smell of blood so heavy in the air, suffocating and intoxicating and metal and sweet. Wet warmth on her hands. That same delicious smell, not far away from her…

She's in the room right next to you. No one will know. She'll never see us coming.

Yua gasped and launched herself to her feet. She opened her window and stuck her head out, hoping to O-Yu that the crisp autumn air would clear her mind.

A kind of drum pounded in her ears, growing more persistent the more she listened. Something was rushing beneath it, but she couldn't figure out what. The coven was near a river—*everything* in Midoka was near a river—but they weren't that close that she could hear it from her window, and that pounding... Her eyes flicked towards her door. She pictured Aza behind it.

Follow the sound. Let it lead you.

Yua wanted to make sure Aza was all right—walk into her room, reach out to touch her, feel her pulse—but she wouldn't risk getting any closer.

She won't suffer. I can make it quick if you let me.

Her legs were heavy, her head light. She shook her head—why wouldn't Aza be alright? Where had that thought come from?—and the movement blurred her room. She wanted to move towards Aza's door, just one step to pacify her shadow's urging, but she knew she wouldn't be able to stop. The drums and rushing became deafening; she could barely hear herself think. But what—

Follow the melody her blood sings. Follow the rhythm of her heartbeat. Remember the taste.

Saliva pooled in her mouth when the memory of hot copper forced its way onto her tongue. She swallowed, but it wasn't enough. She needed more than a memory.

Yua gripped the windowsill until her nail beds rubbed against the wood. She forced herself to focus on the discomfort, scraped her fingers along to rub them raw if necessary. The darkness was loud, and if she took Aza up on her offer, it would only grow louder.

I can be patient, it whispered. *How long can you take this?*

Kei was right—whatever was inside her, it was evil. Yua could barely stop it from tempting her while it still slept beneath her skin; she'd never control it if she let it out. And yet...

What if Aza was right too? What if all she needed was practice? The Seven would never allow it. They'd watch her even more closely if they knew what she and Aza had discussed, and no one wanted the attention of the Seven on them.

But maybe they didn't need to know.

Yua stared at the stars and took slow, even breaths.

Maybe she didn't have to unleash all her darkness in one go. Maybe she could let it out small piece by small piece. This was her body, and this was her mind—surely, she had some control? She had kept this curse locked away for thirteen years, once the Mist Women had taught her how. If even a child could do it...

She opened her window all the way and climbed onto the roof. It was the second highest point in the entire coven after the library tower. She'd hidden here countless times before when the other novices had whispered behind her back.

You can't hide from my *whispers.*

Maishi Hou was a large city, and all of it was visible from up here. The coven was high above near the mountain's peak, so Yua didn't make out any details, just lights far below. During bad weather, dark nights, or fog, the city seemed to disappear completely, and only the encroaching forests were visible. Yua felt more sheltered as well as more cut-off from the world on those days. During clear weather, though, the surrounding countryside and the Asai Nera—the archipelago between Midoka and Krymistis—spread out in the distance, lit by the soothing light of the moon and her stars. Another sea she'd never cross or even knew the name of spread East of Maishi Hou. On the other end of the city rose the royal palace—set high enough into the mountain to watch over the empress's people, but not as high as the coven.

Tonight, grey clouds hung in the air, and a cold breeze tousled her hair. Rain was coming. She wouldn't see any of what lay in the valley when it arrived.

Two *sei*—night wisps—danced nearby. Newai washed his paws near the centre of the roof; his soft purring filled the night with comfort and soothed her internal pain. As loud as her darkness could be around people, it was quiet around Newai, and she loved him even more for it. This was peace, and it was all hers.

Yua pushed up her sleeve and looked at her black veins snaking up her arm and over her shoulder. Under the gentle moonlight, they didn't look so menacing. Aza saw beauty in them, but for Yua, they were just another sign that she was different. The only Midokan without the gift. The only Midokan who failed at being Midokan. Because no matter how much Aza insisted otherwise, she didn't have the gift. That was beauty and creation. This was darkness and death. Yua had seen it herself and remembered nothing before that night. Like she hadn't existed before it.

She held her hand up to the stars and splayed her fingers. 'What are you?' The lines were faintest around her hands, like they grew out of her finger bones into her wrists and spread from there, but they were there. When she didn't see them, she felt them, aching to hurt someone. So, she kept her nails short to limit the danger. She felt its invisible pull even now. It scared her that she sensed it even when she focussed on other things.

'Yua?'

She jumped with a gasp. Aza climbed onto the roof beside

her. Newai glared at the intrusion but didn't budge.

'Why are you up?' Yua asked, heart pounding from the sudden interruption.

'I heard something from your room and came to check on you.'

Yua frowned. 'You couldn't have heard me from your room. I wasn't that noisy, and you were sleeping.'

Aza shrugged. 'Sand Blades sleep with one eye open. And yes, you were. I don't know what you dreamed, but it must have been bad.'

Yua blushed. She didn't remember what she'd dreamed, but she was grateful for that.

Yua let her eyes fall to the roof tiles. 'You don't need to check in on me when I have a nightmare.'

'It's fine. I'd have come in sooner, but I thought maybe you needed a moment.' Aza turned away from her and took in the surrounding view. 'Wow. Good thing I'm not scared of heights.'

Yua turned back to the stars. 'That's why I come up here. No one knows where I am.'

'I don't mean to invade your private haven. I can leave.'

'No. It's fine.'

Yua leaned back and watched the stars. She didn't jump when Aza traced the veins, her fingers almost hot in the cold air.

'I've never seen anything like it,' Aza said. 'Krymistian warriors sometimes get tattoos, but they have to be done by other people. They don't just appear.'

Yua smiled, but it felt more like a grimace. 'I told you I'm special.' She could be herself with Aza. Whatever happened tomorrow, she could enjoy this right now. Nights and moonlight were made for magic.

'What are you scared of?'

Yua was tempted to deflect the question, but she wanted to tell someone. Maybe Aza would understand. Maybe, somehow, Aza would have answers.

'How did you feel after your first kill?'

Aza sighed and lay back beside her. 'Embarrassed. I thought I could have done better. The job was to kill this merchant without being seen and hiding the body so no one would find it until it started to smell, but I was only eleven. I killed him without anyone seeing me, but when I dragged him away, I left this long, bloody smear all over the ground. By the time I got back to my boss, he'd already heard the news. He told me I did well, but I knew the other Sand Blades would have done it better.'

Yua stared at her. This wasn't what she'd hoped to hear.

'Later that day, as it got dark, it sunk in. I'd killed someone. On my way home I saw this child, a few years younger than me, crying for his parents. I don't think it was related, but I kept thinking, what if I killed that child's father? I was too young to realise it, but his tears were an accusation. I don't know who that merchant was, but he probably had a family too.'

'How did you…' Yua wanted to ask how Aza had coped, but that made it sound too insignificant. She wanted to ask how Aza had got used to it, but that felt even worse.

'I vowed to do better, but that night was hard. The child's crying haunted me. I didn't sleep. I jumped at every sound, convinced relatives of the merchant had seen me and followed me home. That was the worst night of my life, but the sun rose again all the same. The next day my boss told me that, no matter how dark it gets, there's always a light, even if that light is just that I'm still alive. I still don't know what the merchant did, but Sand Blades aren't common assassins. We only go after those who are a danger to our country, terrorists, that sort of thing. Whatever he did, it wasn't anything small.' She looked at Yua. 'Your turn.'

Yua swallowed.

'I'm scared I won't find the light again if I give myself to the darkness.' Her eyes burnt. She'd never said the words out loud before, but Aza had been honest with her. It felt good to admit it. 'It doesn't matter who's right, whether it's you or Kei or someone else. There's something bad inside me.'

She hated that she almost choked on her words. Saying all these things out loud—finally, after too many years—made her throat tighten and her eyes sting.

Aza traced the veins all the way to Yua's shoulder. 'Bad things are only bad because people use them in bad ways. Swords are used to kill, but they can kill dictators or save innocent lives. It's the wielder that matters.'

Then again, maybe Aza didn't understand.

'It's not as simple as that. You haven't felt it.'

'Tell me. How does it feel?'

Yua squeezed her eyes shut. They were nearing dangerous territory again.

'Hungry.'

'For what?'

Yua hadn't thought about it. She hadn't thought it mattered.

'I'm not sure. Power. Death.'

Blood, sweet like velvet.

'Isn't the gift the same?' Aza asked. 'That's hungry too. It wants to create, to heal, to save—whatever people choose to do with it.'

There was some truth to that. Mist Women used their gift for the common good, but sometimes a Mist Woman broke her vows and hurt people. There'd been an issue with one in Rifarne some years ago, and a lot of people had died. But this—what Yua had—was more complicated. The power inside her scared her. She wanted to try, but she didn't know if that was her decision or the darkness shaping her thoughts. Her power didn't want to create or heal or save. It wanted to kill. Yua feared she couldn't stop it, only delay the inevitable.

'I don't think it's all the same, but...' She bit her lip. 'There are similarities.'

Aza nodded as if in thought. For a moment, they sat together in silence, and Yua was grateful that Aza didn't push her for answers.

'You know,' Aza said, 'this really is a lovely spot. Does Ichiro know about it?'

Yua raised an eyebrow. 'No. He doesn't have the time to sit out here with me. His work keeps him too busy.'

'What, serving tea?'

'He also helps out in the kitchen.'

'And he prepares rooms for Sand Blades, don't forget.' Aza smiled at the moon. 'You'll laugh, but I thought you two had something special.'

Warmth filled her heart. She was grateful for the ease with which Aza had changed the subject.

'We do,' Yua said.

'Yes, but I meant something *special*, as in kissing and bed sharing.'

Yua blushed. Since the novices didn't talk to her, she hadn't even considered that.

'He's more like a little brother.' And she wasn't sure they were that close yet. 'Although…' Yua sighed and allowed herself a moment to enjoy this moment… this moment which felt as close to normality as any she'd known. 'There was this girl who joined the coven a few years ago. She's older than most new novices. I thought she was the most beautiful girl I'd ever seen, but she fell in with everyone else.'

'Say no more.'

They smiled at each other. Talking to Aza was easier than she'd expected or known with anyone else. She enjoyed this strange new familiarity while it lasted, but she also worried about what she'd tell Aza. She thought all Aza needed to do was ask and Yua would bare her soul to her without meaning to. She'd only been here a day, and already Yua had told her more than anyone else.

'I'm going to bed,' Aza said. 'Don't stay too long, alright?'

'I'll be right behind you. Just one more minute.'

Yua watched Aza climb back into her room and leaned back. If she sat in just the right spot, all she saw were stars and the pale colours of distant suns. The coven, Maishi Hou, other people—they didn't exist. It was just her and the universe. Somewhere, there had to be answers. Perhaps it was foolish, but…

She wanted to find them.

Chapter Ten

Yua was scared to fall asleep after her talk with Aza. Every time she closed her eyes, she sensed the darkness in her like glowing eyes watching from the shadows. It didn't reach out; it waited for her to make the first move, and that scared her more than the thing existing in the first place.

Every theory book she had read talked about the gift like it was a sentient force inside every person, waiting, *wanting*, to be used. Perhaps Aza was right and the power inside her wasn't so different. Maybe it really was just another aspect of the same.

The following day was harder. Kei had called Aza for a brief meeting—Yua assumed to make sure Aza wasn't ready to run back to Krymistis yet—and so Yua had some time alone. She leaned against her window and gazed outside, hoping her thoughts would wander anywhere else. Thinking was the last thing she wanted to do—because, if she was honest, she wanted to try to control this shadow part of herself. It was inside her mind, inside her blood, inside her soul, and she hated that it controlled her more than she controlled it.

Yua jumped when someone knocked at her door. She felt like she'd been caught doing something forbidden. How much more on edge would she be once she and Aza started?

She sat at her table and did her best to look calm. *Deep breaths.* She folded her hands and rested them on her legs like the well-behaved young woman she was supposed to be.

'Come in.'

Ichiro stepped into her room with a tray of tea and biscuits. 'Is this a bad time? Kei asked me to give you and Aza some space, but I just saw her knock on Kei's door. I thought I'd take my chances.' He set the tray onto the table. 'Are you alright?'

'I'm fine. I just—' She wanted to confide in Ichiro, wanted to believe that he was safe to talk to, but this wasn't a small secret. If he kept it and Yua killed someone, he'd lose his job or worse. She didn't want to cause any more pain than she was already bound to. 'I've got a lot to think about.'

He poured her a tea and nudged the biscuits towards her. 'About Aza? How is she?'

Yua shook her head. 'Aza is nice. You were right, she's not scared of me. At least I don't think she is.'

Ichiro smiled. 'I'm happy for you. Maybe she'll stick around.'

'Let's not get carried away just yet.'

But Yua wanted Aza to stay, too, even if she invaded her safe space on the rooftop. She picked up the cup and inhaled peppermint.

'So, what's wrong? You look worried.'

She sighed. 'It's complicated.'

'I work at the head coven in Maishi Hou. Try me.'

Yua hesitated. Maybe she could talk to him about their plan... *if* she phrased it carefully.

'There's something I want to do,' she said slowly, careful not to give any details away. 'But I don't know if it's the right thing.'

Ichiro poured himself a cup, dunked a biscuit, and took a sip. 'Could people get hurt in this thing?'

She began to nod but stopped herself midway. 'It's possible.'

He chewed on his biscuit while he thought. Yua brought her lips to the cup's rim and breathed in the subtle scent.

'This is personal, isn't it?' he asked.

Yua glanced towards the black veins on her arm. They were covered by her shirt, but she felt them all the same like they themselves were alive.

She nodded.

He finished his tea and set his cup down. 'My father died when I was four. An illness the doctors had no name for slowly destroyed his body over the years. Later, he lost his mind to it too. He was still young when he died, but he looked much older. He was broken and fragile. I barely recognised him when I said goodbye.

'In one of the few lucid moments he had, he told me he hated that he had this thing inside him that he couldn't rip out. The illness ate away at him until it killed him, and he loathed himself for not being able to do anything.'

'Ichiro—'

'I think I know what this is about—no offence, but I can't imagine you're up to much in here. Your limited options narrow it down. I don't know much about the magic they teach at this coven, but I think I know you, or at least I'm starting to. Mum always said I'm a good judge of character. You're a good person, and I know you won't hurt anyone. If this thing is hurting you, you have a right to protect yourself.'

She swallowed, but her tea tasted too thick. She put her cup down and watched the ripples fade across the surface.

'But what if my protecting myself gets other people injured?' She thought of that night thirteen years ago. Had she protected herself then too? 'I've hurt enough people already.'

And she refused to become the monster everyone already thought she was.

'Let me put it this way,' Ichiro said. 'My father had no choice. All he could do was wait and go when O-Yu opened the door for him. But you might be able to do something. Kei and the others are scared, but they are Mist Women, not regular sorceresses. If anyone can help and step in if something goes wrong, it's them.'

'I don't want them to know.' The very idea of the Seven knowing made her stomach cramp.

'I promise I won't say a word.' He nodded at her mostly untouched cup. 'Are you going to drink your tea?'

She inhaled its scent again, and the peppermint dispersed her fear. 'Leave it, please. I'll drink it in a moment.'

He nodded and stood.

'Thank you. You really won't say anything?' She thought she could trust him, but she needed to hear it.

'You're my only friend in this place. I'm insulted you have to ask.' But he smiled, and so did she.

Aza returned just as he left.

She sat next to Yua and chuckled. 'Kei is worried that you've scared me too much to stay.'

Yua looked into her eyes. 'Have I?'

Aza snorted. 'You'll have to try harder—*much* harder.'

'You just might get your wish.'

This power, whatever it was, was a part of her. She felt like she was breaking every law just by considering it, but she refused to hide from herself any longer.

'Tonight. I'll ask Kei for help, too.'

Kei feared the gift, but she was Midoka's head Mist Woman. If anyone could at least attempt to tackle this, it was her. Yua prayed to O-Yu that it was a step in the right direction, not towards destruction.

Chapter Eleven

Yua's heart hammered in her chest as she sat in front of Kei's door. She was in a meeting; all Yua could do was wait.

You don't need to wait for anything. Don't you see you can simply take?

Every moment she was alone, the darkness sang louder. She should have asked Aza to come with her, but she'd wanted to do this on her own. She'd never outright asked Kei for anything before, much less her help. If she couldn't do this, she had no hope of controlling the shadow in her veins.

Only, since she had talked to Ichiro and told Aza that she was willing to try, her darkness had grown louder. She couldn't shake the feeling that she had woken a monster that had merely mumbled in its sleep before.

Let me show you what we can do when we're both fully awake... or go to sleep. Surrender. I will have you either way.

Yua swallowed her worries and stood. If she wanted to live without fear of herself, she needed to learn some way to fight the whispers. Pitying herself wouldn't do it. Wishing it away wasn't an answer.

Opposite the three chairs outside Kei's office, framed and behind glass, hung the gift's origin story. Yua had loved it when she was a child, but she hadn't read it in a long time. Her thoughts had wandered there on occasion though. In the story, dragons were the only creatures with magic for a long time. The greedy dragons started a war, and eventually, both sides fell. Where their blood touched the ground, their magic seeped into the world and first infused Midoka with the gift. All things considered, Yua was surprised that Midoka didn't still worship the creatures. Then again, maybe people outside the coven did just that. For all she knew, people came together in the streets every Monday to bow to their long-dead scaly overlords and ask for a prosperous week. Or maybe no one bothered anymore. That seemed more likely to her.

You should be free like those dragons of old.

Yua shook her head and pinched her eyes shut.

You're stronger than any of them.

She was a danger and nothing more. Kei needed to help her learn control, not—

Control is boring. I can teach you to fly.

What happened after the dragons disappeared again? She couldn't think.

They should bow to you. You should be their god, not this O-Yu no one remembers.

The dragons did disappear, didn't they? No one had seen one in centuries, but—

She couldn't think. Shecouldntthinkshecouldntthinkshe—

'Yua?'

She gasped and spun around to face Yoko, one of the Seven. Yua paled—the other six stood behind Yoko.

'Are you alright?' Willow, the Seven who ran the infirmary, asked.

Yua blushed and folded her hands in front of her to hide how much she was shaking.

'I'm fine, Honourable Seven.' She bowed slightly and hoped this was the right way to address them. 'I was hoping to speak with Ohira Kei.'

Willow smiled. 'We apologise for taking up so much of her time. She's free now. You can go in.'

Yua watched as all seven advisers—led by Yoko, Kei's planned successor—left the office. They hid it better than the novices, but Yua could still tell how they felt about her. There was less fear and more curiosity in their stares; she couldn't decide if that was worse. At least none of the Seven glared hatred or terror at her.

'I'm sorry to keep you waiting. If I'd known you were here…' Kei stood aside and waved Yua into her office. 'Is everything alright? Where is Aza?'

'She's in my room drinking tea.' It stung that Kei asked about Aza at all. Yua wasn't here because of her, but she supposed it was a good sign that Kei had asked about her well-being first. 'Don't worry, she's still here.'

'I only wondered because I asked her to stay with you at all times. I didn't expect to see you alone.' Kei gestured to the sofa to the left of her desk. A large painting of a proud dragon hung above it.

Yua sat and reminded herself to breathe when Kei joined her. In a way, she would have preferred a regular meeting to this informality.

'You look troubled.'

Yua nodded. Now she was here, she wished she'd planned a speech.

'I need your help.' She dried her hands on her trousers and exposed her arms. 'I worry what these are.'

'We've always worried,' Kei said. 'What has changed to bring you to my office now?'

Yua couldn't tell her. It was too risky.

'I... I'm eighteen. I can't stay locked up here forever. At the very least, I deserve to know why this happened to me.'

Kei stood to pour two cups of tea from a pot on her desk. She handed Yua a cup.

'This will help.'

Yua let the smell of green tea wash over her, but it didn't calm her.

'Why do you ask now?' Kei asked.

Yua inhaled the fumes again to steel her nerves.

'I can hear it. Every time I close my eyes, the darkness looks back at me.' She shivered when she remembered its taunts outside Kei's office. 'It's getting stronger. I'm afraid of what it will make me do if I can't control it.'

Yua didn't try to hide the waver in her voice. The more Kei saw of her fear, the better.

Kei took a sip of her tea and breathed deep, just like Yua had done. She was nervous too.

'Are you sure you're ready for this talk? It won't be an easy one.'

Yua gripped her cup in both hands to stop her hands from shaking, but inside, she felt oddly numb. She nodded.

'Your power is Mist magic. We've always known. That's why I taught you to suppress it.'

Kei might as well have punched her in the gut.

Yua's voice shook when she spoke. 'If you knew, why the specialists? What was the point?'

'I hoped we were wrong. When no one found an explanation, we decided it was best to keep it a secret.'

'But why?' She felt nauseous. 'You knew. You *knew*, and you didn't tell me.'

'I'm sorry, *chiba*. We did it to protect you. If people had learned too much about the origins of your power, they would have tried to kidnap and study you. Krymistis would have wanted to make you into a weapon. Our own empress might have tried the same. When you were seven, Tramura sent an ambassador.'

Yua's blood froze. Tramura wasn't known for its patience with magic.

'What did they want?'

'He told us to kill you or let them do it.'

She shivered.

Kei reached out and held her hand. 'I wanted to tell you, always. You deserved to know more than anyone. But I was afraid you would try to wake it if I didn't teach you to suppress it.'

Yua frowned. 'Well, I've tried that, and it's waking up anyway.'

Kei smiled. It looked sad. 'I had to try. I had no idea what would happen. The gift grows with the user over time; we hoped that, if we suppressed it, your Mist magic wouldn't develop. It seems I was wrong.'

Like most Mist Women, Kei used her gift to appear younger than her years. For the first time since Yua had known her, Kei looked every one of her ninety. Yua hated that she was to blame.

'You couldn't know,' Yua said. 'As you said, it could have gone either way. We don't know enough about Mist magic.'

She shivered again, and this time, she hugged herself. If it truly was Mist magic in her veins, then her power was a demon. She really was a monster.

'I tried to raise you well,' Kei said. 'I'm glad to see that, despite everything, you are kind.'

'You still should have told me.'

Kei nodded. 'I know. I admit that I hoped to study your magic myself at one point. What you have is unique. It's my duty as leading Mist Woman to understand all kinds of magic.' She placed her teacup on the floor and held Yua's hand with both of hers. 'None of this has changed my love for you, *chiha*. Please believe me.'

She wanted to, but it wasn't as simple as wishes. How often had Yua lain awake at night, wondering? How often had she asked Kei for answers?

How many times had Kei looked right into her eyes and lied?

'It's been whispering louder lately. I feel like I'm losing my mind. I always thought people were just cruel when they called me a monster, but there's an actual demon living inside me.' A nervous giggle escaped her. 'They were right. And you knew.'

'I'm sorry. I should—'

'It's too late for that now. Your specialists didn't understand a thing about me, but I will. I want access to the archives.'

Her goal had been to ask Kei to teach her, but Kei didn't know much more than Yua did. She'd be better off looking for answers herself.

'I don't think that's a good idea.' Kei sounded broken, but Yua wouldn't let that deter her. Not now, and never again.

'So, you won't help me?'

'It's not that simple. You don't know what you might wake.'

'It's too late for what you want—it's waking up whether you like it or not. I won't let it use me.'

Kei nodded, but it lacked energy. 'I can't change your mind?'

'No.'

Kei sighed and dipped her chin. 'Let me think. Please? We're dealing with dangerous magic here. I can't rush into it and possibly endanger our novices or even the whole country.'

Yua nodded. 'Thank you.'

She didn't expect Kei would really do anything, but it was a start.

We could do more than she ever could, if only you'd let me.

The sooner she found a way to silence her demonic shadow, the better.

Yua almost ran back to her room, but she made herself take deliberate steps. She reminded herself to breathe. That everything would be fine, she'd done what she could for now. It was Kei's turn now.

She appreciated that Kei was willing to try, but there was nothing that said the Seven couldn't overrule her if they didn't agree. Kei trying was no guarantee she'd get access to the archives. If she got access, that was no guarantee she'd find answers. And none of this guaranteed that her darkness wouldn't fully wake up five minutes from now and go on a bloody rampage through the coven. Yua had done what little she could, and she trusted Kei enough to know she'd keep her word. But she didn't trust her shadow. There had to be more she could do; she just didn't know what.

A few novices gave her curious or worried glances as Yua rushed across the coven. She tried not to let it get to her—she had a lot of practice—but they had no idea how valid their fears were. Yua didn't hear its whispers right now, but what would stop it from starting at any moment? She wanted—needed— guarantees that no one could give her.

She'd hoped for some relief when they reached her room, but the moment she closed her door and sat on her bed, she was back on her feet. She walked to her window, leaned against the sill, pushed herself off and walked to the opposite wall. Aza watched her from the table, though Yua barely noticed her. Would Aza know what to do if Yua lost all control over her curse? She was so insistent that Yua try, but she had no idea just how wrong this could go. Yua had told her how bad the consequences might be, but Aza still insisted; therefore, Yua doubted she really understood. Or maybe she did but was willing to risk it anyway because the consequences would be Yua's. The murders would be on Yua's conscience. The sentence would be her punishment. None of this would affect Aza.

Yua walked back to her window and looked outside. Was there anywhere in the world where she wouldn't need to worry about controlling herself or hurting people?

Something touched her arm. Yua shot around.

Aza held up her hands. 'I'm sorry. I tried talking, but I don't think you heard me. How did it go?'

'I don't know,' Yua said. 'Kei said she'll try to get me into the archives, but that could take days, probably weeks or longer, and what if that's not enough? What if I lose control in the meantime? You can't stop me, Aza. I don't think anyone can.'

Aza gently took her hand. 'It's alright. Deep breaths, *asta*.'

Yua looked into Aza's golden eyes and tried to focus.

You're alone. If you kill her now—

'No!'

Aza frowned. 'We can try something else if breathing is too hard right now. How many green things do you see?'

'What?'

Aza took Yua's hand, curled her fingers around it, and placed it on her chest. She slowed her breathing—Yua felt it through the fabric of her shirt. 'Breathe with me. How many green things, Yua?'

She focussed on the feel of Aza's rising and falling chest on her wrist as she looked around the room. Her sheets were green. Accents on her table.

'Count out loud.'

'Green sheets. Green accents.'

'Where are the green accents?'

Yua frowned. 'Everywhere. We're in Midoka.'

Aza smiled. 'Good. You sound better, and you're breathing with me. How do you feel?'

Yua swallowed. She did feel better, though she wasn't sure how Aza had managed it. She hadn't even realised how panicked she'd become until Aza touched her wrist and told her to breathe.

'Better. Thank you.' She looked away from the green forest outside her window and into Aza's eyes. They were green too. Usually, their golden specks shone brighter, but Yua chose to focus on their emerald notes for this. 'What did you do?'

Aza shrugged. 'It's an easy technique to calm down panicking new recruits. I wasn't sure if it would work, but I thought it worth a try.'

Yua glanced back at the forest. It'd take her an eternity to count every tree.

'Are there many green things in Krymistis?'

Aza grinned. 'Probably more than you think, but you can use anything—it doesn't have to be green things. You can count circles if you want. Can take a while if you count every grain of sand.'

A nervous laugh hiccuped out of her. 'Thank you.'

Aza nodded. 'I'm glad I could help. Sit and tell me what happened?'

Yua let her guide her to her bed and sat. Aza sat next to her.

'I asked Kei for access to the archives, and she said she'll need to talk to the Seven. There's always more for her to consider, it's never just me.' She hadn't meant to say that much. Yua continued before Aza could comment or pity her. 'She also said… My curse is Mist magic.'

She froze when she remembered how Aza had reacted to the library holding some books on the Mists, to one of the Seven specialising in them. Would this be the thing that drove her away?

But Aza only blinked at her. 'I didn't even know that was possible. No one outside the Mists has ever used Mist magic, at least I don't think so.'

Yua stared into a crumpled corner of her bedsheets. 'This doesn't change who I am. I'm still the same person.'

Aza put one hand on her shoulder. 'I know. But do you believe it?'

Yua gulped. She'd meant it when she said it to Aza, but with herself… It wasn't that simple. Aza didn't hear the shadow whisper to her. She didn't know what Yua was really like.

'They've been saying for years that I'm a monster. I just never thought they were right.'

'They're not.'

Aza sounded so sure. Yua wished she had some of her confidence.

'Do you still want to learn some basics of self-defence?'

Yua blinked. 'Yes, but—'

'Great.' Aza stood. 'Come with me.'

Unsure where they were going but ready to be somewhere else, Yua followed Aza outside her room and down the corridor to the stairs.

'Where are we going?' she asked when they left the building.

Aza turned around and blinked. 'You'll see.'

She stopped when Aza reached the gate.

'I can't leave.'

'Why not?'

'Because…' She was told that she wasn't allowed to leave the coven many years ago. She'd often wanted to, but she'd always thought magic would tear her apart if she tried. 'I'm not allowed to leave. I'm supposed to stay here.'

Aza raised her eyebrows. 'That's not the same as being unable to leave.'

Yua shook her head. 'If Kei finds out—'

'I'm with you. Kei hired me to keep an eye on you, and that's what I'm doing. There's more to looking after someone than physically guarding them. Sometimes you need a day out.'

Yua doubted that's what Kei had meant.

'If you're worried about one of the novices telling on you, look around.'

Yua did. There was no one outside, and it was cloudy. The novices had to be in lessons or otherwise occupied.

'I can't… What if…' Every reason sounded hollow in her head. She had wanted to leave the coven. Aza offered her that, and she wasn't suggesting she run away.

'Just for a few hours?'

Aza smiled. 'Just for a few hours.'

Yua nodded. Carefully, she followed Aza outside the fence. When nothing happened, she took another step. Then another. Not even a mild tug at her limbs.

'I can't believe I could leave all these years.'

'I can.' Aza winked. 'You didn't have a Sand Blade to give you a push. Come on.'

Yua walked ahead of Aza into the forest. The drop was steep, but if she didn't rush into the thicket and watched her feet, she couldn't fall down the mountain. Even if she tripped and lost her footing, there were enough trees in the way that she wouldn't fall far.

'I scouted the area on my first night here,' Aza said. 'There's a small clearing not far from here, but the forest is so thick that you can't see the coven.'

Yua couldn't wait to see it.

'Lead the way.'

For a few moments, she stumbled through the moss and branches after Aza, who moved just as elegantly as she moved everywhere else. Sand Blades had a balance not dissimilar to Mist Women and yet different. Mist Women moved like they secretly owned everything and had every right to be wherever they went. Aza moved with a confidence that spoke volumes about how well she knew her body and its capabilities. Yua, on the other hand, felt like an injured rabbit limping back to its burrow.

'Here we are!'

Aza walked ahead of them. Yua stopped in the centre. Calling it a clearing would have been an exaggeration. She wasn't surprised she hadn't seen it from the roof—more light fell through the branches, but the trees were still thick around them. Still, the ground was relatively even besides a few branches and its natural slope. Yua opened her arms and closed her arms. She didn't remember the last time she'd felt so free.

'Maybe we should wait with teaching you the basics. You look happy to just be.'

Yua responded with blissful silence. A breeze danced through her hair and played with her clothes. Everything smelled earthy and fresh.

'No, I want to learn.' She went to her knees and let herself fall back onto the grass.

Aza laughed. 'Not sure that's the best position for that, but I can give you some trade secrets.' She lay down next to Yua. 'Knuckle to the temple will bring tears to an attacker's eyes, possibly take them out if you hit hard enough. If you shove your palm against their ear with enough force, you'll shatter their ear drums. If they've got you in a tight hold and you can't get out, kick at their kneecaps with everything you've got.'

Yua sucked in air. 'That sounds painful.'

'Good. Don't worry about hurting them, Yua. If they attack you, you defend yourself and run.' Aza closed her eyes and turned her face towards the sky. 'Not that you'll ever need to defend yourself again. You have me now.'

Yua smiled. Aza was still here. Maybe Yua needed to get used to her after all.

'Tell me about Krymistis.'

Aza turned her head to look at Yua and smiled. 'It's hot. There's sand everywhere. If you walk into the desert, you'll likely die of dehydration. That's how visitors see us.'

Yua observed Aza as she spoke. There was an inner peace reflected on her face whenever she spoke of Krymistis.

'And how do you see it?'

'There are markets that smell of spices and are alive with colours. The people are friendly and warm. There are thieves and murderers same as everywhere else, but for the most part, you can count on the locals helping you if you get lost.' She paused. 'I wish I could show you. Descriptions don't do it justice.'

Yua closed her eyes and pictured it all. She remembered some of the Krymistian food previous attendants had brought her—she didn't remember any of the names, but she remembered the smells. Yua pictured a market that smelled just like it only stronger, filled with smiling faces and a cooling breeze from the sea.

'No, they are perfect.' She sighed. 'I wish I could tell you about Midoka, but you've been to more places here than I have.'

How she wished she could visit Krymistis—with Aza or alone, she almost didn't care as long as she got to see different places. They were all new and magical to her. Was there anywhere in the world that hadn't been explored yet? She'd love to see a place like that—somewhere no one else had stepped foot in yet.

Yua didn't open her eyes, but she thought she felt Aza's eyes on her. She wished she had Aza's optimism, too, but this small trip already seemed like a miracle. She knew when to be grateful instead of asking for more.

'Maybe one day. We can explore it together.'

Yua was glad she hadn't opened her eyes. It made it easier to hide the head behind her lids.

Chapter Thirteen

Yua hadn't stepped into the library in years. The other novices had always made her feel like a dangerous criminal or a diseased outcast or both, so she'd stopped coming. The comforting smell of old books greeted her as soon as she entered, and she breathed deep. Coming here before most novices had breakfast made her feel some of the excitement she'd felt all those years ago—a day of learning lay before her, and when she and Aza left tonight, drained and hungry, they'd leave with new knowledge.

From the outside, it looked like a simple extension of the school building. Inside, the walls were lined with shelves so tall they touched the ceiling. While the entrance room itself wasn't massive, the library extended one floor up and many floors below ground with one large room encasing the foyer. Every subject imaginable—magic related or not—was represented. If anywhere held answers, it was here.

She shouldn't have let those other novices put her off—this library was everything she loved about the world.

She took it back when she and Aza entered the room adjacent to the foyer and the awkward stares of three novices greeted her. It was quiet at this time of day, which made her entrance all the grander. She couldn't have hidden from them if she'd tried.

'We're not here for them,' Aza said. 'Don't worry about those idiots.'

Yua nodded, but she still felt their stares even though they had turned back to their books and notes.

'They are smart idiots. You don't get to study here unless you earn it.'

Aza shrugged. 'I meant emotionally. Personally. I don't doubt they can cast spells just fine, but that doesn't make them nice to be around.'

Yua couldn't help a smile. 'Like yourself?'

Aza grinned. 'Like myself. Where do we start?'

Yua looked so high up the shelves that her neck began to hurt. When she had still come here herself, she had looked for basic introductions to the gift, and later she had looked for fiction. The sheer number of books made her head spin. She could spend her whole life reading in here and not crack every spine. Maybe she could take some books back to her room and study more overnight, but for that to happen, she needed to find something useful first.

'I don't think we'll find much up here,' Yua said. 'This level is mostly healing magic and other common uses for the gift, like teleportation magic.'

Aza raised an eyebrow. 'Teleportation is common?'

Yua mimicked Aza's usual shrugs. 'I suppose not. But it's not deemed dangerous enough, and every Mist Woman needs to know the basics to operate the focus points. Most can't teleport without one, but I think Kei can, and I once knew someone else who could.'

That bent the truth a little, but no one had really known Kaida. At least Yua didn't think so. Kaida had been everything a Mist Woman should be—powerful, respectful, and mostly interested in her own affairs. She had never looked down on Yua like the others did, but then they hadn't spent any real time together. Kaida had been just another brief acquaintance Yua happened to like more than others.

'What's the next floor up?' Aza asked.

'Nothing we want—mostly more complicated healing spells. The infirmary is next door, and all the healing classes are taught on the ground floor; the books are here for easy access.'

'You seem to have a section in mind,' Aza said. 'Did Kei give you any hints despite your power being…' She looked around herself and leaned in. '… Mist magic?'

'No, but there aren't many areas those books would be. I didn't ask for access to the archives on a hunch. All the most dangerous magics are down there.'

'I thought we can't get in?'

'Not all the way.' Yua frowned. 'I'm hoping we won't need to.'

Aza nodded, and Yua led the way. A spiral staircase at the centre of the room led down and connected to another at the end. The stairs went all the way down to the last two floors—the restricted archives. Only Kei, the Seven, and a few Mist Women they trusted were allowed inside. Yua would never be one of them. She had a feeling those floors had the answers she wanted, but she wouldn't be defeated so easily. The lower a novice went, the more dangerous the knowledge became until she reached the archives. With their limited knowledge on the Mists, it was possible that Yua was overreacting, that the books she needed weren't dangerous enough to warrant the restricted floors. But she doubted it.

Yua stopped when they reached the third sublevel. 'There should be some books on the darker parts of history down here.'

The air was just as breathable so deep into the mountain as it was outside. The librarians used their gifts to ensure the air didn't get too thick or too thin. Yua had yet to decide whether they did it to allow novices to study unhindered or to preserve the books. All tomes had been enchanted to make sure even the oldest ones wouldn't crumble at a gentle touch, while novices who were stupid enough to try entering the archives without permission… Librarians knew their priorities.

They entered the room through ornate, wooden double doors, and Yua let her eyes swerve over the many shelves. This floor was even more impressive than the ground floor—there were no other novices down here. Yua didn't feel watched. But the number of shelves made a simple browse for something interesting pointless. She didn't know where to start any more than she had known upstairs.

A wooden table large enough to accommodate study groups of ten novices or more stood near the entrance. A thin layer of dust lay over the surface. Darker squares rested in some areas where novices had studied more recently, but dust covered everything all the same. She supposed there weren't many novices interested in history these days.

Aza ran a finger over the book spines on a shelf to their right. 'Out of curiosity, what exactly is on the lowest level? You've mentioned the archives, but that doesn't tell me anything. There are books on destructive magic right here—' she nodded to the shelf to her left—'and you teach people how to set fire to things in Destruction 101. Just what's hiding down there?'

Yua turned her chuckle towards the shelves on her left. The class was called The Basics of Elemental Magic, but she preferred Aza's version.

'The archives hold secrets that could end the world.' She hadn't meant for it to sound so dramatic, but that's what it was.

Aza pulled two heavy tomes off the shelf and blew dust off the covers. 'That's a little over the top, isn't it?'

'Mist magic is on the second to last floor. The lowest one has books more dangerous than that. Only a select few are allowed to enter. I wasn't exaggerating.'

Aza settled down at the table with her two books and an uneasy look on her face. 'What if someone breaks in?'

Yua grimaced. 'Kei herself has set all kinds of wards around the stairs, doors, and shelves. No one gets in there without permission. Her spells would turn an intruder to ash before they set one foot in that part of the library.'

She had seen only one novice who had tried. Shortly after Kei had brought her to the coven, Yua had wandered into the infirmary and seen a novice with hideous burns. The poor woman had barely been able to move, if she had been conscious at all—Yua didn't remember. The wards were likely kinder to their own novices than to any random thief. Yua had often wondered why she had been able to see the novice at all, but she had concluded that the Seven had made an example out of her. The novice had survived, but her injuries together with the word *archives* had been on everyone's lips for days… until the reason Yua was there got out. As far as she knew, no novices had tried since and there'd been no attempted thefts. It troubled her that petty thieves had more common sense than Mist Woman novices.

Aza leafed through one of the tomes. 'Why keep those books at all if no one can use them?'

Yua paused. She had wondered the same thing herself many times. 'Not no-one, just not any novice who asks. Mist Women like knowledge. They probably prefer these secrets here, where they can keep an eye on them, rather than O-Yu knows where. That's the only explanation I can think of.'

Aza sighed. 'Your magic seems harmless by comparison.' She shoved one of the three books towards Yua. 'Let's see what we can find.'

Yua opened the book, but her thoughts were still on the lowest floor of the archives. She didn't doubt that the knowledge down there really could end existence as they knew it. The Seven wouldn't guard it so viciously if the knowledge was harmless. If the books she needed were one floor up from the bottom, what did that say about her power? What was one step up from total annihilation?

After hours which felt like days of fruitless research, all Yua could say for sure was that there was no precedent. It was disheartening to have that part of her suspicions confirmed, but it was reassuring to know that Kei hadn't lied. There was nothing in this library...

At least not on the all-access-granted levels.

Aza breathed a heavy sigh, pushed the tome away from her, and fell back into her chair. 'I hate to say it, but I think we need to go lower. Say, end-of-the-world lower.'

'I think you're right,' Yua said, 'but it's impossible without Kei's permission. We wouldn't live long enough to regret it.'

Aza blinked the dust out of her eyes. 'Well, there's nothing here. What else can we try?'

'Nothing until the Seven have made their decision.' She hated waiting, but at least Kei was talking to them. It wasn't the same as sitting on her bed, alone, not knowing how to fix herself. She still didn't know what she could do, but maybe they were on their way to an answer.

Aza put a hand on her stomach. 'It's got to be almost time for lunch. How about we go back to your room and take a food break?'

Yua nodded. Maybe she'd see clearer after a break.

Chapter Fourteen

Yua felt no more positive about their research when they reached her room. They entered, and Aza's face fell too.

'What's wrong?'

Aza shrugged. 'I thought Ichiro might have brought lunch over. It must be earlier than I thought.'

Yua shook her head. 'I don't normally eat lunch. The attendants used to bring me three meals a day, but I don't do much, so I was never hungry enough for it.'

'Oh.' Aza glanced at her. 'How about today? Studying always makes me hungry. I think I remember the way to the kitchen.'

Yua's stomach rumbled in response, and she blushed. 'Alright.' She bit her lip. 'I should have mentioned it while we were down there. I'm sorry, I'm not...' She sighed. 'Coming straight here is habit.'

Aza smiled. 'It's fine. The more I move, the more I can eat, so you're doing me a favour. I'll be right back.'

Yua nodded. She wanted to offer to go with her, but she couldn't stand to be stared at anymore. They had barely seen any novices in their short time on the library's ground floor, but the garden had been busy with everyone moving from their lessons to the dining room. She was grateful that Aza had been with her. She was grateful that Aza understood. The longer she stayed, the more Aza felt like a shield Yua could hide behind.

And after Kei's confession that Yua had Mist magic and their fruitless research session, she needed a moment to herself so she could think straight again.

She opened a window and breathed in the crisp autumn air. She closed her eyes and breathed deeper, feeling the air fill her nose and her head. Felt her thoughts become lighter with every breath in. When everything felt too much, she could always rely on fresh air to clear out the cobwebs.

Knowing that Aza would find her on the roof, Yua climbed up and sat cross-legged near the centre. Newai had curled up on the end in the shade of a pine but stretched and trotted over to her. Yua stretched, too, inviting the breeze to brush through her fabrics the longer she held her arms towards the clouds. At this time of year, the air always smelled like rain, even when the sun did escape the clouds for a moment.

Newai jumped onto her lap and immediately lay on one leg with his paws tugged under him. Yua scratched his ear and felt his purr against her knee. A breeze caressed her temple and wrist in turn. She already felt better.

Although… It was hard to accept that she had Mist magic. She had hoped to find something in the library that would prove Kei wrong, but she'd known it was a vain hope. Kei wasn't some lazy novice, after all. It was even harder to admit to herself that the theory fit. Even without having the gift herself, Yua knew that it was a benevolent force at best and a neutral force all other times. The user decided what they did with it. But what she'd felt from her darkness… There was nothing neutral or even beneficial about it. The shadow inside her didn't want to heal or help. It wanted to tear and rip. It was selfish, while the gift didn't really have its own personality. That alone was proof enough that what she had wasn't regular magic.

She felt something murky squirm inside her gut.

'Are you annoyed that I'm calling you out for what you are or that I called you a shadow? Do you fancy yourself more?'

It squirmed again, and Yua scoffed.

'*Shadow* it is then. May as well give you a name since it doesn't seem like you'll go anywhere.'

She knew the gift was meant to feel like an orb of light or something like it. Her power had only ever felt dark, like the first tendrils of night on an early autumn evening. *Shadow* was a fitting name.

So, Kei was right. Yua could admit that, hard as it was. But what was she meant to do with it? She couldn't control a part of the Mists, and she didn't really want to try. She had read enough history books to know that whole countries suffered when someone tried to as much as view the Mists. Sometimes, those countries didn't survive. There was a whole desert of cracked regret in the Northern Reaches. How was she supposed to do any better?

Surrender and you'll see how much better we can be.

She closed her eyes and shook her head.

But her Shadow had reacted to its new name—no, *his* new name. When she sat like this with her eyes shut and the breeze soothing her fears, she felt a definite male energy from it. Or maybe that was her imagination, and it was just that its voice sounded male. Or did it? It had a strange quality of being neither male nor female and yet both at the same time. Yua didn't know what to call it, only that calling it a *he* personified it, and she felt like that gave it power. It had enough of that without her help. Likely too much for her to handle if she tried to coax it towards the surface. It wasn't a fight she thought she could win, but maybe giving it a name was a start. Her Shadow had been a nameless terror all her life. Maybe this would help.

She heard her door open and close. Moments later, Aza stuck her head out of the window.

'I've got sandwiches and biscuits!'

Yua smiled and leaned towards the window to help, but Newai gave her a look. 'Interesting combination. I'd help, but the cat…'

Aza climbed onto the roof and passed her the tray. 'Say no more. His comfort is more important than me not dropping our lunch down the roof.' She smiled at Yua, and Yua relaxed. 'What's the point of growing up if you can't have biscuits for lunch? Besides, I did also get sandwiches. I'm responsible, see?'

Yua laughed and took her half. 'That's very mature of you.'

Aza winked at her. 'That's what I thought.' She sat next to Yua and petted Newai's head. He leaned towards her and closed his eyes. 'We're spoiling him.'

Yua blushed. 'Since when is he *our* cat?'

Aza gave her that look that said she knew better than Yua. 'He's a cat, and he's tolerating me. I'm pretty sure that makes me one of his humans. Cat law is very clear on these rules.'

Yua's chuckle escaped her lips in a happy sigh.

Enjoy it while you can. It won't last.

She pulled her sandwich in two and bit into one half.

Aza raised an eyebrow. 'That seems excessive. What did that sandwich ever do to you? Don't you like cheese?'

Yua shrugged. 'Just making a point.'

Although, she wasn't entirely sure what point that was. She doubted she could intimidate her Shadow, but that didn't mean it had to intimidate her. She knew how to keep it locked away, and nothing would change about that until she was ready.

'Thank you for lunch,' Yua said.

'I'm always happy to provide food.'

Aza took a big bite out of her sandwich—chicken and lettuce, from the looks of it—and eyed the biscuits. They had a caramelised brown sheen to them. Yua guessed they were ginger biscuits and hoped the breeze would waft their smell her way, but they lay in the wrong direction for that. But it didn't matter. Aza had brought her food—no, Aza had gone out of her way to do something nice for Yua. Aza could insist this was for her benefit all she wanted; it didn't change how much it meant.

'How are you feeling now? You were restless this morning.'

Yua nodded. 'I'm still nervous about what any of this means, but I don't feel like I'm about to lose control over myself. I don't think I'm much of a risk right now. Between you, me, the Seven, and Kei, we'll figure something out.'

Won't we? She didn't have the energy to voice her doubts. She needed to be confident going forward.

'Trust me, I'm a Sand Blade,' Aza said. 'We're good at solving problems.'

Yua snorted. 'I didn't realise you took contracts on Mist demons this often.'

Aza offered her a biscuit, and Yua gladly accepted. She smelled the ginger moments before she bit into it.

'This is my first, I'll admit,' Aza said. 'But Sand Blades are good at adapting.'

Yua let the biscuit melt on her tongue and savoured the smooth blend of sugar and spice.

'The way you talk, you seem to be good at everything.'

Aza thought a moment. 'Not everything. If I were a good baker, I'd be eating these all the time.'

'Yua?'

She spun around. Newai complained at the sudden movement with a long meow. Kei never visited her unless it was to talk about her new attendant or to chide Yua. She couldn't have talked to the Seven about her archives access already… could she? Yua had only seen her a few hours ago.

'We're up here,' Aza answered.

Yua's eyes flew to Aza.

Aza hid behind a biscuit. 'I'm sorry, were we hiding? She doesn't sound angry, but if I shouldn't have said anything… I won't next time.'

Yua shook her head. 'It's fine, I just wasn't expecting her so soon.'

If they were already done discussing it, they could only have reached one conclusion. It must have been a unanimous no.

'I'll wait up here to give you two privacy, but shout if you need me. I can be down there in seconds.'

Yua nodded with a lump in her throat. She wasn't ready to have her only chance at answers rejected so soon after their failed research session.

'I hope I'm not interrupting?' Kei said when Yua climbed back into her room.

'We're just having lunch.' She couldn't get herself to ask.

'One of the librarians told me she saw you in the library earlier.' Yua's heart plummeted so close to the topic at hand, but Kei smiled. 'It's nice to see you take your research so seriously. We couldn't ask for more from our novices.'

Yua frowned. 'Only I'm not a novice now, am I?'

Kei's smile faltered. 'No, I suppose you're not. I think my news will interest you all the same. Even our most successful novices rarely earn such privileges as what we're granting you.'

Her heart jumped. Kei couldn't mean—

'I have spoken with the Seven, and we agree that your request is not only reasonable but also shows responsibility. If Aza accompanies you, we have decided to allow you access to the archives.'

Chapter Fifteen

Yua had been curious about the archives for so long she had thought she'd be ecstatic if she was ever allowed inside. Instead, she felt a silent dread now she was here, and it lay heavy in the dust on every cover. The novices' whispers and stares had felt more sinister as Yua had walked through the library with Aza. She felt like they knew where she was going, what she was going to find, and they judged her for it and for dragging Aza into the forbidden unknown with her.

And for all Yua knew, they were right. Everything behind the heavy ebony-wood doors was behind them for a reason. They guarded forbidden knowledge, and while they weren't adorned with intricate decorations promising certain death, Yua knew they would hurt her if she didn't have permission. But Kei allowed it. The Seven knew she was here and allowed her inside.

So, why did she feel like she was breaking every coven rule?

'I feel it, too,' Aza said next to her. '*Kelsos*. No door has ever made me feel so unwelcome.'

'It's the spells the Seven have placed on it. If we didn't have permission, we'd feel a lot worse just for being down here.'

The stairs had led them into an unassuming round room. The only light here came from the green flames on the wall, one on each side of the doors, and they cast flickering emerald shadows. Yua had never seen a Mother, but she had read about the infernal servants of the Dark One and imagined they looked like this… right before they formed into some grotesque humanoid mist-shape and stabbed her.

Besides the lights and the doors, there wasn't anything here. The doors crackled with power. A green glow ran through the wood's rings. The gift inside them—or perhaps the promise of what lay behind—had sparked a fire in her darkness.

Let's see what's on the other side…

Yua shivered. The corners of her mouth tugged up as if her Shadow tried to convince her to grin. She set her lips into a tight line and crossed her arms.

'I'm not sure about this.'

Aza stepped closer. 'Why not?'

'Let's just say I have a bad feeling.'

'Your Mist magic?'

Yua nodded. Aza reached out, and Yua placed her hand in Aza's. The whole coven could have come down around them, and she knew Aza would have got them both out to safety. She could walk into one room and look at some tomes.

'That's a good sign if you ask me,' Aza said. 'If your power recognises whatever is behind these doors, we're on the right track.'

Yua glanced at Aza. 'Or the wrong one, depending on how you look at it.'

'I'm looking at it positively. Are you ready?'

Yua gulped. In her mind, her Shadow was a blurry figure with a mean grimace, and it rubbed its hands together. *Go on.*

Yua nodded. 'Let's see what has my Shadow so excited.'

She put her hand onto the ebony and pushed. Was it her imagination or did she smell burning?

The door buzzed with warmth under her palm as if to welcome them. They entered.

The library above was grand, a marvel of Midokan architecture. The builders had laced the gift into every surface and even into the air to help novices focus. The archives weren't any of that. Some might have called them boring or plain. To Yua, they were more beautiful than the main floors.

Down here, the Mist Women hadn't tried to hide the tomes' ages. They could have preserved the books, refreshed the colours on their covers, kept dust off them, placed comfortable chairs and ornate furniture in the reading spaces, but instead, every book, every corner, looked and smelled old. Spells preserved all the books, but quite a few looked like they'd fall apart if she breathed on them. The whole room—or what she could see of it past the first rows of shelves—had a strange heavy feel to it, like it was burdened by the knowledge within its walls.

Aza brushed two fingers over a row of book spines and inspected the thick film of dust. 'You'd think they'd renovate every century or so,' she said. 'I know not many people use this space, but I still expected more. The fabled archives of Midoka—one grand dust trap.' She blew the dirt of her fingers.

'It's to remind you of the danger and age in these tomes,' Yua said. It was a guess, but it felt true. 'If everything looked cheerful, people wouldn't respect these secrets enough.'

'I think I'd respect them just fine from a cosy sofa. Where should we start?'

'I've no idea.' Yua was roughly familiar with where various subjects were upstairs, but no one had given her a tour of the archives. Any direction was a good start. 'There are more floors below this one.'

'Sorted by subject?'

'Sorted by danger. The books here are the safest.'

Aza gazed over the many rows spreading before them. 'Let's hope that your power isn't at the bottom, then, or we'll never find it. There must be thousands of books here.' She pointed towards the back between the shelves. 'I'll start over there.'

'Shout if you find something?'

Aza nodded and left Yua alone.

Yua huffed once Aza was out of hearing distance. 'No preference?' she asked her Shadow.

No. I want to savour these last moments.

A shiver ran down Yua's spine. She told herself it was trying to scare her into letting her guard down, but it didn't quite silence the doubt. What if something terrible was about to happen? They were alone down here. If she called for help, no one would hear her.

Kei had offered to send someone with them to supervise, but Aza had waved her off. *They are just books*, Aza had said. No one had ever got hurt by reading. At the time, Yua had agreed—the Seven had left her to come into her own so long, she could do a bit of research without their help too. They'd done enough by allowing her access. But an uncomfortable sensation snaked up her back, and Yua wished someone had accompanied them after all. She might have felt less watched from the shadows with a Seven here. If they didn't come back, she was sure Kei would eventually come to investigate, but how long would that take? How long before anyone noticed they hadn't returned? There was no limit on the amount of time they could spend down here—once someone had access to the archives, it went without saying that the Seven and Kei trusted them.

This will be easier if you don't fight me.

Yua swallowed and reverently placed a hand on the shelf ahead of her. These books were so old. All this ancient knowledge… at her fingertips. She didn't mind too much if they didn't find answers right away.

Then it hit her.

Aza had disappeared behind the shelves, but over the dust and the vellichor, Yua smelled the sweet metal of Aza's blood. She heard it, too—three rows ahead, to her left.

'*Stop*,' she hissed. Her jaws ached. 'I'm in control. You will not have her.' Every word was difficult as the scent became stronger. Richer.

You only need to take a few steps and you're there. You'll be even faster if you let me fly.

'No.' She gritted her teeth. Even the one word was hard. She felt like her jaws locked together to stop her from speaking while she also wanted to rush across the room and—

You've been in control long enough. It ends now.

'No!'

Her head felt like it wanted to split open. Or was that her chest? Her whole body felt about to split in half. What would pour out of her when it did? Would her blood still be red or had her Shadow turned it black?

Aza stuck her head out from behind a shelf. 'Sorry,' she said as she sucked on a finger. 'I cut myself on one of the pages. Did you say something?'

Yua blinked. Aza sounded closer. Her Shadow had led her closer, and she hadn't even noticed.

She gulped. 'No, but let's hurry.'

'Hurry?' Aza laughed. 'Have you seen how many books there are? We'll never get through all this today.'

'I know, I just… Let's see if we can find anything. I don't care what, just any starting point, maybe a reference.'

Yua hadn't come to the archives just to leave without anything again. Kei had taught her all these techniques to suppress her power—it had to be good for something. Yua took slow breaths. Focussed on the feel of air flowing through her lungs, into her mouth. All it did was add to the pressure around her heart.

'Are you alright?' Aza asked.

Yua ground her teeth, but it made her discomfort worse.

You need to bite into someone, feel flesh tear against your teeth. Let me show you how.

Yua shook her head so hard the floor spun. She wouldn't let it be Aza. Never.

Haven't you wanted a teacher all these years? I could teach you quite a bit.

Yua ran her tongue over her teeth and focussed on Aza. 'I'm fine. Did you find anything?'

'Not yet.'

Yua stepped around to search Aza's shelf. The urge to search anywhere but here overcame her—her Shadow didn't want to be here. That had to mean something.

'I don't think my Shadow likes this. I think we're on to something.'

Aza didn't take her eyes off the spines. 'It doesn't like this shelf, this row, or this whole floor?'

'It got excited when we came in,' Yua said. 'What I feel now is too different. There's something here—there must be.'

If only it had a strong aversion to a specific book.

'You search this shelf,' Aza said. 'You never know, I might have missed something. I'll look over there.'

Yua nodded and scanned the titles, but most of it was history. There was a ringing in her ears that blurred the titles, like her Shadow was trying to annoy her so she'd stop. She had to stare at the spines a little longer to read them, but the more she prevailed, the easier it got. Her Shadow didn't stop, but she felt more in control again.

She'd have to ask Kei for a list of which subjects she could find on which floor. If they continued like this, they might as well move their beds down here. Kei's words after Himari had left rang in her head—anger would get her nowhere. If nothing else, she could be angry with the Seven *and* ask for their help. They didn't need to pick the books for her—who knew what they'd keep from her that way?—but a floor plan, at least, would help.

'I've got something,' Aza said.

Yua rushed around the shelf to Aza.

'*Dark Manifestations of the Gift Throughout History*,' Aza read with her finger running over the golden letters. 'Sounds promising, yes?'

Yua nodded. Aza carried the heavy tome to the table. Yua sat on a chair, and Aza pulled another around to sit next to her.

'Where shall we start?' Aza asked.

'I don't know.' The table of contents alone spanned ten pages. 'It's a shame we can't take it with us.'

'We can't?'

Yua shook her head. 'Too dangerous. If a careless novice found one of these books and attempted a forbidden spell, it could be disastrous.'

Aza sighed. 'I see your point. Anything look good?'

Everything. Yua wanted to take this book with her, hide it, and not return it until she'd memorised every single page. All her life, she'd been different, but this book was full of people who had odd talents, in whom the gift manifested in unknown ways. It was filled with stories like her own. She gently brushed her hand across the page. She was so used to feeling alone, like the world was against her. So used to the whispered, hateful accusations behind her back. Had all these people in this book gone through similar hardships? Would she finally find someone she could relate to? She doubted any of them had dealt with this branch of Mist magic, but she couldn't deny the kinship she felt towards every name.

Aza pointed at a chapter heading on the final contents' page. 'Look at this.'

'The Banishment of the Dark One by Queen Rachael of Rifarne, annotated by Mist Woman Kaida. That was two years ago. How could Kaida have annotated it?'

'Did you know her?' Aza asked.

Yua shook her head. 'I saw her around a few times. She seemed nice, but she died during this battle.'

Aza thought for a moment. 'She must have sent notes to Kei.'

Yua nodded. 'They were close, I think. I wonder why Kei never asked her to examine me.'

'Why would she have?'

'Kaida wasn't any Mist Woman. She was rumoured to be even more talented than Kei. Even I felt the power around her, and I don't feel much of anything where the gift is concerned.' Yua shivered when she remembered it. Kaida had radiated so much power, she had barely seemed human. 'It was like… Kaida was the eye of the storm and her gift the tornado.'

Aza sat back to listen. 'Then why wasn't she in charge? I didn't think Mist Women settled for second best.'

Yua shrugged. 'It's not an obligation or a law. I guess Kaida didn't want to lead.' She had often wondered how different things might have been if Kaida had found her that night, but those were all just daydreams. There was no more point to them than to wishing she was a normal Midokan. 'Anyway, let's keep looking.'

Aza nodded, and they leaned over the pages again. It didn't take long before she spotted something.

Aza noticed it too. 'Shall we?'

Yua nodded, and Aza opened the book on the right page. The Mists in People—A Theory. The title's font was thick and grim, like someone had written it in blood.

It's not, her Shadow whispered. *I'd know.*

An ink drawing adorned the left side of the text—a person, gripped tight by a shadow rising out of their chest and head. It looked like a nightmare. Would this happen to her if she lost control?

Only if you keep fighting me.

Yua shuddered. But she sensed her Shadow shudder, too, and wondered how true its last threat really was.

The text was hard to read, written in a fast hand and interrupted here and there with ink blots where the feather had dripped.

'I'm not sure how useful this is,' Aza said. 'It's only a theory.'

'If that's all there is, we'll have to work with it. Besides.' The picture stared up at her, and she remembered her Shadow's reaction. 'This is right. Something's here.'

They scanned the text in silence. To her disappointment, there was no record of another possessed like her.

But there was something else.

'It's been tried before,' Aza said at the same time as Yua read over the paragraph. 'Several times.'

'But it's never been successful… Why now?' Why her?

Aza shrugged. 'Maybe you're just lucky.' Yua scoffed. 'Or maybe the people who did your ritual were better at it.'

'Or maybe it's all part of the old Midokan belief of balance.' She had read about it before. Mist Women held the same belief to an extent, but she knew the people of the Red Wastes—what they now knew to have been Ar'Sanciond, thanks to Queen Rachael of Rifarne—had held the laws of balance dear. She thought she'd read something about Vistria still following those beliefs. The gift did seem to work on similar principles, but Yua only had her self-taught knowledge to work with.

'I've never heard of it,' Aza said. 'What is it?'

'Don't they teach it in Krymistis?'

Yua had figured that everyone knew about it since even she did, and she hadn't had a teacher.

'Maybe other children learn about it,' Aza said. 'They taught me where to stick the pointy end of a blade.'

'I don't know much myself, but I think the basic theory is that the gift requires balance. Maybe there's great darkness in me because there's great light somewhere else.' Although, why *she* had to carry that darkness was beyond her. So maybe it wasn't that.

'And what should we do with that theory?' Aza asked. 'Find the light? Extinguish it? Ask it to be less bright?'

Her heart missed a beat, and warmth spread from it. Was this what it felt like when her Shadow laughed?

Yua frowned. 'I don't think that's it.'

Aza yawned, and Yua stifled her own.

'I think we should take a break,' Aza said. 'This is progress, but I'd rather nap before we dive any deeper into whatever we'll find here.'

Yua nodded. Excited as she was to be down here, she had access to the archives now. They could come back. After everything she had learned today, she felt mentally drained. It'd be easier to think once she was rested. She'd struggle to sleep tonight as it was because she was now certain of two things:

Her power was unique, and it was one of those secrets that could destroy the world.

Yua turned over in her bed for the tenth time in the last thirty minutes. They had spent all morning in the archives, and she had struggled to take her mind off their findings for the rest of the day. Exhausted as she was, she couldn't sleep. She didn't dare to nod off for even a second. Her Shadow's whispers had been too loud and too insistent in the archives, and she didn't trust its silence now. She worried that she hadn't kept it back at all, but that it had retreated to ambush her another time. Down in the archives, she had been alert, but it had been a struggle nonetheless. How would she fare if it struck now she was this tired? Aza had excused herself to her own room as soon as they got back. Yua tried to ignore it, but she heard Aza's soft breathing from the other side of the wall, sensed how unprotected and unaware she was. If she lost control right now… If she as much as went to check on Aza… Even with her Sand Blade training, Aza would be too slow.

You're faster than all of them. Take what is yours.

She gritted her teeth and gripped the duvet in both hands. Aza's blood wasn't hers. How could she convince a Mist demon of that?

A slight tremor went through her; she imagined her Shadow laughing.

Everyone's blood is yours. You just need to take it.

Yua shook her head and wrapped a leg around her duvet for better grip. How long could she fight this? If she didn't get any sleep tonight—and she wouldn't, it was too irresponsible— she'd be weaker tomorrow. She was alone with Aza most of the time. Could she endure the stares for the sake of Aza's safety? Would a few novices make a difference, or would she kill them all like she'd killed her family that night?

You don't have the strength to fight me. Surrender, and this pain will be over.

Her head shot around when she heard more than Aza's breathing. A teasing rush. A scarlet promise. Aza's blood hummed its melody loud and clear. Yua feared what would happen if she closed her eyes for too long. Now that her

Shadow had given up on hiding, it was safer to not close them at all.

She should go to Kei. If anyone could help her, it was the most powerful Mist Woman in the world. But that would take her past Aza's room, and she was still in enough control to know that was a terrible idea.

It wasn't only Aza either. Every door she passed would be a struggle. The rushing grew louder as everyone's blood joined Aza's melody. The novices on the floors below, tucked into their duvets and feeling safe. The servants on the ground floor. Ichiro. Their refrain created a steady buzz like bees in summer around a pollen-rich flower. Yua's heart raced with their song. Her eyes grew heavier every second. She was so tired.

Close them. Haven't you earned a break? A second of peace?

Yua threw her duvet off herself and jumped out of bed. She wrapped a thin nightgown around her shoulders and hugged it tight. It wasn't enough to steady her, but at least she was holding onto something. When she slid open her window to climb onto the roof, the sound it made scraped against her mind.

The moment the autumn breeze hit her, she felt herself calm. Newai greeted her with a long yawn-stifled meow and a generous stretch. Yua sat next to him and scratched his ear. She didn't hear his blood in his tiny veins—a small blessing. Everyone else's was quieter up here too. She closed her eyes and felt the cool wind caress her face, hug her arms, stroke her ankles. Felt the air fill her lungs and quiet the dark storm inside her.

Newai climbed onto her lap and settled on her legs. He preferred his own space, but he must have felt that something was wrong. Soft. Warm. Mercifully quiet. Yua stroked his back and enjoyed his comforting purr until the sun rose over Maishi Hou and she couldn't keep her eyes open any longer.

Yua leaned back in her chair and sighed. She and Aza had spent the whole morning and most of the afternoon on opposite ends of one table. Even here, on the bottom floor of the archives, they'd found only more of the same—whatever had been done to Yua had been attempted before, but as far as they could tell, she was the first successful result. Clearly, Kei had contacted the wrong experts or they'd have been all over her. Or those experts had never known this much about her condition in the first place, and the coven had grasped at straws. That seemed more likely to her. After all, she was the only successful experiment—how much knowledge could these experts really have had? She'd never thought about it this much, had just hated their involvement, but Kei and the Seven must have been... not desperate—despair was beneath Mist Women— but something close to it.

She didn't like what that said about her chances of finding answers now.

'Look here.' Aza turned a book around and moved around the table so they could both see.

Yua blinked the exhaustion out of her eyes; her sleepless night was catching up with her. 'Found something?'

Go to sleep, Yua. You know you need the break.

She couldn't tell whether her Shadow was growing more insistent from hunger, lack of sleep, or because they were close to something.

'Hmh. It's… disturbing,' Aza said. 'I don't know what to make of it.'

'"Blood Magic in the Mists".' Yua gulped. She had a feeling she wouldn't like this. '"Yesterday's peek into the Mists was fruitful." I thought that sorcerer from Ar'Sanciond was the only one who tried something like that?'

'Someone here must have dabbled,' Aza said. 'The Dark One has never invaded Midoka, so this one either didn't take it as far or was just better at it. But never mind that, keep reading.'

Yes. Keep reading.

Yua felt like her very heart twisted into a grin.

'"Yesterday's peek into the Mists was fruitful. I was able to record…" Hmm…' Ink blots forced her to skip some of it. She hoped those parts weren't anything important. '"… a new species of demon. It is by far the… I ever encountered. I watched it before it noticed me and had to close the window in a hurry. If I am correct, it—"' A chill ran down her spine. 'No, that can't be right.'

'What does it say?' Aza craned her neck. 'His handwriting is atrocious from this angle.'

'It says he watched one of those demons leech off another demon. When it noticed him, it dropped the other, which sank to the ground and didn't get back up. It sounds like it took its life energy.'

The grin around her heart stretched into a grimace. She shivered.

Aza's forehead creased. 'But you don't do that. You…' Aza sighed and scratched her head as she struggled for words. 'How did you kill all those people? Do you remember anything at all?'

She was grateful that she didn't.

'No, but I…' She couldn't get herself to be blunt about it. 'I… hear your blood. I think. And other people's. My Shadow wants to…' She didn't remember how she'd killed her family, but she did remember the smell of blood. She remembered being covered in it. 'I think it wants to… drink…' She gulped. This was too difficult. 'We don't know what Mist demons eat or what's inside their veins if they have veins at all. The Mothers don't seem to have any blood, from what I've heard and read—they're all shadows and fog. I don't think it's an unrealistic assumption that other demons don't bleed either.'

Aza leaned back and absent-mindedly twirled her dagger through her fingers. 'Maybe it's a Mist equivalent. Maybe they bleed more Mists or a kind of black blood we thought was shadows.'

Yua's skin crawled. With this demon inside her, did she still bleed red? 'But why give *me* that power, or whatever you want to call it? I was a child. Why give it to anyone? None of this makes sense. I know I'm not possessed—it was the first thing Kei tested.'

Aza slowly nodded to herself like she was trying to apply reason to all this. 'So, this demon the author describes probably isn't inside you, at least not the demon itself. What about its hunger? You said it wants to drink my blood.'

Yua blushed. 'I didn't say that.'

'But it's what you meant.' Aza shrugged. 'Isn't it?'

'How can you be so matter-of-fact with that?' Yua gritted her teeth. Aza was too calm about this revelation. 'Why aren't you more worried? You don't know this demon any better than I do. It wants to hurt you.'

Aza gave her a long, calculating look. Finally, she smiled. 'How should I react? I'm sure I've mentioned this, but I'm a Sand Blade. We're raised to adapt. This isn't ideal, and I'd prefer it if you didn't kill me to bathe in my blood, but it is what we've got. Wishing for something easier won't change facts, so let's work with what we have.'

Yua swallowed. It made so much sense when Aza put it like that.

'Alright.' She sighed. They were both committed. Now they just had to make it work. 'What you said about it not being the demon itself but its hunger seems more likely, but how does that work? What happened to the demon? Unless…' Was it her imagination or did her Shadow feel giddy in her veins? 'I just remembered. Years ago, I read somewhere that creatures of the Mists don't die like we do. They return to the Mists and reform there. What if the people who did this to me somehow caught a demon's life energy and trapped it in me?'

But that suggested that she and her Shadow weren't two separate creatures. What exactly would that make her? She wasn't ready to entertain that thought.

You'll have to accept me sooner or later. Or should I say us *since you know the truth now?*

She didn't feel like she knew the truth. She felt like she had barely scratched the surface. The more they figured out or suspected, the more questions she had, and she was beginning to fear that there were no clear answers.

'This is all very troubling,' Aza said, 'but *why*? What did they hope to achieve?'

And they were back at the beginning.

Yua exhaled a heavy sigh and put her head into her palms. 'I don't know. Things like this usually only exist in the Mists for a reason. This shouldn't be possible.' I *shouldn't be possible*. The realisation spun her head and made her feel less human. 'Who knows what went through their heads? What motivates a Mist demon besides killing?'

Kaida had seemed like the kind of person who'd have known, but Yua couldn't ask her. Kei had no answers either. If there were other options besides searching these archives until her hair turned grey and fell out, Yua didn't see them.

Aza intertwined her hands and stretched her arms above her head. 'I don't know about you, but I'm ready for a break.'

Yua nodded. Their search had masked the melody Aza's blood hummed for a while, but now she wasn't looking through the tomes, it grew louder, and there was no one here to help either of them. The faster they could get amongst more people—more witnesses, more help—the better.

Her head spun from the new insights, but even so, she felt deflated. She no longer felt completely human, but she wasn't a Mist demon either. She was a nameless monster, some new terror the archives would lock away to be forgotten, and no amount of chamomile tea would make that better.

Chapter Sixteen

Yua sat on her roof and hugged her legs to herself. There was no sign of Newai, so she hugged herself harder. Aza had gone to get food. Yua was grateful to be alone, but she could have done with the cat's warmth.

She had always known that she was dangerous, but she had hoped that more knowledge would somehow help. Aza's insistence and stories of Krymistis had let her hope that maybe, if she knew enough, practiced enough, she might control the darkness in her veins, but she now knew that the opposite was the case. She wasn't just dangerous; she was the danger itself. No amount of knowledge would change that. Throughout history, there had been a few attempts to study the Mists, and none of them had ended well. In all those ill-fated attempts, someone had brought a part of the Mists into their world and let it loose. This time, it wasn't loose but imprisoned inside her, and the more Yua dwelled on that, the less she knew how to contain it.

How could she, a Midokan girl without magical ability, control something as inherently evil as the Mists? O-Yu expected too much from her. She'd never been religious, and every new piece of information solidified her conviction that the Great Dragon was a myth. It didn't matter, though, because Kei expected too much too. Aza expected too much. Yua herself, who had known better deep down, had dared hope for too much.

She had killed so many when she was five. The Mists had leaked out of her and controlled her rather than the other way around—that had to be what had happened. She hadn't made any progress since. If she concentrated, she felt the evil crawling through her veins. She felt it near her heart, her mind, ready to grip both if she gave it half an opportunity.

Who would die then?

She pulled her legs into her chest, and a sob escaped her. Her parents must have hated her to have done this. Had they worshipped the Dark One? Had her entire family?

Had they expected the same of her?

She had no idea how she could ever hope to win this, but she knew that she would rather die than let something so evil control her.

Ignoring her Shadow all these years had accomplished one thing: no one else had died or been hurt. But didn't she matter at all? She hadn't been happy. She had been a scared prisoner in her room as well as in her own body. Yua thought that had to count for something. Even so, she couldn't value her happiness above everyone else's lives. They mattered too. Perhaps they mattered more since there were more of them and only one of her.

She could either go on as she had been, continue to protect everyone else through inaction but be miserable, or she could risk practicing control one day at a time, one thread of sanity at a time, but put too many people at risk who wouldn't even know the danger they were in. She wasn't convinced the latter would really make her happy either. The responsibility of something so irresponsible was too heavy.

Yua balled her hands into fists and gritted her teeth.

Maybe there was a third option.

If she closed her eyes and focussed on it, she felt the Shadow inside her veins. It was a part of her, not the other way around. Maybe the darkness would die if she did. From what she'd read in the archives, she guessed it needed a host to exist outside of the Mists, but she had no idea if it could jump between people if necessary. She had to hope that keeping her alive was in its best interest too. It hadn't claimed her mind yet, and she was still controlling her movements. Maybe she could use that.

Maybe… Her heart hammered. An idea had begun to form. She couldn't tell anyone or they would try to stop her. Aza would insist on at least being there, and Yua couldn't guarantee what would happen then. So, she had to do this alone.

And she had to do it tonight before she lost her nerve.

Chapter Seventeen

Yua lay on her back and stared at the ceiling, where faint moonlight slow-danced with the shadows of clouds. She tried to calm her breathing. Her Shadow had been loud over the last two days and nights, and she knew what she had to do.

But that didn't make it any easier.

Because Yua had struggled with her Shadow in the archives, Aza had offered to stay the night in case Yua needed help. Yua didn't like to be babied, but she *was* scared, and her bed had always been too large for one person. So, Aza lay curled up in Yua's bed, the blanket kicked off one leg and held down by the other. She'd considered telling Aza and taking her along, but that would only introduce more issues. Or more solutions? Yua no longer knew which thoughts were here own and which ones her Shadow had put into her head. One more reason to stop fretting over possible outcomes and get on with it.

Yua slid out of her bed and stood. She moved carefully so she wouldn't wake Aza. She had a feeling Aza was watching her even while asleep, but Yua wouldn't chance her luck tonight. She couldn't afford to waste any.

Yua stopped by her window and looked back on the Sand Blade. She decided to stop tiptoeing—it wasn't luck that would see her through tonight, but skill and determination. Luck was only a nice illusion when you had nothing else to fall back on.

This was her body, this was her mind, and she would claim both tonight. If her Shadow wanted to stay, it would have to adjust… though in truth, she had no idea what she'd do if it wasn't willing to cooperate. If she had learned anything from the archives, it was that they weren't two separate beings but one—she couldn't exactly make it leave.

Yua climbed through the window onto her roof and took a moment to enjoy the comforting moonlight and the gentle breeze. If this went wrong, it'd be the last time she felt either. Despite the autumn chill, she felt warm tonight—from adrenaline, she suspected, though she didn't feel excited, only determined.

Her Shadow tugged and prodded her. She closed her eyes and felt it within her. A living thing that had been imprisoned for too long. She could understand its pain, at least.

Unless it was more like a worm inside an apple, rotting it from the inside out. In that case…

She sighed. It couldn't change her determination.

'Just you and me.' She didn't whisper. She wouldn't cower or hide. Not anymore and never again to something that took her own mind hostage in her own body. She smiled when her Shadow rose through her and reached for her mind. 'Do your worst.'

It didn't whisper either. It grinned. Yua shivered; it seemed they were both tenacious.

She spared a look at the room where Kei would be asleep right now. The curtains weren't drawn, but they never were—Kei preferred a breeze as much as Yua did. The room beyond was dark and still. If Yua didn't come back, no one would have seen her leave.

Tonight, she might well die alone.

At least she wouldn't take innocent people with her.

That's not up to you.

The small clearing Aza had taken her to wasn't far away, and it wouldn't take her into the city. The farther away from people she was once she started, the better.

Every step through the coven's corridors and outside the gate felt like she moved towards her doom. Thanks to the late hour, no one else was outside. It made leaving easier, but part of her wanted someone to stop her. Part of her didn't want to do this, and Yua didn't think that part was her Shadow. She was scared, more so because her Shadow was watching every uncertain yet firm step. Tonight wouldn't allow for mistakes, but this wasn't something she could have practiced. Her stomach coiled when she stepped into the forest. Physically, she could still have turned around, but mentally, she was committed. It was too late for doubts. No matter what happened, this struggle ended tonight.

Her vision blurred when her Shadow reached for her mind again. She shoved it back down and gasped from the effort. It was getting harder to control. If her attention slipped now, it would have her.

'I'm… not… your prisoner,' she forced out through gritted teeth.

Think of what we could be. Free me. We can be more than this.

She hated that her Shadow spoke clearly while her own voice was strained, but she was afraid it would escape if she opened her mouth too wide.

We're the same—you know we are. Free me and you'll never have to sneak around again.

'No.'

When Yua reached the clearing, she kept walking to the other end. If this went wrong, she didn't want to be too close to the coven, and the next neighbourhood was still a long way down the mountain. The few extra steps wouldn't make any difference that mattered to her Shadow, but at least she'd tried. If she didn't survive tonight and unleashed the evil inside her veins, she'd die knowing that she'd done everything she could, no matter how small.

You think this will stop me? I'm too strong for you. Surrender. I promise it won't hurt if you do.

Yua was shaking when she reached the other end of the clearing. A few *sei* danced under the moon and didn't shy away from her. Yua swallowed—they might become her first victims in thirteen years.

She breathed deep and exhaled in one long sigh. She'd either go home victorious… or she hoped that someone would kill her before she could claim another victim. The city wasn't prepared for her—nowhere was. Failure wasn't an option.

'Alright.'

Yua closed her eyes, hoping to let the darkness in sliver by sliver. She imagined a steel barrier around her mind and felt the many trees at her back. Maybe O-Yu would smile on her and let her borrow some of their strength.

She opened her eyes.

Pictured a gap in the barrier.

'Do your worst.'

The pain was instant.

Her Shadow's Mist magic tore her into the air and pulled her limbs in opposite directions until her heart was exposed and vulnerable. Yua couldn't move one finger.

'N—' It hurt too much to speak.

The darkness laughed, an odd vibration around her heart. *Oh, yes!*

She pushed against it, but the Mist magic was stronger and too unknown. It ripped at the barrier around her mind and filled her conscience with an endless dark void. If this was the Mists, she didn't understand why anyone would want to go. Their hopelessness seeped into her and suffocated her.

You can't win. Surrender or don't—I will have you either way.

A scream tore out of her lungs. It hurt, like darkness itself squeezed her neck, but her control wasn't gone just yet. As hard as she could, she shoved her will against the darkness.

'You—'

It retreated from her mind but laced tighter around her heart.

'—won't—'

She saw more clearly but felt less. She strained her muscles so tight she was afraid she'd burst. If she could never move again after tonight, would it have been worth it?

'—have me!'

Everything Kei had taught her, every technique to keep the darkness at bay she'd ever learned—Yua took it all and threw it against the darkness around her heart.

It let go.

She fell to the ground, panting and exhausted. She'd never put this much energy into anything. A nervous laugh escaped her, but her eyes fell on her arm. The empty skin between her markings was filling in as the darkness leaked out of her pores and wrapped around her.

You think you've won? I don't tire like you do.

But she sensed the lie behind the threat. They were both exhausted, and her Shadow wasn't as brutal this time around. It gave her just enough time to steady herself. She'd read enough about the gift to know the theory behind its use. Since she didn't have magic herself—at least, not in the regular sense—she'd never been able to apply it, but now… Her Shadow had to live somewhere inside her. Maybe it really did live inside her veins, or maybe the rules about the gift could work for her too.

So, Yua turned her attention inwards and looked inside herself.

Why do you fight me? We could rule the world.

She no longer knew if the Shadow was talking to her or if these were her own thoughts amplified by exhaustion— exhaustion because of the effort she was putting into this and because this fight had lasted a lot longer than one night. She refused to let it end with her death.

'You're evil.'

Her jaw would likely hurt for days from the effort. She gritted her teeth and clamped her lips shut when a trail of dark fog slithered out.

I am you. You are me. We are the—

'We're *not* the same.'

We are. Just look at your arms.

They were pure obsidian. Not an inch of ivory left. Yua hadn't even noticed.

Yua gasped for air. She'd never liked her markings, but she'd always been able to see herself between the lines. Now, she didn't recognise herself.

Listen.

Aza's blood. Yua whipped around and heard it behind a shrub not far from her. One leap, two leaps, three, and her teeth could be in Aza's neck. For all her Sand Blade training, her soft skin wouldn't protect her. A faint memory from a night thirteen years ago pooled around her tongue, made her taste copper.

You'll be stronger than you ever knew you could be. Let us have her.

Every muscle in her body ached. Not moving had never been so hard. The whispers were fainter, though—more insistent, almost desperate and pleading, but tired.

But every time Aza's blood sang a new note, she was thirsty enough to run around the world just to sink her teeth into Aza's neck. Her heart hammered with the thought of a hunt.

Yes. Move. She's right there.

Yua swallowed.

Gripped the soil in her sweaty, shaking fingers.

And refused.

She made herself take deep breaths. What had Aza told her to do? Count green things? Yua's eyes darted from tree to tree and wondered how many leaves it would take before the world was silent again. She didn't just hear Aza's blood, she smelled it. She shook from the effort of staying where she was. She'd come too far to give up, but she didn't have much fight left in her. The bustle of Maishi Hou, even at this hour, was too far away, but there were other things she could focus on.

The light of the stars, so bright they burnt her eyes.

The smell of grass and moss, too weak against the melody Aza's blood hummed.

The pressing feel of fresh soil under her nails, oddly uncomfortable.

None of it was enough, but she focussed on them regardless.

Yua clenched her teeth, stared right into the moon, and drew strength from it.

She took one steadying breath…

… after…

… another…

… forced the darkness back with every ounce of her will…

…

and felt her heart return to normal.

Chapter Eighteen

'Yua!'

Her relieved sigh left her lips in a worn-out gasp. She rolled over and watched Aza run towards her. Her Shadow had calmed. Her heartbeat was returning to normal.

But Aza's voice was still too loud in the night's perfect silence.

Aza fell to her knees beside Yua and helped her sit. It hurt every bone in her body, but the pain wasn't as bad as it had been. Aza kept an arm around her shoulders, and Yua felt better for it. Her eyes darted to the vein in Aza's neck, and she forced herself to look into Aza's eyes instead.

'How did you find me?' Yua asked.

Aza shrugged. 'I followed you. I knew you were struggling more than usual earlier, so I slept with one eye open and one ear against the wall.' Aza stroked Yua's arm. 'Look. This is how I knew it was safe to come over.'

Yua followed Aza's finger, and her breath hitched. Her markings were gone. For the first time she could remember, her skin was… empty. She had wanted this for so long, but now she had it… For the second time tonight, she didn't recognise herself.

'When did they leave?'

'It was hard to see from over there and in the dark. They only disappeared after you fell to the ground.'

Yua nodded. Slowly, like it was too much effort, her markings began to return. She was surprised that she was relieved.

'Oh,' Aza said. 'Guess I spoke too soon.'

Yua gently traced one darkening vein from her wrist to her elbow. 'No, it's fine.'

As much as she had hated them, her skin looked wrong without them. Maybe the moonlight distorted her view, or maybe she was too drained to think clearly, but she was beginning to see the beauty Aza had seen all along. No one else had these marks. They were hers, and she no longer hated that they stood for everything that singled her out. If anything, they'd be a reminder that she had fought her Shadow and won.

They were also proof that she hadn't defeated her Shadow forever, but Yua took that as a good sign. She could control it. This power had originated in the Mists, but now it was her unique type of magic, and she would own it.

Aza sighed and sat back. 'What exactly happened here?'

'I called my Shadow. It almost overwhelmed me.' Her eyes flicked back to Aza's neck. To her wrists. 'I can... hear you. Your blood. It sings to me.' Goosebumps crept up her arms, and she shivered. 'It was so loud when my Shadow almost had me.' She hated that her voice wavered. She had to be stronger than this or she wouldn't win next time.

'Hey, look at me.' She did but found Aza's neck again. 'At my eyes, Yua. Honestly.'

Yua smiled. She had no idea how Aza could make light of this, but if Aza was still comfortable around her, it could be easy for Yua, too… or at least easier. No more fear. With Aza's help, on her own, maybe even with Kei's assistance, she'd be in charge. No other forces would ever move her body ever again.

No one else would die.

'It will take me a while to gain full control over this,' Yua said. 'You won't be safe near me until I do.'

No one else was safe, either, but no one else had treated her with the same acceptance and respect as Aza. Apart from Ichiro, and maybe even Kei, who had hidden the truth from Yua all these years to protect her. With a pang of guilt, Yua realised it must have been difficult for her too.

'Are you telling me to leave?' Aza asked.

Yua shook her head. That was the last thing she wanted, but until she knew what she was doing, it couldn't matter what she wished.

'I want you to have the option,' Yua said.

Aza cupped Yua's face with one hand and gently turned Yua's face to her own.

'Now you listen to me,' Aza said. 'Tonight, my blood sang to you, whatever that means. I saw how much you were struggling. I can't imagine what you've just gone through, but if I guess correctly—and don't correct me, I always do—then you wanted to hunt me across the world and bathe in my blood or something equally dramatic.

'But you didn't. You fought it, and you won. You underestimate yourself, Yua. Whatever this is, whatever it takes, you can do it.'

Tears stung Yua's eyes, but she wouldn't let them fall. Control started right now. Not trusting her voice, she nodded.

Aza pulled Yua into a hug. 'Who knows? There's a gifted queen in Rifarne, I hear Tramura is going easier on the gifted, and now this. Maybe the world is changing. Maybe it's time for something new here too. It's about time Midoka experienced a kind of magic it's never seen before, don't you think?'

Yua smiled. Now that would be something to marvel at.

'Besides,' Aza said, 'if you can't control yourself after all and throw yourself at me, I can always knock you out.'

Yua laughed and lay back. Now that her Shadow had settled, the stars were no longer too bright. They were beautiful. The night was a comforting blanket holding her tight. As much as she wanted to return to the coven, fall into her bed and sleep for a week, she craved the peace of this moment more. She had earned a bit of quiet, and she would enjoy it while she could…

Because she had a feeling it wouldn't last long.

Chapter Nineteen

Yua fell onto her bed as soon as they were through the door. Aza closed it behind them and stood by the window. She was grateful that Aza had convinced her to return before the novices usually headed to breakfast. The coven was still quiet, and they had sneaked back in without anyone noticing, but the first novices had passed them inside the corridors and on the stairs. If they'd waited another thirty minutes, they wouldn't have been as lucky.

'Do you want to talk about it?' Aza asked.

'There's nothing more to say,' Yua said. 'You saw.'

The truth was that she did want to talk, but she didn't know how to put her feelings into words. Now they were back in her room and her victory was beginning to sink in, she felt nothing and everything at the same time. Sorry and grateful. Proud and empty. Scared. Brave. And underneath all that was the song Aza's blood was still humming—would always be humming—for her dark magic. She was in control right now, but O-Yu help her, it didn't like that it had lost. Even now she felt it squirm under her skin and through her veins like it was searching for a way out.

'That doesn't mean I understand it,' Aza said. 'I can't imagine what must be going through your head.'

Yua didn't know either. She wondered if she ever would.

'Maybe later,' Yua said. 'Right now, I want to sleep.'

Aza wouldn't argue with it. People never did.

'I'm not surprised, and I'll leave you to it. But I also think you need to talk to someone.'

Everyone except Aza, it seemed.

Yua sat and drew her legs up. 'I told you, there's nothing to—'

'Nothing to say, I know. I don't believe it. Are you honestly telling me that you're fine? You fought your Shadow and won. Your magic raised you into the air at one point, your skin looked charred from where I was hiding, your eyes were darker than the night, and you're telling me there's nothing to say? Don't tell me you're fine.'

Yua sighed—Kei wasn't her biological mother, but it seemed she had inherited some things by observation—and stood.

'I don't know what to tell you. I *am* tired. I'm also scared of myself and impressed with myself.'

Aza smiled. 'That's a good start.'

Someone knocked at her door. Yua asked them to enter, and Ichiro entered with a tray of tea and a selection of bread, cheeses, and hams. Aza's stomach rumbled loud enough for the whole coven to hear. Yua laughed to herself. What would it be like to unapologetically be herself, like Aza?

'You're a saint, Ichiro,' Aza said. 'We've had a long night. How do you say *star* in Midokan?'

'*Tahou*,' Yua said.

Ichiro grimaced. 'Please don't—'

'I'll call you *tahou* from now on.'

'It's just tea.' He set the tray onto the table.

Aza made a ham-and-cheese sandwich and narrowed her eyes at him. 'Blasphemy.'

Ichiro poured a cup and handed it to Yua. 'You look tired. Did you spend all night in the archives? I've heard some of the novices talk about it.'

Yua didn't want to know what rumours they had invented over it, but she imagined the Blood Wisp being allowed free rein with the world's most dangerous secrets would keep them busy for a while. If she was lucky, it would be more exciting than her sneaking out last night, just in case anyone had seen her leave after all.

She took a long sip of chamomile. Ichiro had no idea what she'd done last night or what she could have done. She was happy to leave it at *tired*. Details would only complicate an already complicated subject.

'I'm fine. Your tea will help. Would you leave us, please? You're right, I am tired. I'll have a nap.'

'Good, you look like you need it,' Ichiro said. He moved the food and tea off the tray and picked it up. 'You *will* have a nap, right?'

If she dared. The worry that her Shadow would seize the first opportunity to overwhelm her was still there, but she needed to sleep eventually.

'I promise.' It'd be easier to think once she was rested. Now that she'd won the first fight, she knew there were steps she needed to take, but she was too exhausted to figure out what those were.

'Good, then I'll leave you to it.' He walked to the door. 'But if I find you anywhere near the archives, I'll drag you right back to your room.'

Yua smiled. She doubted her Shadow would take her to do some reading if it took control, but that was one more thing she couldn't say to him. The less he knew, the more likely he was to bring her tea. It was selfish, but hadn't she earned two friends by now?

'Stay with me?' Yua blushed even as she made the request. It was a simple thing. She wasn't asking for anything unreasonable. But she'd never asked anyone to stay before, and that she felt safer with Aza was new too. The question felt unnatural on her tongue, and her mouth went dry.

Aza downed her tea and stood. 'I'll just use the bathroom, but after that I'll stay for as long as you want. Go lie down. You might already be asleep when I come out.'

Yua wasn't so sure. She felt tired enough to fall asleep standing up, but her mind was also too busy. Maybe Aza could help her make sense of some of her insecurities.

She sat on her bed as Aza disappeared in her bathroom and fell back into the sheets. Newai jumped in through the window and meowed in greeting. He stretched out next to her, and she scratched his ears. He purred into her hand. She didn't know if all cats had the uncanny ability to know when their humans needed them, but she was grateful that he did. Maybe she was even luckier than she'd realised—it seemed O-Yu had granted her three friends.

'You can sleep on my bed if you like.' The ginger cat looked at her with big eyes. For a moment, she wondered what it'd be like to fall asleep with someone warm cuddled into her. 'My friend will be here in a minute. I hope you don't mind.'

Newai rubbed his head into her hand. Yua took it as agreement.

The coven didn't allow pets so she couldn't give him an official home, but perhaps it was better that way. He had the freedom to go wherever he wanted, and she wouldn't tie him to any one place.

Aza joined them on the bed. 'I'm surprised you didn't get changed.'

'Hm?' Yua looked down herself. She still wore the same clothes she'd worn yesterday. There wasn't much variety in the trousers and shirts all novices wore, but now Aza had made her aware of it, clean clothes would have been nice. Yesterday's fabric seemed to stick to her like it was caked to her marked skin with mud and blood and something itchy. She scratched her arm but wasn't convinced she had the energy to get up again now she was lying down.

'I'm sorry I didn't talk before,' Yua said.

Newai regarded Aza with narrowed eyes but didn't greet her. Yua thought it wasn't that he didn't like her but rather that his survival instinct made him suspicious of strangers. He had shared the roof with Yua for about three years now. Aza was still new.

'That's okay,' Aza said. 'I'm struggling to put what happened into words, and I can't imagine it's any easier for you.'

Yua gave her a tired smile. 'It must have looked strange from where you were.'

Aza raised an eyebrow. 'You were *floating*, Yua.' She looked away. 'I wasn't close enough to see your features well, but I knew you were in pain. I saw you struggle. The way your skin darkened until it was nothing but ink… I don't know. I'm glad you didn't attack.'

Yua looked at her hands, pulled up her sleeves and regarded her arms. Her veins were still black, but they were their usual thin lines.

She trembled and hugged herself. 'Your blood… sang… to me. I don't know what I'll do if it gets this loud again.'

Aza looked at her, but Yua didn't meet her eyes. She still expected to find the usual fear and disgust in Aza's features. After what had happened last night, she'd accepted that today was likely that day. Everyone had limits.

'Don't think about it while you're tired,' Aza said. 'Thinking is hard when you're tired.'

Yua couldn't argue with that.

'What do you think I should do?' she asked.

Aza shuffled closer. The bed dipped a little from the shifting weight, and Newai glared at her for it. 'Right now, I think you should keep your promise to Ichiro and take that nap. Afterwards? Use the archives. If answers are anywhere, they're there.' Aza half-climbed over her until Yua had no choice but to look at her. 'Can you hear it now?'

Yua felt the bit of colour she had drain from her face. What was paler than ivory? She didn't have to concentrate to hear the melody. It simply was there, like stars at night or puddles after rain. It wasn't loud, but it didn't need to be. She was worried it was forever stuck in her head, a particularly catchy song that promised pain.

She nodded.

'And do you feel in control?' Aza asked.

Her eyes burnt. 'I don't know.'

Seeing Aza's face so close to her own did terrible things to Yua. Her Shadow had always whispered that Aza's neck was right there, but in this moment, she wouldn't have to cross a room or a clearing to get to it. She only needed to lean forward. Grab Aza's head and pull it down to her lips.

Yua was grateful when Aza sat back.

'Then why waste time?' Aza asked. 'You can take a nap, I'll wake you after an hour, and then we go back to the archives. You'll feel better once you know that you're doing something proactive.'

Yua nodded and slid off her bed. 'It's too early to sleep anyway.' She patted Newai's head. 'I'll see you tomorrow.'

He meowed and huffed.

'What?' Aza jumped off the bed after her. 'I said we can go after you've napped.'

'You also said I'll feel better.' She was still scared to close her eyes, let alone let go enough to fall asleep. If being proactive helped her feel better, she'd go to the archives and research until she was so out of it that Aza had to carry her back.

Although, that would put her head close to Aza's neck again, and she couldn't risk that.

'Sleep will make you feel better too,' Aza said. 'Let's go later. The archives have been there for how long? They'll still be there in an hour or two.'

She knew sleeping first was the responsible thing to do, but despite her fatigue, her heart raced too much. Her mind was too vivid with visions of Aza bleeding out in her arms and Yua licking the blood off her skin, out of her hair. If she went to sleep now, her Shadow would overpower her. She knew it with a certainty she'd never felt for much else. Focussing on reading ancient texts now wouldn't be easy and she was sure she'd miss things, but at least she'd be awake. If she was awake, she could control herself.

Yua glanced at her. 'Please? We don't have to stay all day. I just need to know that I'm doing something.'

Aza sighed. 'Fine. I'll be with you, so if you fall asleep, I'll carry you back.'

She smiled. It was nice to have someone who understood her.

Yua opened the door and held it open for Aza. 'Thank you.'

Once again, Aza had been right—Yua already felt better just from taking steps towards her goal. She felt like she was waking up for the first time, and it gave her the boost she needed to stay awake for the next few hours. Part of her was scared of what they would find, but a larger part was excited to see what else the tomes could offer her.

And a smaller, ever-growing part inside her dared her to suck Aza's blood from her veins and bathe in the leftovers.

The archives were a good idea. You'll be alone down there. Just you and her, no witnesses.

Yua couldn't tear herself away from the vein pulsing in Aza's neck. When had her eyes flown to it? She'd left her room, Aza had left after her, and then… It was so close. There was no one else in the corridor.

No one would know.

She'd be quick. If she surrendered to her Shadow, it would be easy as breathing.

Yua blinked and forced herself to look away.

'Can you do something for me?'

'Sure,' Aza said. 'What do you need?'

Yua stared at the wall, but she still heard the memory. She had won the first battle, but she couldn't shake the feeling that her Shadow was preparing its counterattack. Maybe being alone with Aza in the archives wasn't a good idea. Maybe focussing on her research was just what she needed to take her mind off it. How was she supposed to know which path was right? Either way, her Shadow whispered promises of disaster. She had to choose one option and hope it was the right choice. She would *make* it the right choice.

No matter how loud her Shadow screamed, she wouldn't hurt Aza.

'Can you find Ichiro and ask him for more tea?'

'Good idea. What will you do?'

The itch was getting worse. Yua tugged at her sleeve, but that made it prickle worse.

'I'll take a bath and get changed—you're right, it's about time I got out of yesterday's clothes.' She backtracked into her room and slipped behind her screen, stripped off everything as if the fabric were burning her, and handed her clothes to Aza for washing or incinerating, whatever Aza fancied. If the clothes never touched her skin again, she'd be happy.

'You know,' Aza said, 'I've changed my mind. You don't need to do more research today. You need a day off.'

Yua frowned. 'It doesn't work like that. I can't—'

'Maybe I can convince Kei to give us some space, hm? You go have a bath, I go talk to Kei. I'll be quick, I promise.' Aza edged closer. 'Don't argue with me. After what you achieved last night, you deserve a day off.'

Yua sighed. Aza had been right so many times before, maybe she had a point now too. A break did sound nice, even if she still didn't believe that she could just take time off from her darkness.

'But don't stay away too long?'

Aza grinned. 'Promise.'

Once Aza had left the room, Yua traipsed naked into her bathroom and sank into the bathtub. She'd never been one for taking long baths, but today it felt like the right thing to do. A long time ago, Kei had gifted her lavender oil to drip into the water. Maybe an infused soak was just what her tired mind needed. Because they were in the coven, the water was always the perfect temperature—O-Yu forbid the novices had to make do with cold water or burn their delicate flesh—and caretakers had worked out a piping system so she could pour as much water as she wanted. Some invention from the continent, she was sure—maybe Vistria. From what she'd heard, Vistrians revered magic, possibly even more so than Midokans, and they placed much importance on beauty. This seemed like something they would come up with.

But it didn't matter. Pondering how their water system worked wouldn't help her control her Shadow. She appreciated Aza's suggestion, but she wasn't naïve—the chance of Kei agreeing to anything like a day out, whatever Aza had in mind, was zero. So instead, Yua considered where to pick up her research until the lavender filled her senses and even her next predicament no longer seemed important.

Yua didn't know what to say when she took the first step onto the long stairs down the mountain into Maishi Hou. Aza had convinced her to leave the coven grounds and sneak into the forest, but that hadn't been the same. They had done that in secret. This, though… the cool breeze and weak warmth from the autumn sun that kissed her skin felt like freedom.

'This is the happiest I've seen you,' Aza laughed.

Yua realised she was smiling and grinned wider. 'I—' She wasn't sure how to describe it without sounding childish or like she'd never been outside before. 'I've never left the coven, at least not with Kei's permission. How did you convince her?'

Aza shrugged. 'It wasn't that hard. Kei agreed that you've been working hard and deserve a break. The neighbourhood immediately around the coven is close enough that the Seven can keep an eye on you—something about Lena feeling for you?'

Yua paled. Lena was one of the Seven and had a gift for empathy, which apparently also allowed her to… what? Tune into Yua's energy? This day felt less like freedom if she would be watching their every step.

'Relax,' Aza said. 'They're only watching in case something goes terribly wrong. No one is trying to limit your fun.'

But it's the things you find most terrible that would be the most enjoyable. Why don't we have some real fun? They won't be able to stop us.

Yua shivered and rubbed her arms.

'Is the breeze too cold?' Aza said. 'We can do this another day; although, I'm not sure if it'll get any warmer for a while.'

Yua shook her head. 'No, I just don't like being watched.'

Whether it was a Seven or her Shadow, there was always someone observing her. She didn't know which one was better—either could be devastatingly dangerous.

'I'm sorry,' Yua said.

Aza grinned. 'So, this is Yua's big day out, huh?'

They smiled at each other, and Yua wasn't ashamed of the sting in her eyes. It would only last for the day, but for these hours, at least, she'd belong only to herself. She could pretend that neither Lena nor her Shadow were there if it meant a day away from the coven. If her Shadow stayed quiet, this day had the potential to be the best day she'd ever had.

And still, it troubled her that her Shadow was silent at the thought.

Yua breathed deep and cast her eyes out over the valley. The stairs leading up to their coven had been chiselled into the mountain itself and had natural curves, which would make walking treacherous at times. She had read somewhere that all covens sat above their towns and cities, but she'd never been to or even seen another. Standing just past her coven's gates, the whole world lay open to her, and it sent her heart into a manic frenzy.

Aza stood next to her. 'Are you going to take another step or is this as far as you dare to go?'

'I'll go, just… in a moment.'

'As slowly as you want.'

Yua nodded and moved onto the next step down. Her experience was limited, but as far as she was concerned, this was the most beautiful place in the world. To her right, the mountain fell into the valley. The Seven and Kei had put spells in place to stop anyone from taking one step too many, but as they were invisible, they didn't stand in the way of the view. To her left, the forest stretched down the mountain and around the coven's foundations. The library extended deep into the rock, its secrets buried out of sight like corpses. The occasional royal empress trees painted patches of purple into the otherwise green landscape. Leaves rustled. The fountain splattered behind her. As much as she hated being a prisoner here, she could admit that there had to be worst places to be stuck in. She had never felt more peaceful.

Yua took another step, then another, savouring the experience which was so common for everyone else.

'Tell me more about Krymistis,' Yua said. Today was a good day to learn about the world outside the coven.

Next to her, Aza kept Yua's pace. 'What do you want to know?'

It was hard to think of something specific when she knew so little about the place. Aza had talked a little about the market and their swords before, but for all Yua knew, there was nothing more to say on either.

'I've never seen the sea. Is the place you're from by the beach?'

Aza smiled, and her eyes glazed over. 'Most places in Krymistis are. There isn't much food or shelter out in the desert, so our towns and cities developed near water. I don't think we're very different to other places in that regard, though. We just rely on water more since the desert doesn't offer much.'

Yua couldn't imagine anything so dry. She'd always imagined Krymistis exotic and colourful.

'Is your home far from here?'

Aza nodded. 'I'm from the capital, on the other end of the country. Paranossa has one of the biggest ports in the world.' She turned her smile onto Yua. 'You'd love it. Maybe one day I'll take you.'

Yua's smile didn't feel as happy. The chances of her leaving the coven and even the country for such a long time felt like little more than a daydream.

'What are the beaches like?'

'More sand. Also, a lot of ships.' Aza looked out over the valley to their right. 'It's not exotic like Midoka.'

Yua blinked. 'You think we're exotic?' She was desperate to explore the world at her leisure, but Midoka was all she knew. It hadn't occurred to her that someone from another country might think of it as unusual. Then again, she hadn't known anyone from other countries until recently.

Aza laughed. 'The way you use the gift is amazing to me. It's everywhere. It's like you Midokans can't take one breath without weaving magic into it.'

Yua focussed on the uneven steps under her feet. 'Well, other Midokans maybe.'

'Sorry,' Aza said. 'I didn't mean it like that. I just meant that at home, we lace the gift into our weapons and sometimes we play with it, especially children, but we don't use it as freely as Midokans do. Like there's no other option. Like you'll die if you use your hands. That's what's so different for me.' Aza walked ahead and blocked Yua's path. 'I think it's a good thing you're not like that. When I arrived, I saw people use their gifts to bring objects closer, to work their gardens or to entertain their children. It's like most Midokans are above physical labour. You're not like that.'

She'd never seen it like that. The gift, or lack of it, had always been a cause for shame to her.

'And that's good?'

She doubted the novices and Mist Women would agree.

'*Kyastra*, you're a gem amongst charcoal.'

Yua blushed. It was the nicest thing anyone had ever said to her.

'Shall we?' Aza asked. 'It's a long way down.'

Yua nodded and led the way down the stairs. With every step away from the coven, she felt lighter. Even her Shadow seemed quieter out here. Could it be that a change of scenery was all she'd needed? Could it have been that easy?

Aza stopped dead beside her and stared into the woods. 'Is that what I think it is?'

'Hm?' Yua followed Aza's eyes to a *sei* dancing through the foliage and low-hanging branches. 'It's just a night wisp.'

Aza frowned. 'It's not night. It's pretty sunny for autumn, actually.'

'I didn't name them. They are more often seen at night, but really they live in shaded areas like forests.' She turned her attention away from the small blue glow and back to Aza. 'Why are you so suspicious of it?'

'I've mistaken them, I think. We have something similar in Krymistis, but ours lure travellers into the desert where they die of thirst.'

A chill ran down Yua's arms. '*Sei* are harmless. A little mischievous, maybe, but not mean. They're a bit like children—mostly playful.'

'Can we get closer?' Aza took two steps closer to the forest. The *sei* stopped. They had no eyes, but Yua felt like it watched them.

'They're shy,' Yua said. 'Set one foot into the forest and it'll hide.'

Yua had seen new novices from other countries sneak out at night to scare them. To those novices, they weren't living creatures because they had no eyes or limbs and didn't communicate like humans did. To Yua, they were better than people. Respect for all things was taught early on at the covens, and the novices who delighted in scaring them soon stopped.

Aza backed away with a frown that spoke of a lifetime of learned suspicion. 'Huh. In Krymistis, if you see one and set one foot into the desert, you die.'

'Come on,' Yua said. 'As you said, it's a long way down.'

The autumn sun had gained a little strength by the time the first sounds from the city carried up to them.

Dread coiled around Yua's throat.

'It sounds so busy,' she said. 'What if… What if I can't…' Her Shadow was quiet right now, but what if it was a trap? Was it capable of that? If she started to hear their blood when she was surrounded by people on all sides, her Shadow would overpower her—she wouldn't even try to tell herself otherwise. Kei would never let her leave again if she killed or injured someone, no matter how many Sand Blades volunteered to come with her.

Aza twirled her dagger between her fingers. 'Then I'll whack you over the head with Desma. She's pretty persuasive.'

Yua smiled. She genuinely felt better; if Aza said she'd stop her, she would. Yua didn't know how, but maybe trust was less about knowing and more about faith. Aza had undeniable skill with her daggers, and she had seen Yua several feet in the air while her Shadow tried to devour her. Maybe that was enough for a Sand Blade.

'Where do you want to start?' Yua asked.

'I'm not sure. I didn't see much from inside the carriage. They brought me right up to the stairs, and it was still dark when I arrived.'

'But I saw you arrive. It was late morning.'

'Kei briefed me first.' Aza's stomach rumbled. 'I wouldn't hate something to eat?'

Yua nodded. 'I don't know what we'll find, but I'm sure there's something.'

Aza shrugged and gazed down the stairs as if she could smell the food already. 'This isn't the capital for nothing, right?'

The closer they got to the city, the more even the steps became. The forest thinned to both sides as nature gave way to neighbourhoods and the everyday bustle of Maishi Hou. The steps finally ended in a quiet road with a small fountain as the centrepiece. The road curved around it like the fountain had been here first and the architects hadn't wanted to disturb it. Two-storey houses lined the quiet street on both sides. A woman was sweeping outside her door and humming to herself. Two children were drawing on the road with chalk, laughing when their runes came to life and glowed before their magic flickered out of existence again. They were so young— Yua guessed around six—but even they had some control over their gift.

How different would her life have been if she hadn't killed her family? Would they have been able to teach her? For a moment, she resented them for their lack of preparation. Maybe, if they had done their research better… She blinked the thought away. No one knew much about the Mists. It wasn't fair to wish more knowledge onto her parents when no one else would likely have done any better. It was more likely that she would never have had the same carefree childhood.

In the archives, she had questioned what she was. These innocent children, who had nothing to do with her internal struggle, made it worse. In the eye of any Midokan, she wasn't even that—less than a regular Midokan child, and less than a demon from the Mists. She was something in between. Not quite human, not quite monster.

'Are you alright?' Aza asked.

Yua realised she'd been staring at the children's play runes and snapped her head back to Aza. 'Yes. Where shall we go from here?'

Yua had always imagined the steps to come out in the middle of a lively market. She hadn't expected the end of their trip to be so… mundane.

'I can still hear a lot of people,' Aza said. 'We can't be far.'

'I'll ask.'

It'd be nice to talk to people who weren't scared of her. Everyone likely knew about the Blood Wisp, especially this close to the coven, but they had no way of knowing it was her.

Yua approached her. The woman continued to sweep but looked up.

'Excuse me,' Yua said. 'What's the fastest way to the market from here?'

She felt ridiculously nervous. It was just a normal question. People had conversations like this all the time. She wore long sleeves, so her black veins were covered. Yua took a deep breath in for confidence—this woman had no reason to fear her.

The woman smiled. She wore a well-loved, simple dress with fading blues and greys. It looked like she'd had it for years, had swept the space outside her door in it for years. Sand had permanently stained the bottom. The little traces of use—a patched hole on one arm, frayed ends on the sleeves—suited her. Unlike the Mist Women, she wore her few wrinkles and greying hair with pride. Yua felt deep within her that she'd never look as caressed by life as this woman did. Her Shadow would either end her, or she'd learn to control it and would grow used to hiding her age like all Mist Women did. She envied this woman for her boring life; it must have had its own hardships but was free from the whispering darkness Yua fought every day.

'Are you alright, my dear?' the woman asked. 'You don't look well.'

Yua blushed. She must have been staring while the woman had explained the way... and Yua hadn't heard any of it.

'I'm sorry. You reminded me of someone, that's all.' She reminded Yua of the woman Yua could never be. Of the woman her mother might have been. Of all the little things she'd never have and hadn't realised she wanted. 'Would you mind repeating yourself?'

'Follow the road ahead and turn left at the crossroad. If you follow the voices from there, you can't miss it.'

Yua folded her hands before her and bowed. 'Thank you, ma'am.'

'Such manners!' The warmth her smile brought to her features made Yua envy her even more.

The door opened and a man stepped out. Children were laughing inside. He whispered something in the woman's ear and gently pulled her inside. His eyes didn't leave Yua.

Aza stepped closer. 'Is something wrong?'

'Please leave us,' the man said. 'We don't want any trouble.'

The woman looked torn but didn't object.

Aza scowled. 'We'd never—'

'It's okay,' Yua said. 'I'm used to it. We know where to go now, so let's find something to eat.'

The woman opened her mouth to speak, but the door closed before she could say whatever was on her mind.

'I don't understand,' Aza said. 'How does he know who you are?'

'We don't know for sure that they recognised me. They might just be wary of strangers.' But Yua knew the look on his face all too well. 'I don't want to talk about it. Let's go.'

It didn't leave her mind as they followed the woman's directions. Yua could have led such a different life. A life filled with the laughter of her children, boring every-day chores, and a husband who cared enough about her to step into perceived danger and pull her out of it. But did she even want that? Children? A husband? She already knew daily boredom, and it would be difficult to find a husband in a coven full of women. She thought of the way Aza smiled at her, the way Aza saw beauty in her most hated features. She'd made Yua feel better about herself than anyone else ever had. Maybe she didn't need a husband or children. Maybe she needed...

Yua swallowed, suddenly too warm in the chilly breeze. She'd never considered anything so normal as a relationship before. It had always been something that existed in fiction but not in her life. She'd never known a Mist Woman to get married or even take a lover, but then she'd never asked.

'Look.'

Yua followed Aza's nod.

'Your sleeve has ridden up your arm a little and exposed your veins. That must be how they knew it's you.'

Yua pulled her sleeves over her wrists and gripped them so they wouldn't shift again. Her face, at least, was as plain as anyone's. If she kept her arms covered, she'd be invisible in the crowd.

'Maybe we should go back.'

They'd barely left the coven, and she'd already let strangers see her blackened veins. Would she do any better in a busy market? If someone saw her for what she was in the crowd, she doubted they'd leave her alone as easily as the couple had done.

Aza shook her head, took her hand, and lightly pulled her onwards. 'Don't let one man put you off. His wife was nice to you. There'll be more like her, and besides'—she nodded to Yua's finger gripping her sleeves—'hold them like that and no one will get a long-enough look at your arms.'

Yua hesitated. She didn't want to spend the whole day worried about how much skin she was showing. She was hardly indecent—if she didn't hold on to her sleeves, they still came down to her wrist. In the coven, she wouldn't have thought twice about it. But if a gust of wind got into the fabric...

'Yua.'

She looked into Aza's eyes.

'I won't let them hurt you.'

Yua believed her. Slowly, she nodded. Aza let go of her hand and led the way.

They followed the road until it split. From there, the excited chatter of marketgoers showed them the way. More people passed them, many with bags or newly bought items floating behind them like the world's most loyal dragonfly. Aza was right, people here used magic for the most mundane things. It was odd to her that, right above them, novices practiced magic that could heal or destroy, while people down here in the city used it because they were lazy. The coven's teachers made new novices use their gifts for ordinary chores so they'd get used to how the gift felt faster, but they didn't encourage it once the novices' control was good enough. They'd scoff at the blatant use she saw now.

Amidst all that, no one gave her more than a glance. Yua suspected Aza's presence had something to do with that too. More so than ever, Aza looked and felt like a bodyguard. She stood taller, straightened her shoulders, and took long, deliberate steps. Her golden hair and bronze skin earned them a few curious looks, but none lingered. Yua had hated that Kei had hired an assassin to watch over her, but right now, she was grateful.

Yua turned a corner...

And stood in the middle of the market.

Stalls were left and right of the street. It was wide enough for more sellers in the middle, which created four rows in total. Yua didn't see the end for all the people crowding around them or rushing past. Was this the chaos she'd yearned for atop her roof? She was surprised that she already missed the silence and Newai.

Aza stepped in front of her with a grin. 'Everything you hoped it'd be?'

Yua took a tentative step back. 'No. It's too much, I don't know where to—'

'Don't worry about it, you've got me. I lead, you follow.' Aza took her hand and clasped it with her warm fingers. 'I won't let you get lost.'

Yua nodded and Aza rushed head-first into the thick of it, pulling Yua along like a dog that was scared it would get stepped on. Every other step, someone bumped into her. Sellers were shouting out their wares from every direction. Small children ran through the crowd and made her trip. There was so much noise, so much confusion, so many more people than she'd ever seen in one place…

And not one of them looked at her or cared she was here.

Yua's heart skipped. She'd never felt so intimidated, but more than anything, she felt free.

'Look!' Aza almost tore her arm off when she took a sharp right through the ever-moving mass. 'What's that? I've seen pictures, but no one told me what they are.'

Yua smiled. 'Why don't you try one? They are good, I'll have one with you.'

Aza winked, and Yua's stomach fluttered. 'I knew there was a mischievous streak in you.'

Yua ordered two and waited while Aza paid with a sparkle in her eyes. She ate as she watched Aza bite into her own.

Aza sighed. 'So good. What are they? The taste is familiar, but I'm not—'

'They are octopus balls.'

Aza choked. 'When you say *balls*—'

Yua giggled. 'You know, because of their shape.'

Aza swallowed and laughed. 'Oh, *aste os*. I thought—never mind. They're yummy. Who cares what they are?'

Yua laughed. Now *this* felt like the freedom she'd imagined. She wouldn't let anything spoil this day for her.

After their early lunch, she allowed Aza to pull her into whichever direction her Sand Blade fancied. Yua had never known there was so much variety to everything: beautiful dresses of the finest silks and brightest colours; more food and sweets than she could ever eat; jewellery imbued with magic. One stall sold books of all genres, their covers clean and new rather than yellowed and worn.

The crowd no longer frightened her. Aza's confidence was rubbing off on her, and she didn't care where Aza took her next. Yua wanted to see it all.

She hadn't received new clothes in so long, and the ones she did have were the same trousers and shirts all novices were. Yua hadn't chosen them; her heart turned to stone when she realised that she'd never picked her own clothes before. The colours and fabrics here easily beat what she had. She touched the fine materials, allowed merchants to hold them up so she could see herself in them, and almost agreed to try one on behind a partition inside one of the larger stalls.

Before she could regret trying a dress she couldn't buy—and showing everyone her black veins for a moment of normality— Aza pulled her to a table with sharp daggers, swords, and other weapons Yua didn't have names for. There was no crowd around this seller. Midokans didn't use traditional weapons, but it seemed some Krymistian traders tried their luck anyway. Aza looked as enchanted with the sharp edges as Yua had felt feeling the fabrics.

Before she knew it, the sun no longer stood high in the sky and the shadows were growing longer. Would Kei allow another day like this if she asked nicely? Nothing had gone wrong. Surely, she'd proven that she could control herself? Her Shadow had been quiet for once. Even better, Aza had guarded her without feeling like a bodyguard for most of the day. Once Yua had got used to the bustle and accepted that no one was looking at her, Aza had felt less like a protector and more like a friend. Yua's heart warmed at the thought.

'We should probably head back,' Yua said. 'It'll take a while to climb all those stairs back up to the coven.'

Aza didn't reply.

Yua looked behind herself, to her left and right, and over the heads of the thinning crowd, but there was no sign of her. She was alone.

Yua's eyes flitted to her arms. Her skin didn't look so well covered anymore. Was that man staring at her? Did this woman hold her child's hand just a little tighter when their eyes met?

'Aza?'

The market had been so noisy a moment ago. Now the voices had thinned, and another sound washed over her.

Blood.

There were so many people. The song rose over the chatter, over the last-minute shouts of sellers as they packed up for the day. And then it was no longer just inside their veins.

Someone was bleeding. She smelled the difference—fresher, somehow, like the first autumn breeze after a stifling summer, but still warm. Its song was clearer, too, like she finally heard it in person after having pressed her ears to walls before.

Find him. Follow the scent.

Her eyes darted over the people until she found a crying boy. It dripped off his finger. Red, teasing droplets going to waste on the pavement.

Yua felt herself inch forwards. She knew she should stop, should at least try to turn away, but a part of her didn't want to.

Lure him away from these people. Rip open his neck.

'Yua.'

Her head snapped around and found Aza's concerned eyes. Her own flitted back to the boy, but Aza placed a hand on her cheek and moved her head back.

Don't let her spoil it. Drink her blood instead and she'll never stop you again.

'Breathe. Calm down.'

'I'm not—' She was panting from the effort and the blood lust.

Under her sun-kissed bronze, Aza paled a little. 'Let's get you back.'

A woman gasped and pointed at Yua's arms. The markings had started to spread—just her pinkie left and her whole hand would be ebony.

More people had stopped to stare, first looking at the woman's brand-new dress, which she had dropped in shock, and then at her. Yua had never thought she'd miss the coven's safety.

Aza put an arm around her shoulders and hurried her away from the market. Tears stung her eyes. She'd known it had been too good to be true.

'Where were you?' she hissed. It came out sharper than she'd intended.

'I swear I only turned around for one second and you'd disappeared.'

Neither of them said another word. The damage was done. She could have lost control and killed that child. It wouldn't matter that nothing had happened. That woman would complain to Kei since her new clothes lay dirty in the street and she would no doubt blame Yua. Worse, she'd complain that Yua had been allowed out at all. The boy's parents must have noticed where her attention had been too. Her day of freedom had been nice, but it'd be a miracle if she ever got another.

And while Aza led her back to the coven, their blood sang up to her, filling her feet with lead and her head with nightmares.

Chapter Twenty

Yua marched up to Kei's office and barged in without knocking. She wasn't angry, but she was nervous and running on adrenaline. As far as she knew, what she was about to demand had never been done before, at least not in this coven.

After she and Aza had returned from the market, she had spent another sleepless night too scared to close her eyes. The whispers had been relentless, and Yua was tired of being afraid. She couldn't afford another night without sleep, but her Shadow had promised her what it would do if she drifted off.

Maybe her lack of sleep and her adrenaline made her too bold, but she didn't care. It was time she took charge.

Kei opened the door from her bed chambers and peeked into her office.

'Yua? Is something wrong?'

Yua blinked. Kei was in her nightgown. She stared out the window—it was only dawn. Yua blushed. She had got too carried away with her plan to notice the time.

'I'm sorry,' she said, her eyes still on the pink light on the windowsill. 'I'll come back later.'

'Nonsense.' Kei sat at her desk and beckoned Yua to sit opposite her. 'This seems important, so let's not waste time. What do you need?'

Her heart jumped. Kei had always put the needs of everyone

else first, but where Yua was concerned, that usually meant keeping her away from others. To protect others from her. It felt nice to hear the words aimed at her for once.

'Has Aza told you what happened in town?' Yua asked.

She was worried her demand would come out as a garbled, confused mess if she didn't take a moment to breathe, but she was more worried that the words wouldn't come out at all if she hesitated.

Concern ghosted across Kei's face, but she steeled her eyes.

'She hasn't. Did something happen that I should know about?'

Yua swallowed. They had been together the whole night—after Yua's reaction to the boy's blood, Aza had stayed with her in case Yua needed help—but Yua had half-expected her to report everything that happened to Kei.

Yua gripped her trousers in her lap.

'There was a boy. He was bleeding.'

Kei nodded for her to continue, but it wasn't as easy as that. Yua still couldn't get herself to say the words, and she already needed all her resolve to make her demand.

'I… smelled it. I…'

Kei was quiet for a moment. Yua stared at her feet, hoping she didn't need to elaborate.

'I see,' Kei said. 'Then you did well for getting away. I take it Aza played a part in that?'

Yua nodded.

'You understand I need to reconsider whether you—'

'I didn't come here to confess.' She felt bold, interrupting Kei like that, but she needed to get it out before it ate her whole. 'I want lessons. Shizue studies the Mists. You said yourself that my power comes from there. I want her to teach me how to control it.'

Yua took Kei's stunned silence as her chance to take a deep breath and steady herself. Asking that one of the Seven teach her, privately, was terrifying, but she was more scared of her Shadow.

To her surprise, Kei chuckled. 'I admit, I didn't expect this. You know even I can't order Shizue to do anything, least of all take on a private novice?'

'I know, but I think—'

'But that doesn't mean I can't speak to her and try to convince her.'

Her mouth went dry. She no longer felt brave enough to look into Kei's eyes. Instead, Yua stared at her feet and willed her hands to stop shaking.

'Thank you.'

'Don't thank me yet,' Kei said. 'Shizue rarely takes private novices; of course, the subject matter might have something to do with that. I think she'll jump at the chance, to be honest, but I don't want to get your hopes up.'

Yua felt her lips tug upwards. No matter what happened, Kei was willing to try. Kei hadn't argued or tried to change her mind. Her support meant everything.

'How would you like me to plead your case?'

There it was—the scariest moment of all… or rather, the moment that would lead to it.

'I want to ask her myself.'

Kei raised an eyebrow. 'Then why come to me at all? I'll ask her here now if you're ready.'

Yua nodded. Kei would contact Shizue immediately, one

mind to another. It didn't help her nerves though. She felt safer in the relative familiarity of Kei's office. Shizue herself was enough of an unknown; Yua didn't want to sit in her space, too.

'Because you're my…' Even after all these years, it felt odd to call Kei her mother. Not wrong, just… weird—her real mother lay dead because of Yua. 'You're this coven's leader. I thought you would have to approve it.'

'This may be technically true, but all Seven have been grown women for a very long time—centuries, in some cases. If they want to ignore my advice, they can, but I'd like to think that we have a tighter bond than that. In any case, it will be up to Shizue to decide whether she accepts you. I can support your request, but I can't force her.'

A polite knock came at the door. Kei gave Yua a look that said, *See? This is how you enter someone's office.*

'Come in,' Kei said.

Yua steeled herself. She didn't remember the last time she had been this nervous, if ever.

Shizue entered. She was the very picture of calm all Mist Women had perfected with a hint of curiosity robed in black satin.

'Good morning, Kei.' She looked at Yua. 'And good morning, Yua. I didn't expect to see you here.'

'Yua is the reason I called you here,' Kei said. 'Please sit. Yua has something to ask of you.'

Every Seven was terrifying to Yua. They held so much power over the country, if not the entire world, but Shizue scared her the most. Shizue studied the Mists, the one subject that was as good as taboo even for a coven that loved secret knowledge. Yua had no way of knowing how old any of them were, but she suspected Shizue to be the oldest, if only by her too-collected demeanour. She moved slowly and looked at everything, other people included, like they were beneath her—with acceptance of their existence, mild curiosity or perhaps amusement, but otherwise disinterest. Like this world held no more surprises for her and had grown boring a long time ago. Yua had wondered if that was why Shizue had chosen to specialise in the Mists.

Shizue sat next to her. Her nearness made it worse. It felt too much like they were equals. Yua would have preferred it if Shizue had towered over her. Sitting beside her like this made her feel like an arrogant, presumptuous novice who didn't yet understand the unwritten rules of this coven.

'I'm listening,' Shizue said.

O-Yu give me strength.

'I've come to ask you to teach me. I feel my Sha—' She blushed; no one else knew that she had named the evil inside her—'*my darkness* inside me, and I know it's awake. I'm worried if I don't learn how to control it, it will overpower me.'

Tears burned her eyes, but she forced them back down. She'd known this was personal to her, but until she had voiced it out loud, she hadn't realised how deep her fear ran. Loss of control and herself was no longer just a worry at the back of her mind. It was a real possibility that she needed to address, a real monster she needed to defeat.

Shizue smiled. 'I like you, Ohira Yua. You have a determination and courage I respect and expect in my novices. But I don't know how much help I can be. You are right that out of all of us, I know the Mists the best, but I know them in theory only. You have already experienced more of them than

I ever will.'

Was she wrong or did she hear regret in Shizue's voice? Yua bit her lip. If Shizue respected courage…

'Don't pretend. We both know you would give anything for a chance to study me.'

Something lit up in Shizue's eyes. 'You are right about that, but I wouldn't be studying you, would I? I would be guiding you, and I don't believe I'd be a good guide. As I said, you have experienced more—'

'Yes, I know. Trust me, I know what I have and haven't felt.' She blushed; was she really arguing with one of the Seven? 'With all due respect.'

Shizue laughed. 'From what Kei told me, you like to take matters into your own hands. It was brave of you to battle your Mist demon outside to enforce your authority, but Kei wasn't aware of your actions until after the fact, was she? None of us Seven knew. What you did was brave, yes—it bears saying again—but it was also dangerous and dancing on the border between responsibility and stupidity. If I were to accept your request, I would expect you to work with me, not against me or without my knowledge.'

Yua swallowed. She was so close to getting what she wanted, but…

'And if I had told you about my plan, would you have agreed to it?'

'No.'

Yua's heart sank. Shizue was the only one who could at least try to teach her, but if they didn't agree on things like this, would she be better off on her own after all? But then what would happen? She couldn't go on as she had done. Something had to change. Now that her Shadow was awake and watching, she had to make sure her control over it improved. She had to be able to keep it down or death would follow... either her own or that of many others. More likely both.

'At least,' Shizue said, 'not so soon. I would have prepared you more for it. I would have insisted on being there in case something went wrong. What would you have done had your Mist demon overpowered you? Could you have lived with yourself if you had killed a hundred people because you were impatient?'

Yua blushed deeper but made herself hold eye contact.

'No. But I wasn't there alone. Aza was there, and she was ready to interfere.'

The look on Shizue's face made Yua's insides boil, but she couldn't decide if it was pity or sympathy.

'And do you really believe that Aza would have been able to defeat this darkness?'

Yua wanted to say that yes, of course Aza would have beaten it, but she couldn't get herself to lie. Not before Shizue as well as Kei. Not when she had wondered the same thing often enough.

'I admire what you did,' Shizue said, 'but I also can't condone it given that you rushed into it. Nevertheless, I understand why you acted.' Shizue exchanged a glance with Kei. 'Very well. I will teach you. But I expect you to trust me and do as I say. I will not go easy on you when you're tired or coddle you when you don't want to hear what I have to say. Can you accept my terms?'

Yua's heart was in her throat when she spoke. 'I can. Thank you.'

Chapter Twenty-One

As soon as Yua got back to her room, she asked Aza to get tea and cake. Shizue had agreed to teach her, and Yua felt like celebrating. It felt like an even bigger achievement than winning the first fight against her Shadow.

If only she could talk sense into her Shadow like she had argued with Shizue. Her life would have been a lot easier.

While she waited, Yua leaned against her windowsill and breathed in the fresh air. Pure. Untainted. Nothing like the dark threat in her veins.

She reminded herself that she had made progress. It wasn't much, but any knowledge was more than she'd started with, and she hoped that Shizue would add more. Yua now knew where the monster inside herself came from, and she knew the ritual used to merge human and Mists hadn't succeeded before her. It confirmed what she'd always known—she was different—but it also gave her confidence. Some of the mystery had begun to unravel, and she and Aza had achieved this much on their own.

You could achieve so much more if you let me in.

She took a deep breath. Fresh air in, worries out. It didn't calm her. Even now, her Shadow reached out beyond her room. She knew exactly where Aza was—two floors down and walking slowly, probably because she was balancing a tea tray.

Suddenly, Yua was grateful she'd sent Aza away, and she hated herself for the same.

Aza was safer away from her.

Aza might have been able to help.

But Aza would be back soon, and they'd know either way then. Her gift was starving, and if she couldn't force it down... Did she even want to anymore? No... no, of course she did. Everything else would be wrong. She had fought for this scrap of control. If she let go now, it would destroy Aza and Kei and Ichiro and all the other novices here and it would be her fault, hers alone, and then her friends would be dead and *theirbloodwouldbeonherlips.*

Wispy shadows rose from under her skin and into the room, like fog at night in autumn but infinitely worse. Her Shadow was leaking out of her, and she couldn't stop it. Couldn't even breathe. Her chest felt tight, like something big and heavy was sitting on it and refused to get up. She tried to take deep breaths, but they turned into desperate gulps for air. She wanted to bury her face in her hands, but when she raised them, her nails had grown into claws and her teeth strained against her gums like they, too, had grown longer. Her hands shook, and she didn't know how to calm them. She didn't want to see her claws, scrape her skin on her too-long teeth, cut her legs open if she sat on her fingers to steady them. Tears burned her eyes. She felt so childish, so stupid for reacting like this, but more than anything she was terrified of what she might do, horrified of what she was becoming.

She gripped the windowsill as hard as she could, her claws scraping against the window, and slid down against the wall. Her arm still reached up to the window after she sat on the floor. The room was spinning, the ground no steadier than the swaying walls. A sad, little whimper escaped her lips.

This is beneath you. You should rule them, not cower to protect them.

Hands gripped her shoulders. Someone spoke, but she couldn't hear. There was a noisy rushing in her ears that blocked out everything else, and it grew worse the more her vision blurred.

Someone shoved her head down. Yua tried to turn away, but the hands were stronger and forced her head between her knees. She took panicked gulps of air, but the hands didn't let go.

'Breathe for me, Yua. I've got you. There you go.'

Her next breath was longer. A sob escaped her, and her chest shook. Aza sank down beside her and gently pulled Yua into her lap until she was lying on her side.

'There you go. Keep breathing, Yua. You're doing great.'

She didn't feel like she was doing great, but the floor and walls had steadied, and her breaths were interrupted only by her sobs, not blind panic. Her fingertips and gums felt less tense, but she didn't dare look.

Her lips quivered. 'I'm so sorry.'

'There's nothing to apologise for. Talk to me. What happened?' Aza stroked the hair out of Yua's wet eyes and away from her hot cheeks. It felt nice; it was embarrassing. She was a grown-up, not a child. She shouldn't have reacted like this.

Yua still didn't want to talk about it, but that had done her no good before, and she was already weeping on the floor. She couldn't get any lower than this.

'I'm scared I can't control it,' she said. 'I'm scared I'll hurt you and Kei and Ichiro.' She sat up and leaned against the wall.

Aza's golden eyes didn't let hers stray. 'I can hear it, even now. Your blood sings to me. I don't know how to stop it or what I am or if this is what the people who did this to me had in mind.' Panic tightened her throat again, but she couldn't stop. The words were coming with or without her permission. 'And what if I shouldn't stop it, anyway? This is what I am, isn't it? I wanted to embrace what I am, but I don't know what I want anymore. It's all I can think about, all I can taste in my dreams and all I can hear when I'm awake. I don't know what—'

Aza cupped her face and kissed her, lips warm and full of sunshine. Did she taste honey? She didn't know anymore. It didn't matter.

Just as she was about to close her eyes, Aza pulled away and cleared her throat.

'Good. You've calmed down.' Was that a blush on Aza's sun-kissed cheeks? 'How are you feeling?'

Yua focussed every bit of her attention on the floor. She never gave the servants credit where it was due—the floorboards were spotless. Her eyes flew over her hands—her nails were back to normal. She assumed her teeth were, too, since her gums no longer felt like they were about to burst.

She swallowed. 'Better.' And then, because it didn't seem enough somehow, 'Thank you.'

Aza smiled. Their eyes found each other even though Yua tried to look anywhere but at Aza.

'You're welcome. Next time you feel whatever that was, tell me, okay? You don't have to do this alone. I want to help.'

'How can you? Neither of us knows what we're dealing with.'

Aza grinned. 'No, but I do know how to shut you up now.'

Yua returned the smile and the blush. Had she liked the kiss because it had taken her mind off the panic, or for some other reason? She liked Aza, but she hadn't felt that instant love so many books spoke of. Where did this leave them? Would Aza expect more or would things go back to the way they'd been? Which did she want?

'If you're feeling better,' Aza said, 'would you like your breakfast now?'

And the moment was gone.

Chapter Twenty-Two

Yua felt like a heavy blanket was pulled over her head until she didn't see anything beyond the fabric. Its soft weight suffocated her. She tried to push it off but couldn't find a grip on the non-existent cloth. Her Shadow rose beneath the illusion.

Through her heart.

Into her head.

And stole its way into her mind, where it held tight and didn't let go.

Her Shadow wanted her to see. She dreaded to think what it would show her.

Yua watched herself get up, move away from Aza who had offered to stay with Yua, and leave her room.

Once, many years ago, she had read a book about mind manipulation. It had described how a sorcerer or Mist Woman could use their gift to sneak into the mind of another and control them. It had also explained why the practice was forbidden. Moving through the coven against her will, Yua wished she'd paid more attention to solutions should she ever find someone else inside her mind. She hadn't thought it would ever apply to her or that she, ungifted as she was, would have the power to do anything about it.

She tried to shove her Shadow back down, but it didn't respond. It had nestled itself deep in her mind, finally in control after all these years… and after her recent attempts to subdue it, her Shadow wasn't happy.

Then, she smelled it.

Blood.

And then she heard it.

Blood.

Sweet. Sharp.

Just around the corner.

Her Shadow was no longer the only force that directed her. Yua's own instincts moved her forwards, towards the promise that beckoned her forth like a naked lover wrapped in satin sheets.

Yua opened a door and picked up a knife from the bedside table. It was still wet with apple juices. It didn't matter.

She wanted to scream at herself to stop before she couldn't undo what was about to happen, but if any sound left her lips at all, it turned to silence long before it reached her Shadow.

You should have worked with me, Yua. We could have reached a compromise.

She doubted it, but it was too late for regrets.

Yua carefully straddled the sleeping novice and placed her hand over the novice's mouth. The young woman's eyes fluttered open.

So much fear. Yua pushed against her Shadow, against herself, but it was no use.

So much fear. She licked her lips, her excitement only partially her Shadow's.

The novice's blood sang notes of terror and sin.

Gripped by the same terror as the novice beneath her, Yua tried again to push her Shadow away, but it didn't care. It knew better. Yua wanted to continue. Whatever she had been able to hold on to before was gone, her Shadow turned to shapeless, ungraspable mists inside her.

The novice raised her hands to cast a spell, but Yua didn't let her. Her fingernails had turned to claws while she savoured the woman's fear, and she threw the knife aside. She didn't need petty tools. Yua drew her elongated nails across the novice's throat, felt the flesh rip and give way under her. She closed her eyes when hot blood sprayed over her. An animalistic moan escaped her throat.

Yua no longer knew where she ended and her Shadow began. Here, at the end of her sanity, there were no more whispers, no more promises. Only instincts. This was her truest self. She wouldn't deny her nature any longer.

She lowered her head to the wound and drank. After several deep mouthfuls, she sat up and washed her hands in the spreading pool of red. Much had soaked into the sheets, but there was too much for the linen to absorb it all. Slowly, Yua spread it over her arms, her shoulders, her chest. The warmth felt good on her skin. Like a bath after a long day…

And this day had lasted thirteen years.

She spread the novice's blood over her body until something blunt and heavy hit her over the head and plunged her vision into the abyss.

Birds chirped outside her window and sunshine flooded her room when Yua woke up. She sat up with a start. It must have been a nightmare. She clutched the clean sheets of her bed and the clean nightgown she was wearing. Her eyes burned.

'Oh, thank you, O-Yu.'

She hadn't killed a novice. Everything was fine. She hadn't—

She hadn't gone to bed in a nightgown. Aza had offered to stay and Yua had been grateful not to be alone. Neither had got changed. Yua had still been wearing her novice's clothes.

'Hey.'

Yua turned her head to find Aza watching her from a corner, arms crossed and daggers in one hand.

'Are you alright?' Aza asked. 'You, erm, were pretty out of it.'

'It wasn't a dream.' Yua choked on the realisation.

She had killed a novice. No matter what she'd thought of her life before now, it was about to get much worse, if they didn't simply end it. The novice's family would want justice. They'd be right to demand it.

'Afraid not.' Aza sheathed her daggers and sat next to her. 'What do you remember?'

'Why are you still here?' The words left her lips before Yua could stop herself. None of this made sense. She had committed a terrible crime last night, and Aza had witnessed it. Previous attendants had run for much less.

Aza reached out and squeezed her hand. 'I don't know what happened last night, but I know it wasn't you.'

'But it—' Too much saliva filled her mouth when she remembered the blood. 'It was me. I enjoyed it. I *wanted* to do those things.'

She'd moaned when she'd felt the first spray of blood, like it had been some twisted sexual revelation.

'Listen to me,' Aza said. 'Whatever that was, it wasn't you. This right here in front of me, trembling because she's scared of herself, that's you.'

'I bathed in a novice's blood, Aza. I killed her.'

Aza shook her head. 'The novice is injured, but it sounds like it's not as bad as you thought. Your excitement must have affected your perception. Willow believes she'll survive.' An uncertain smile entered her eyes. '*Aste os* that you don't know what you're doing, hm? It would have been a lot worse if you hadn't got carried away in the moment.'

A sob escaped her. 'She's—'

Aza nodded, and Yua collapsed against her. She clung to Aza with both arms like she would drown if she let go, and Aza held her close.

'Oh, Great Dragon. I thought I had… I thought…'

Aza made soft cooing sounds. 'Your Shadow did that. Or do you fancy killing me and bathing in my blood?'

Yua paled and shook her head. 'No.'

'Then it wasn't you.'

Aza made it sound so easy. Yua wanted to believe her. Instead, fresh panic washed over her.

'The sheets! A-and if she's in the infirmary, other novices will see what happened. Kei's word won't mean anything. What will I—'

Yua had daydreamed, but she'd never truly thought about it since she'd never had a choice. She had nowhere to go. The coven was a prison, but it was also her only home, and the other novices hadn't made it easy. What would they do now that Yua had proven them right? Would they still stop at whispering behind Yua's back, or would they be too scared of her for even that?

Aza stroked her hair. 'It's okay. I've taken care of it.'

Yua's heart missed a beat. 'You have?'

'It took most of last night, but while Willow treated the novice, I cleaned the room. Ichiro took the sheets to be washed or maybe disposed, I'm not sure.' Her eyes darted to Yua's. 'I think the official story is that some experiment the novice worked on went wrong. I don't know what Willow and Kei will say to her once she's awake though. She probably remembers you, and she'll know she wasn't working on anything that would hurt her like this.'

The tears tightened her throat so much Yua almost couldn't talk.

'Why?' she croaked out.

Aza shrugged. 'I came here to protect you. When Kei briefed me, I thought you'd be arrogant or difficult in some way, but you're scared. You're just another victim. And besides, this is *the* head coven in Maishi Hou. Everyone knows that experiments go wrong here all the time. Kei and the Seven know what they're doing.' Aza nodded at her. 'You're shivering. Make room.'

Yua was in no frame of mind to argue, so she moved over and let Aza lie down next to her.

Aza opened her arms. 'Come here.'

Yua obliged, grateful to hide her tears for a moment. Aza's arms were warm and soft. When she closed her eyes and inhaled, she smelled vanilla—Aza must have eaten biscuits while she waited for Yua to wake up. She couldn't remember the last time someone had held her.

'It'll be okay,' Aza said.

Yua wanted to believe it, but after what she'd done, she didn't know how anything could ever be alright again. Her Shadow had shown her what it was capable of, and she wasn't sure it was worth the risk. How many more novices would get hurt before she learned to control herself?

You think I've shown you everything? I can do so much more. We can be so much more.

And then there was the uncomfortable truth that she had liked it. Even now, saliva pooled around her tongue and goose bumps raised on her arms when she remembered the smell and the taste, the feel of it on her skin.

'What's wrong with me?' she cried into Aza's side.

Aza held her tighter. 'Nothing. You're not sick; you're not violent. Your magic is just different, that's all. If you want to suppress it again like you did before, that's fine.'

Yua nodded against Aza's neck. Control cost too much. She didn't want to feel that lust for someone's blood ever again.

Chapter Twenty-Three

Breakfast—a selection of cheeses, hams, and fruit—tasted like nothing. Yua rolled it around on her tongue, but everything tasted… boring. None of it was offensive to her taste buds, but none of it was inviting, either. The mixture of smells was pleasant enough, she just wasn't drawn to any of it.

'Still not hungry?' Aza asked.

Yua shook her head. 'Why can't I get excited for this cheddar?'

'Can you get excited for my blood?'

Yua frowned, even less interested in the food than before. 'Don't put it like that. I'm fine right now.'

Aza shrugged and ate a grape straight off the vine. 'Then I guess you're just full. I wouldn't worry about it.'

'Easy for you to say.' She sighed. 'What if I'll never want normal food again?' She hated herself for phrasing it like that, like people were food now. She didn't see Aza like that. Did she? Aza was still her friend—in fact, Aza was the most loyal friend she'd ever had. Seeing her as something so… so weak, so degrading and inferior, was an insult.

'Then that sets your path, doesn't it?' Aza asked between grapes.

Yua worried her frown would become a permanent feature on her lips. 'Does it?'

Aza slowly nodded and straightened. 'You feel better right now, right? What if—and bear with me on this—what if you drank blood on purpose?'

Her Shadow stirred.

Yua paled. Aza couldn't be serious.

But Aza continued. 'You can try a tiny bit of mine, just to see if it works. If you do it regularly—'

A nervous laugh escaped her. 'I can't just drink your blood every day.'

Let's not be hasty.

'Maybe you won't have to,' Aza said. 'Honestly, I'd prefer it if you didn't drink my blood every other day too. I'm pretty sure I'd die from that much blood loss.'

'How can you be so casual about this? You're not seriously suggesting what I think you're suggesting!' Yua had no idea how she'd have felt had their roles been reversed, but she doubted she'd have been this calm about having her blood sucked out of her neck by her half-feral Mist demon friend.

We're friends now, are we? Her insides twisted as her Shadow grinned. *She's offering, Yua. Take her up on it. Think how easy it would be.*

Aza ate the last grape from the vine and put the barren stalk back on the platter. 'I'm a Sand Blade in case I haven't mentioned that. We're taught early that life doesn't always happen like we want it to. Plans often don't work as we wanted. Things get complicated. You can either complain about it or you can take the situation as it is and work with it. I could worry about this better, more dangerous you, but that wouldn't help you adjust, now, would it?'

Yua envied how everything was so clear for Aza. If this really was her life now, complaining about the good old days wouldn't help her move forwards, and if she was honest with herself, the good old days hadn't been all that good. No one had lost any blood because of her, but she hadn't been happy, either. What she felt now wasn't perfect happiness, but it was a big step towards it. The idea of needing blood to survive was terrifying, but…

This is right. It's who you are. Embrace it.

Yua had wanted a solution for so long. She felt petty ignoring it just because it scared her.

Yua smiled. 'You think this me is better?'

Aza returned the smile and winked. 'Absolutely.'

Chapter Twenty-Four

Aza had brought a variety of chocolate cake, a raspberry sponge, and a poppyseed cheesecake. She silently thanked O-Yu that she could still enjoy desserts. She didn't care if it was because desserts weren't meant for nourishment but for comfort—at least, that's how she had always thought about it—because it made her feel as good, if not better, than the kiss… and it didn't leave her conflicted. She had worked hard to get this far—if she wanted breakfast cake, she had earned it.

They were finishing the last crumbs when a polite knock came at her door and Shizue entered. Yua was surprised she hadn't simply walked in. She'd always thought of the Seven as the ultimate power that went wherever it wanted and did whatever it pleased. Shizue had knocked at Kei's door, too, but Yua had figured that even the Seven gave their leader some respect. Yua, on the other hand, was no one, at least not when compared to one of them.

Yua started to get up, but Shizue held up one hand to stop her. 'Don't let me rush you. Finish your breakfast. The strength won't hurt.'

'It's fine,' Yua said. 'We were pretty much done.'

Aza nodded and stood.

'Are you staying for the lesson?'

Aza gathered their plates on the tray and picked it up. 'I would prefer to if that's all right. I'll just return this to the kitchen so we have more space.'

Shizue inclined her head. 'We will begin, but I won't do anything we might need you for until you've returned.'

Aza nodded and left, but the promise left a sour feeling on Yua's tongue. What would Shizue do to her that Shizue alone couldn't control? And if Shizue alone wasn't enough, how much help would Aza really be?

Yua wrung her hands. 'What should I do?'

Now that Shizue was here and she was about to receive her first lesson, she was nervous. She felt like she should have prepared for this, but she didn't know what she could have done.

'Sit comfortably,' Shizue said. 'Before we begin, I want to clarify a few things. You'll be pleased to hear that the novice you attacked is recovering.'

Yua felt herself pale. 'I…' She knew she should apologise, but Shizue wasn't the person who needed to hear it. Still, she couldn't think what else to say that would match her guilt.

Shizue held up one hand before Yua could overthink it. 'It was an accident, I'm sure. We practice dangerous magic here, after all—accidents happen all the time. Novices have put themselves in worse conditions plenty of times. I assure you I've been here long enough that this incident doesn't faze anyone except the newer novices. What I want to know is this: what do you intent to do about it?' Yua was about to respond, but one look from Shizue silenced her. 'We will get to that in a moment. For now, tell me: how does your Mist demon feel?'

'Thirsty,' Yua blurted out before she could stop herself, but perhaps that was for the best. If she wanted Shizue to teach her control, Shizue needed to know everything without reservations.

'Is this thirst like what you feel when you have tea?'

Yua had never dwelled on it. Her Shadow had always just felt... well, thirsty. Longing.

Yua shook her head. 'I don't think it is.'

'How is it different?'

'It's hard to describe.'

Shizue smiled in understanding. 'Then let's take a step back. What do you feel when Ichiro or Aza brings you tea after a long day?'

'My mouth might feel dry. I might salivate more.' She blushed. This felt oddly personal.

Shizue nodded. 'And when your gift is thirsty? Does your mouth go dry then?'

Yua blushed deeper—this was even more intimate. She'd never thought she'd discuss her Shadow with anyone except maybe Aza. Even when she had demanded lessons, she hadn't expected to be questioned like this.

'Yes, but...' She swallowed to buy time, but her heart beat faster all the same. 'I can also smell it. The blood, I mean. No matter how many walls are between me and it, I'll smell it and I... There's more saliva then, too.' It was awkward to say out loud, like she was confessing to something forbidden.

'There was an incident, wasn't there? When you went to the market?'

Yua gripped the hem of her sleeves. She should have known Kei would tell the Seven. Of course they had to know.

'Yes. There was a boy. He was bleeding, and I… I wanted to…'

'Not you, Yua. The Mist demon. I won't say you wouldn't have been accountable had you attacked him, but I won't deny that this is partly our fault either. It can take a long time to learn control with things like this. Some of us wanted to teach you sooner, but we all agreed, eventually, that it would be more dangerous to act before you were ready to control the Mist magic. You did well to walk away.'

Yua dreaded to think what would have happened if Aza hadn't found her in time. Would she have killed a child? Would she have drunk his blood in front of his parents? Tears filled her eyes at the mere thought.

'I don't deserve your kindness, Honoured Seven.'

'Please, call me Shizue. Is it not true that to control our limits, we must test them first? How will you know what you can and can't do if you don't push yourself?'

'I'm not—this isn't—' Her mind was blank. 'This isn't weight training or hand-to-hand combat! A child—'

'Could have died, I know. But your continued guilt over what might have been won't change what was. You can punish yourself until the day you die of old age, but it won't change that nothing happened, and it won't change that your Mist demon will crave blood. We need to figure out how we can stop your demon from taking it too far.'

Yua nodded. 'That's what I want.'

'Good. You said the smell of blood causes more saliva to form. Anything else?'

'Yes.' Yua did *not* want to go into detail, but if Shizue was to help her… She bit her lip and got it over with. 'I'm physically drawn to the blood. My Shadow focusses on it until it's all I can hear, see, smell. I would do anything to reach it.'

'Like an obsession?'

Yua paled. 'Yes. Exactly like that.'

Shizue nodded like this made perfect sense to her. 'The forces of the Mists are single-minded in their purpose. From what we understand—which isn't as much as I'd like, to be honest with you—even the Dark One only wants to control. The Mothers serve Him without question, but it's all they want. They have no goals or aspirations of their own. Your power is the same. It wants blood, nothing else. Are there any physical signs that would help me and Aza identify when you need help?'

'My markings fill in the more I lose myself. My nails grow. I think my teeth grow, too, but I can't confirm it because… well, because they are my teeth.' Her sight didn't extend to a spot so close to her eyes—a simple matter—but it had still come out more clumsily than she'd intended.

'Alright, last question. After you… what do you call it? When you take blood?'

She blushed again. Shizue had made her more comfortable, but now Yua felt more awkward than ever. She couldn't possibly say it out loud.

'No matter,' Shizue said. 'That's not what I wanted to know. How did you feel after? Did it lessen the thirst at all?'

Yua was embarrassed to admit it but nodded.

'Interesting. Do you sense your *Shadow* now?' Shizue pronounced it like Yua shouldn't have named it. Like she'd named a lamb she knew she'd have to slaughter.

Yua looked away. 'Yes. It's there most of the time.'

'How do you control it? I remember we taught you a few techniques, but I'd like to hear what you do from you.'

'I see inside myself and force it back down. I can feel it, like… like other novices sense their gifts and direct them, but I doubt it's anything the same.' She couldn't compare it, but in her mind, the gift was light while her Shadow was darkness. She couldn't see her power working in the same way.

Shizue raised an eyebrow. 'Now that's unexpected.'

'Is that bad?'

Had she said too much? What if Shizue changed her mind and decided it was safer to keep her locked away forever? Now they had begun to work together, Yua wanted the chance to work at it.

'Truthfully? I don't know. Perhaps, had we acted the day Kei brought you here, we could have drawn the demon out of you and sent it back to the Mists, but Kei wouldn't hear it. She said the chance it might kill you was too great. I did agree, even though it was my suggestion.'

Yua's heart missed a beat. Shizue had suggested banishing her power even though it could have killed her, a five-year-old girl at the time. Yua didn't know how she felt about that.

'Understand, Yua, that we always knew your power was dangerous, but we didn't know how it might evolve. If there was a chance it got loose and claimed more people, we had to prevent it, no matter the cost. No matter the life lost.'

A shiver ran down her arms. 'Then why didn't you?'

Shizue's eyes softened. 'Kei stood between us and you and forbade us from harming you in any way. She said we had a unique opportunity to study something extremely rare. The coven is the safest place for you, so we agreed to leave the darkness be and let you handle it when you were ready. I know you're angry with that decision, but Kei was right. Trying anything at such an early stage could have killed you, and we don't kill children.'

Yua didn't care if she sounded bitter—she was a person, not a thing. 'And you wanted a test subject.'

'Yes.'

Yua cringed.

The door opened and Aza entered. 'What have I missed?'

Shizue nodded to the empty chair. 'We've been talking. I'm sure it's nothing Yua hasn't already told you.'

Aza sat and looked at Yua. 'Have you told her about our idea?'

Her mind was still reeling from their conversation. She'd forgotten all about it.

Shizue looked at Aza. 'What idea?'

Yua was relieved Aza was leading this conversation. Her stomach felt far too unsettled for this one.

'I thought it might help if Yua drank from a willing person on purpose. She could—'

'No.'

It sounded final.

'But if we—'

'No, Aza. Yua. You cannot do this. Not with me to supervise, and certainly not without me. Not until I know more. Maybe not even then, depending on what I find.'

Disappointment hit her hard. She hadn't realised that she wanted a yes so badly. She knew it was dangerous, but she had hoped, with supervision and with her initiating it rather than her Shadow forcing her into it… She'd hoped it would be a rather large step in the right direction.

Yua hung her head. 'We promise.'

'Good. Now, as Yua will tell you, some of her answers weren't what I'd expected. I will return to my chambers and sort out a training plan that fits what we discussed. We'll begin tomorrow.' She stood and walked to the door. 'Don't do anything stupid in the meantime.'

'No. That's not good enough.' Yua wasn't sure where her bravery was coming from, but she wasn't about to let Shizue walk away. She had asked for lessons, not for a discussion she could have with Aza any time.

Shizue turned around. 'Pardon me?'

'We train now.'

'I'm glad you're eager, Yua, but as I said, it would be unwise to rush.' That Shizue looked and sounded amused made it worse. 'I need to prepare.'

'You had thirteen years to prepare.' Thirteen years in which they had locked her away and kept her hidden from the world. Thirteen years in which she had questioned everything about herself. Thirteen years of hatred and fear from the novices and her attendants.

'As I explained, some of your answers weren't what I—'

Yua shot to her feet. 'I'm sorry, is this unexpected for you? Because I've been living with it, enduring it, this whole time. You might have the time to prepare, but I don't. I can hear Aza's blood calling out to me, can hear my Shadow begging me to rip her throat out, but you expect me to be patient because you need to read a book? I'm right here. Ask me whatever you need to know, but walk out that door right now and Aza and I will do what we think best.'

Her heart was hammering so hard it almost drowned the sound of Aza's blood. Aza stepped behind Yua, ready to defend her and protect her, and Yua felt stronger for it.

Shizue closed the door again and sighed. 'This is what I get for choosing the Mists as my subject. I suppose I shouldn't be shocked to see you're as determined and wild as the source of your power. Like calls to like, does it not?'

'Does this mean you'll stay?' Yua asked.

Shizue nodded. 'Yes, Yua. How could I not with that threat? I will not let you harm Aza.' It didn't sound like a warning but like a promise.

'Good, then we agree,' Yua said. 'No one gets hurt because of me.'

'I vow it on my honour as a Seven. I will stop you with everything I have should it become necessary.'

Grave as Shizue's words sounded, Yua felt better for hearing them.

'Since you're so keen to learn control today, I think we should start with a breathing exercise. This won't be like the others we taught you years ago, however. While you focus on keeping your demon where it belongs, I will attempt to draw it out. It won't need much convincing, so ready yourself.'

Her blood ran cold. This was too much too soon.

'Shizue—'

'No. You're right, you need to learn control. I'm afraid the wrong kind of power has chosen you if you want something without risk. Don't worry, I'll stop the Mist demon if it gets too far. I'm sure Aza will help as well.'

Aza nodded and twirled her daggers. 'Ready to knock you out whenever.'

'Now, call your power,' Shizue said. 'Can you hear it?'

Yua felt her Shadow grin and hated that it was silent otherwise. It, too, was getting ready. She hoped this was more than Shizue's way of teaching her a lesson.

'Do you think you can control it?' Shizue asked.

This was a mistake.

'I don't know. It's fine right now.'

'Good.'

Aza's dagger ripped out from her fingers and into Shizue's waiting hand. Aza opened her mouth to protest Shizue's use of magic, but before one word left her lips, Shizue cut her palm.

Yua's Shadow roared, too starved for words. The room closed in until there was nothing but the beautiful red drop, teasing her like a lover and beckoning her forth with just as much promise.

Yua jumped to her feet.

Over the table.

She threw herself at Shizue, fuelled by the suddenly desperate dark.

Shizue waved her bleeding hand in an arc. A shimmering shield appeared between them and sent Yua tumbling back into the chair. Something dug into her back. Yua jumped back to her feet, focussing on the crimson offering. Nothing else mattered. Not the pain in her back, and not the dread in her heart.

'Force it down, Yua. Now.'

Shizue's words cut through her mind. Her Shadow tried to hide them behind a thick veil of primal want, but Yua had heard them.

Down, she ordered. *Don't you dare.*

Her Shadow rippled through her—its version of laughter. It crept forwards and infected her mind, snarled, snapped its fangs like a rabid wolf. Yua pushed against it with all her willpower, but her Shadow didn't care. Her tongue darted out. She realised her teeth had grown again when it flicked against them. The taste of metal on the air killed the last chains of her restraint. There was fresh blood right there, and she needed it.

Yua threw herself over the table at Shizue.

Yes! So close. Just a little—

She couldn't move. Shizue's gift held her in place in mid-air.

'Force it down, Yua.'

A deep, guttural scream tore from her throat. Obeying was impossible while Shizue was bleeding. The smell was too raw, too close.

'Look at me, Yua.'

Her eyes darted to Aza. Her insides twisted as she and her Shadow hoped for easier blood together.

'Imagine that's me. Imagine I cut myself and Shizue isn't here.'

Oh, yes! Her blood is even sweeter! Let it be her!

Yua screamed again, reached for Aza…

And froze.

Because Aza looked afraid—no, she *smelled* scared. It was unmistakable beneath the practised look of calm. Thick and inviting and utterly wrong.

Yua couldn't look at her. Her eyes fled down her blackened arm, which was still reaching for Aza, and got stuck on her hand. Her fingernails, normally trimmed, had grown. There wasn't the smallest trace of doubt in her mind that they would cut deeper than Aza's blade.

And Aza just stood there, inches away from them, and stared Yua down.

'You can do this,' Aza said. 'Force it down. You're stronger than this, I know you are.'

She couldn't allow this curse to touch Aza. If her nails grew just another two inches and cut Aza, she'd never be free of this want again.

'*Go. Away.*' Every word was a struggle as her elongated teeth scraped against her lips; the only blood she'd taste today was her own.

Yua had thought the night in the clearing had been a battle, but it didn't compare to this. What would have happened if she'd smelled fresh blood then?

No! Don't give up now. Please, just a bit farther. You don't have to choose, you can have them both, just please *don't stop now.*

Yua shoved every ounce of willpower she had against her Shadow. Slowly, the marks on her arms thinned and revealed alabaster skin. Her nails and teeth retracted. Her Shadow screamed with as much ferocity as she had moments ago, when she had told Shizue to stay. She was deaf to its pain. She could do this. She had to. Shizue was holding her back physically, but she wasn't aiding her internal struggle, and Yua didn't want her to. She had to do this by herself or it wouldn't matter.

With one last scream, she pushed against her Shadow—
And won.

Shizue gently lowered her onto the table. The restraints lifted, but some light touches were still there in case Shizue needed to tighten them again.

Aza took her hand, but her face was pale. 'Are you okay?'

Now Yua knew Aza's fear was there, she couldn't pretend otherwise. She closed her eyes. Maybe now she'd be able to sleep without worry, at least for one night.

'How do you feel?' Shizue asked.

'Exhausted.'

'You've done well. I would like you to rest today and tonight. Don't leave your room unless you absolutely must. Aza, bring her food, if you would?'

Yua shook her head. 'I'm not hungry.'

'You've pushed your mind and body to the very brink of their abilities. You need to eat.'

Yua sighed and felt like she was sinking into the table. She could barely feel her muscles, let alone move them. How was she supposed to sit upright, pick up her food, chew, swallow? It was too much effort.

Aza squeezed her hand. 'I'll be right back.' Next to her head, the door closed.

'I will stay until Aza has returned,' Shizue said. 'You should be proud. I wasn't sure if I put you through too much too soon.'

'No, it's fine. I need to do this.'

'I'll visit tomorrow to see how you're doing. Will you be alright today?'

'Are you asking me if I'll attack Aza the moment you're gone?' Shizue's hesitation was her answer. 'I'll be fine.' She doubted she could move even if her Shadow overpowered her.

'Sleep once you've eaten. We'll talk tomorrow.'

Yua didn't remember what Aza brought her. She only remembered the soft feel of sheets, and the best sleep she'd had in days.

Chapter Twenty-Five

It was dark safe for a thin beam of pale moonlight visiting her room when Aza's blood song woke Yua. Aza sat in her favourite spot in the window with one leg hanging down. Much too close. Her veins pulsed with crimson promise until Yua's ears rang. She swallowed, again and again, but there was too much saliva. Yua felt herself sit, eyes fixated on Aza's neck.

She wanted it so badly it hurt.

How could she ever hope to win when such a great part of her didn't want the victory? The blood was everything, and it didn't matter whose it was. She wanted Aza's, but Aza was right there. Anyone would do. Yua could practically taste it. Her Shadow writhed inside her when she imagined its metallic tang on the tip of her tongue, its warmth embracing her throat, its—

Yua had to fight back before she hurt Aza, but she was still weakened from her session with Shizue. She was rested enough to wake up, but rested enough to force the darkness back again? Every thought was a struggle.

She should have known that her Shadow wouldn't just forget Shizue's blood, would be encouraged by its smell, but it hadn't crossed her mind then. She had been too tired to think.

Aza smiled at her. 'Can't sleep?'

Aza froze when Yua stepped into the moonlight, and it took all Yua's willpower to stop there. Her marks had filled in again, another shadow within shadows.

'Do you need me to call for Shizue?' Aza asked.

Yua wanted to urge Aza to do just that or to run away or both, but it came out a growl as feral as any starving animal.

Yes! Tell her to run. Let us hunt her.

Aza gripped her dagger and slipped down the windowsill. 'I'll knock you out if I have to. Tell me what you need.'

Shizue had needed so much magic to hold her down earlier. Aza's knife wouldn't do a thing.

Yua smiled. Aza couldn't run anywhere that Yua wouldn't reach first.

'Look at me, Yua.'

Her name on Aza's lips cleared her head. She blinked, but grasping any one clear thought was still difficult.

'Come on,' Aza said. 'Let's sit.'

Yua let Aza drag her onto the bed. Nice and soft. So comfortable. Yua focussed on that.

'How are you feeling?' Aza asked.

'It hurts.' Her voice broke into a sob. 'I can't bear it. This pain is too much.'

Aza gently pulled her down until they were lying on their sides, Yua cradled in Aza's arms like the vulnerable girl she really was. Her Shadow could tempt her with power all it wanted; it meant nothing if she couldn't control it, and she couldn't control *this*.

'It's okay. I've got you.' Aza's voice was so soothing that Yua couldn't stop her tears from falling. She didn't deserve this comfort. 'Any better?'

Yua shook her head. 'It burns. It feels like it'll rip out of me if I don't— If I—all I can hear is your blood.' She was ashamed of the admission, but Aza's arms felt safe. She could admit to anything here and be alright at the end.

'Force it down,' Aza said, 'like you did earlier.'

'I can't. It's—' Yua's sob died in a scream.

Everything hurt. Her limbs were aching to get up and run, and hunt, but she was afraid of where her feet would carry her while she was like this. Her fingers felt like they'd rip out of her hand. Even her teeth hurt. She wanted to sink them into something, anything, to make the pain stop. Her instincts told her it would make the agony go away.

Aza kissed her hair. 'Let me help.'

She rolled Yua onto her back and straddled her. Yua didn't realise what Aza offered until her hand was on her dagger.

'No.'

Yes!

'No, Aza, please. I'll kill you if you do. I won't be able to stop.'

Aza smiled, a soft lie in the dark. 'I trust you.' She cut her finger.

And Yua's vision went dark.

She threw herself upright into Aza's lap, ignored the bleeding finger, and bit into her neck. Aza hissed. Warmth poured into her mouth, and Yua moaned. Inside her veins, her Shadow moaned with her. This was everything—everything she'd ever wanted; all she'd ever need. Why had she denied herself this… this… peace?

This is your right. Don't let anyone take it from you again.

She wouldn't. She'd sooner kill any who tried to stop her and bathe in their blood.

Aza placed her hand on Yua's head. 'Is this helping?'

Aza's blood was unlike anything she'd ever tasted—warm, comforting, invigorating. Her Shadow wanted to tear Aza to shreds—no words were needed; she felt its want like her own—but her strength returned with every drop she swallowed. Finally, she was the stronger half.

Aza sucked in another sharp breath, and Yua tried to be gentler. She wouldn't hurt Aza. If she was careful like she was now, she could have both—herself and her Shadow. Because it was a gift, she saw that now. She felt stronger, faster, *more* of everything.

Aza sighed and sagged against her. Yua drew away—just like that—when Aza's hand on her hair grew weaker.

'Yua—'

She licked the wound, not willing to waste a single drop. She was positively buzzing with life, high on the feeling.

Aza guided Yua's face away from her neck. 'Yua, I—'

Yua kissed her. Aza held her close as she kissed her back, hard and fierce like a long-overdue downpour in summer. All the awkwardness between them was gone. Aza leaned into her and pushed her down into the sheets, one hand wandering between Yua's legs.

She'd thought she didn't know how she felt about Aza, but she'd been lying to herself because it was easier than the truth... and with her mind still heavy with the scent and taste of Aza's blood, nothing but truth mattered.

Yua didn't know where to go from here. So, she surrendered to Aza and hoped her door and floorboards kept their moans where they belonged.

A knock came at her door. The warmth Yua had felt in Aza's sleep-heavy arms turned into nervous cold.

'Just a moment!' She looked at Aza. 'What do I tell Shizue?'

Her new teacher had been very clear where she stood on Yua drinking Aza's blood on purpose. If there was one thing Yua didn't want, it was the anger of a Seven, much less one who had chosen to believe in her.

Aza shrugged. 'The truth.'

Yua wiped her clammy hands dry on her legs as they both threw on yesterday's clothes and sat at the table. What if Shizue wouldn't teach her anymore since Yua had broken two promises to her in such a short time? She had agreed that she wouldn't bite Aza. She had agreed that she would do everything Shizue said.

Yua braced herself and asked her inside.

Shizue entered the room with a warm smile and sat at the table with them. 'You're looking well. I didn't expect you to recover so fast.'

Straight to it, then. Yua supposed it was better not to let it fester.

'I drank from Aza last night.'

Shizue's smile died. Yua had never seen a Mist Woman be anything but calm, but Shizue didn't look happy right now. She didn't look angry, either, but her relaxed features didn't fool Yua. A Mist Woman only looked this composed when she was raging inside.

'Well, both you and Aza are here, so I take it neither of you killed the other. But to go against my express instructions—'

'I made her,' Aza said. 'She was struggling after what you put her through yesterday. To make her smell blood, knowing what it would do to her, was cruel. You couldn't expect her to just sleep it off.'

Yua couldn't imagine that anyone had ever interrupted Shizue before or talked to her like that. To her surprise, her face didn't turn into a more-forced calm. She dreaded what anger might be hiding under the surface to lure Aza into a false sense of security.

Shizue sighed. 'I apologise if I put you through too much too soon, Yua. I thought you could handle it, but perhaps we need to take a few steps back.'

'We don't,' Yua said. 'I could have killed Aza last night, but I stopped myself before there was any danger.' She wouldn't remind Shizue that everything about it had been dangerous. 'I controlled my Shadow, and I feel better than I've felt in years because of it.'

Shizue looked at Aza. 'I don't know if you're good for her or if you're a bad influence.' Aza grinned like both were compliments. Shizue turned back to Yua. 'I came here today to continue your training, but I need more time to think after this. I'd ask you to wait until I return, but I have a feeling it would fall on deaf ears again. Do you think you can go one day without ignoring my advice?'

Yua nodded. 'Yes. As I said, I feel better than ever.'

She did, too. Yua had never considered herself athletic, but this morning, she felt like she could run the length of Midoka without getting tired. The colours in her room seemed a little brighter, like she had never truly noticed them before. She saw every speck of dust dancing on the sunshine that fell into her room. Her exhaustion was gone. Yua didn't know what she'd do with her new-found energy, but she was confident that her Shadow was as satisfied as she for the moment. For once, she didn't think the day ahead would be a struggle.

'Good,' Shizue said. 'Then I will take my leave since I need to adjust your training schedule again. I'll be back tomorrow.' Shizue stood but stopped by the door without turning around. 'Please, don't do anything for a day. I don't want to have to adjust your schedule a third time in as many days.'

'I promise.'

Shizue gave her a look that told her how little her renewed promise meant. Yua did feel bad. Shizue had agreed to teach her, but so far, Yua hadn't been a good novice. She'd sit tight today and wait for tomorrow. No more experiments of any kind. No more blood. No more incidents. Just a normal day researching in the library and getting her thoughts in order. That's all today would be.

For the first time in a long while, Yua wasn't worried when she went to bed that night. They had spent all day researching in the library but hadn't found anything useful. It had worn her out, but she didn't feel physically drained. She still felt like she could run for miles without needing a break, but she had promised Shizue she wouldn't do anything rash, and she intended to keep this promise. She had earned an early night.

Aza slid under the covers with her, and Yua couldn't tell anymore whether she was awake or dreaming. Aza's warm desert skin calmed the chill Yua had felt since the market. Aza's humming blood was a lullaby, cradling her and whispering sweet nothings.

Then Aza caressed her face and kissed her with all the love written in the stars, and Yua didn't care whether it was a dream. It felt good. It was soft and comforting. Hadn't she earned a little respite? While Aza's lips were on hers, her Shadow was silent and her mind empty. Nothing else mattered.

Aza slid a hand under the duvet, under Yua's nightgown. She'd never felt another's skin on hers until the night before, not like this. The intimacy of Aza's touch was exactly what she'd needed but hadn't realised she craved. Aza's hand sank lower, and a moan escaped her.

Her vision blurred while Aza felt her way around under the sheets and under her skin. Everything begged for release. Aza craned her neck to look at her, the pumping vein on her neck such an invitation.

'Please.'

Yua obeyed. She leaned in and sank her teeth—when had they grown so sharp?—into Aza's flesh. Aza didn't scream. Aza didn't try to shove her off.

And something dark pulled her under. Yua drank until Aza was no longer moving, her smile slowly dying in her darkening eyes.

Yua licked the blood from her chin. Nothing compared to this purity. A warmth unlike any she'd ever known chased away the last remnants of the chill. This couldn't end, she wouldn't let it. She finally knew what she was, what she could be. This was right, this was her, and nothing would stand in her way ever again.

She stood, not caring that Aza's blood stained her clothes—she'd learn to be less messy—and left her room. Now she'd accepted herself, everything was clearer and Yua heard it all. Two floors down, a novice got into bed and pulled the covers over herself. The soft rustle of the sheets was gentle in Yua's ears. On the ground level, the metallic clanging of the cook's pots and pans rang in her ears.

And all around her, their blood sang an anthem.

Almost everyone was asleep.

No hunt? No fun.

Someone was coming up the stairs. Ichiro.

Yua smiled. Inside her veins, her Shadow mirrored it. He'd never suspect a thing until her fangs ripped him open.

She approached the stairs with confidence. Never would she cower before anyone again. She'd be the Blood Wisp they were so terrified of.

An unsettling thought tickled the back of her mind. Ichiro hadn't talked behind her back. He'd been kind. She'd be kind in return and make it quick.

She waited by the stairs and slid behind him before he knew she was there. Her hands were around his neck in an instant, itching for that snapping sound—

But something wasn't right. Something didn't feel… what? Like a dream? She'd known it wasn't a dream, hadn't she? She'd been pleased with herself and her progress. This was right. This was—this was—

Not a dream.

She chased the whisper away.

'Yua—'

She smothered Ichiro's lips with one hand and sank her teeth into his neck. If he screamed, the sound didn't leave her palm. All she heard was the beautiful hymn his blood sang for her.

He struggled. He whimpered. Finally, he sagged towards the floor.

Again, that feeling that something was off scratched at her mind.

Yua stepped away so forcefully, Ichiro collapsed on the floor. His blood pooled around him, but his heart was still beating. Yua heard it fighting. If anyone found him…

What's the point of hiding the body? They'll know it was you. They should fear you.

If she left him, he could serve as a message: the hunt had begun, and no one was safe.

Another's blood called out to her from across the courtyard. Kei. Her uncaring adoptive mother. Would a true mother have subjected her to all those specialists? Would a mother have locked her away like a criminal? Would a mother have kept her from the lessons every other novice took? Kei could make all the excuses she wanted, Yua didn't believe them.

She deserves to be punished, to feel the pain you have felt.

Faster than she'd ever known she could run, Yua flew across the garden. She didn't think her feet touched the ground once. No doors stayed closed for her. No windows remained locked. Their magic couldn't keep her out—she was above even that now.

The night welcomed her home, and the breeze caressed her as lovingly as Aza had done not long ago. But Yua couldn't stand still to appreciate it. Not when Kei's blood was this loud, practically shining a beacon for her to follow.

Yua rushed into the building and up. Kei's door was closed with more magical seals than any other in the coven. Only Kei could pass, allow others to enter or remove it.

But Kei had never encountered anyone like Yua and her Shadow before. Not like this.

Yua opened the door and stepped inside without any trouble. Kei had allowed her inside not long ago, but Yua hadn't been sure if the seals would still recognise her. Her markings were all over her... only, they were no longer black but the purest white, paler even than her alabaster skin. Her eyes felt odd, too, like a curtain lay over them, and Yua knew her darkness showed in them.

Kei wasn't in her office, but she heard her blood's chorus loud and clear from behind the door on the right. Kei's private chambers. Yua had never been inside.

The door opened before she got the chance.

Kei paled. '*Chiha*. What happened to you?'

Yua barely saw the room behind Kei. Her eyes had locked on to her prey, and her prey looked scared. Kei was skilled—it's why she was their leader—but she could never hope to be as fast as a Shadow. Yua fell on her and pierced her neck, but she barely had time to lick at the wound. Kei shot a wave of magic into her that flung Yua into the wall. It cracked under her, but she felt no pain.

Yua's smile turned into a thirsty grin. Her Shadow appreciated the challenge, and therefore, so did she. Yua charged, fast as falling stars. Kei erected a magical barrier before her, the gift shimmering around her. Yua stepped through it. Kei gasped and put up her hands for another attempt, but she wasn't fast enough.

Yua pounced, clung to Kei with her legs and arms wrapped around her, and sank her teeth into Kei's shoulder.

The Mist Woman whimpered. *Pathetic.*

Kei screamed. Her gift exploded. It tore Yua along and threw her across the room. She landed on the floor with a heavy thud. Kei raised a hand and trapped her beneath her shining gift, too bright for Yua's Mist eyes.

'How dare you claim my daughter.'

Yua had never heard Kei so furious. Her carefully controlled voice shook with rage. Yua was glad it wasn't directed at her.

She frowned.

No. It *was* directed at her. Of course it was. Why would she think—she and her Shadow were one now. Didn't Kei see that? Didn't Kei see the difference?

Blood ran down Kei's shoulder from the gushing wound. Yua struggled against her prison, all senses trained on the crimson river.

Use me. Let me show you why they should fear us.

If Kei could use magic, so could Yua.

Take it down, she whispered to her Shadow.

It flew from her pores against the golden cage around her and ate at the bars, weakening their hold. She broke through before they were fully dissolved. She was stronger than anything Kei could throw at her. With her Shadow working with her rather than against her, no one could stop her.

Surprise ghosted across Kei's face, but she was still sluggish from the recent blood loss. She didn't struggle when Yua wrapped herself around her middle.

Something's not right.

Why wasn't Kei fighting? Yua had never known her to give up.

How disappointing. Finish her, then find us someone else to hunt.

Kei's blood was too rich for her to care. It wasn't as wild as Aza's, but Yua tasted experience and so much wisdom that it gave Kei's blood sweet undertones. She wouldn't waste a single drop.

Something blunt whacked her over the head and knocked her to the ground.

The world spun in a confused haze as if she had jolted awake from a dream. How long had she slept? Aza was already up and leaning over Kei. What was she doing in her room so early?

Yua blinked. This wasn't her room. It was Kei's. She swallowed and tasted metal. Buried deep in her thoughts, her Shadow laughed.

Cold dread choked her. Kei lay unconscious on the floor. Yua remembered Ichiro. She wished the world would spin again and take away the clarity.

'Help!' Aza shouted into the corridor beyond Yua's nightmare. 'Kei needs help, *now*!'

Doors flew open. Feet rushed through the corridor. Yua wanted to hide, but she wouldn't. She had done this. Ichiro. Kei. O-Yu help her, if they died...

A tear ran down her cheek, hot and ashamed and horrified. Her hand was too heavy to wipe it away. Her whole body was numb. She'd stay right here and never move another muscle.

The Mist Women were too busy tending to Kei and taking her to the infirmary to spare Yua more than a glance, but Aza came over. Her steps were cautious. Yua couldn't bring herself to lift her head only to see fear in Aza's eyes.

'Yua?'

It didn't matter that she hadn't looked up—she heard Aza's fear under the thick caution just fine.

Yua didn't answer. It was too much effort, and now that Aza's fear had surfaced at long last, she was too afraid a sob would fall out with whatever excuses she might have uttered.

'Are you alright?'

Better than ever.

She'd never be alright again. But maybe she'd get lucky, and this was a dream too. She'd killed Aza, after all. If Aza was here, then maybe...

'Come on.' Aza tried to help her up. When Yua put no effort into the movement, Aza forced her to her feet. 'Can you stand?'

Even nodding was hard. No part of her wanted to move. No part of her felt able to.

'Let's get you back to bed, hm?' Aza said. 'You need to rest.'

For once, Aza was wrong—rest was the last thing Yua needed. Her Shadow was quiet. She felt healthier. Her body was numb now, but new energy pulsed within her. She remembered why and wanted to throw up.

Yua didn't have it in her to argue with Aza, so she let her Sand Blade lead her back to her chambers for the last time. She'd never see the outside again.

Chapter Twenty-Eight

Yua lay under her covers and closed her eyes for good measure. She felt childish hiding like this, but more than anything, she didn't want to see anyone. If she was lucky, they would exile her. If she wasn't…

She would die for what she'd done.

It was bad enough that she had attacked anyone at all, but to have attacked one of her only friends and Kei, her adoptive mother who had given her a home when no one else would have dared… The Seven would never forgive her for this. Yua would never forgive herself.

Admit it: you enjoyed it.

Yua pulled her pillow over her head and squeezed her eyes shut tighter. Her Shadow was quiet for the most part, apparently happy now it had drenched her lungs in blood, but it liked to remind her that yes, she had liked the taste. She had liked the excitement of the chase.

They were more reasons to hate herself now she was painfully sober again.

Yua had never drunk alcohol or taken drugs. Stuffed away in her chambers, there hadn't been an opportunity, but even if she had been able to, she didn't think she'd have tried any. But the high she had been on last night, stalking Ichiro and cornering Kei… She imagined it was like being drunk. She had felt alive.

She had been the monster everyone had always accused her of being.

Only now, they had proof.

Yua didn't know which sentence she preferred. If they exiled her, she'd be free to go wherever she wished if she didn't come back here— she wasn't sure whether *here* meant this coven or the whole country—but she'd still be a slave to her Shadow. She didn't doubt for one second that it would manage to overpower her again, and then who would die? There was nowhere she could run where her Shadow wouldn't be this strong. There was nowhere in the world where she'd be at ease with her Mist demon.

It would be a struggle, but she was used to those, and at least she'd be alive. Maybe Aza would even come with her. They could travel the world together, just like they'd talked about.

If they killed her… she might finally know peace. She didn't want to die, but she didn't think anyone would care what she wanted. No one attacked Ohira Kei and got away with it.

A knock came at her door.

'Yua?' Aza asked. 'May I come in? Do you want to talk? Tea? Cake? I can just sit there if you don't want to be alone.'

The fear was gone from Aza's voice, but her warmth was worse. Yua didn't deserve it. There was nothing she wanted more than for Aza to come in with tea—any tea, so long as she came—sit on her bed together and lie to her about how everything would be alright.

Aza tried once more, and then everything went quiet again except for her Shadow. It was done teasing her for now, but she felt it watch, and that was the heaviest noise of all.

She had always thought herself imprisoned, but she saw now that it hadn't applied before today. At least before last night, she could go to the library. She had been blessed with one beautiful day in town with Aza until her Shadow had ruined that too. It was more than she could have asked for.

Yua crawled out from under her sheets and heaved herself to the door, hoping that Aza was still there. She knocked.

'Aza?'

'Yua! How are you feeling? Can I come in?'

Yua opened the door and stepped back. Aza threw herself into her arms and held her for a moment, but Yua didn't hug her back.

Aza cupped her face. 'Are you hurt?'

Yua tried to frown, but every muscle in her face was too tired.

'Can you do one thing for me?'

Aza's worry softened into a smile. 'Of course. Anything you want.'

'Take me to the infirmary.'

Yua had caused a lot of suffering. She needed to apologise and say goodbye to the two people she had hurt the most before she died.

Chapter Twenty-Nine

Yua paled when she saw Ichiro. Willow had given him his own room since his case was more serious than most. The silence drew attention to how frail he was. Even lying down, covered by a thick duvet and soft pillows, he looked like any movement would snap him in two. How could she ever hope to apologise? Nothing she could do or say would make it better.

Yoko and Shizue had greeted her when she'd crossed the garden and asked to speak with her right away, but Yua had brushed past them and gone straight to the infirmary. If they worried she'd attack anyone else in the meantime, they could follow her for all she cared, but they had stayed away. Aza had talked to them when Yua had ignored them, but she'd caught up to her now.

'Go on,' Aza said. 'I'll be right here in the door. Don't worry, I can see you just fine.'

Yua nodded, a heavy lump in her throat. She sat on a chair by his bed, and he opened his eyes. They lit with a smile she didn't deserve.

'Yua. You came back.'

There it was—his smile couldn't hide the fear in his voice, just like Aza hadn't fooled her.

Her eyes stung. 'Of course I did. I—' No words could do her feelings justice, but she had to say something. 'I'm so sorry,

Ichiro. This is my fault.'

He reached for her, but his arm lacked the strength and fell to the bed's side. His hand was icy when she took it.

'It doesn't matter whose fault it was,' he said. 'It happened. That can't be helped. What are you going to do about it?' His voice trembled, not from emotion but from weakness. Willow and her novices would kick her out if she took much longer.

'Shizue has started to teach me.' If she hadn't changed her mind about that. 'I will control this. I swear it.' It would be harder without Shizue's help, but she'd make it work. She had to.

'I know you will.'

'I wish I had your confidence.' She blinked the burn in her eyes away. 'I don't know what I'm doing. I don't know how to fight this. It controlled me while I slept. How can I defend myself against that?'

'I don't know, but you will. Do you remember the story I told you about my father?'

Yua smiled through unwanted tears. 'I do.' She had the choice Ichiro's father hadn't, and she wouldn't waste it.

Ichiro tried to squeeze her hand, but it was more of a soft touch. She didn't squeeze back; she was scared she'd shatter what was left of him.

'I'll be up and bringing you tea again soon. Maybe they'll let me watch your lessons.'

She stifled a sob. He brought her *tea*, for O-Yu's sake. This wasn't what he'd imagined when he took the job. He deserved better.

He glanced towards Aza by the door, and a tired smile prodded his features. 'I'm glad you have someone else to look after you.'

A novice wearing the healer's white coat stepped in. 'Our patient needs rest. Please return tomorrow.'

Yua nodded and ignored the novice's hurried escape. Talking about Yua behind her back and calling her Blood Wisp for all these years had been one thing—their rumours had been based on more rumours. She had resented them for their prejudice, but now she was glad the young nurse didn't stick around. Sometimes, fear was perfectly healthy.

'Will you visit me again?' Ichiro asked.

Yua stood. 'If I'm… able, I'll be here.'

She didn't want to tell him that the odds were against her; he needed to focus on getting better, not worry about Yua's fate.

His smile didn't reach his eyes.

Yua and Aza left the room and closed the door.

'Are you sure you're up for facing Kei?' Aza asked. 'I don't doubt your determination or your courage, but I'd understand if you'd rather not so soon after… you know.'

'Yes,' Yua said. 'I need to see her.'

She couldn't be sure she'd get another chance once she met with the Seven.

'It's nice of you to visit your friend.'

Yua jumped at the sound of Willow's voice. She sounded friendly, but Yua didn't believe it. Willow hid it well, but the way she looked at Yua had changed. She—all Seven—looked at Yua and saw the power in her veins, wondered how they might study it, maybe even use it. Yua had no intention of becoming another experiment, but she was all too aware that she wasn't able to negotiate after what she'd done.

The Seven smiled. 'I'm sorry, I didn't mean to sneak up on you.'

Yua wasn't sure how to behave. Willow seemed friendly enough, or as normal as was possible for Mist Women—more powerful than anyone else in existence, but perfectly human otherwise. The novices working in the infirmary gave Willow warm smiles, and everyone else regarded her with respectful reverence. No matter how approachable she seemed, she was still one of the Seven. Yua wasn't sure if she should bow or get to her knees. She inclined her head and hoped it was enough.

'I didn't see you,' Yua said. It sounded flimsy to her ears.

'I saw you enter and wanted to see how you're doing. Who did you come to see?'

'Ichiro and Kei, Honoured Seven.'

Willow's smile put Yua at ease. 'So polite! Please, there's no need to be so formal. We're all Mist Women here.'

Yua grimaced. 'I'm not.'

'Perhaps, but you aren't without power. Not all Mist Women specialise in the same area. You can't command fire or convince flowers to bloom, but you possess a type of magic no one else here understands. In fact, they fear it.' Willow inclined her head to Yua. 'To send Ohira Kei to the infirmary is no easy feat. Don't underestimate yourself because of a few novices' ignorance.' She put a hand on Yua's shoulder, and the tension drained from her. 'Your gift is of the Mists. That makes you the only true Mist Woman if I'm not mistaken.'

Yua didn't know how to respond. She hadn't thought of it like that. All Mist Women had perfect control over everything down to the tiniest hair on their heads. Yua would be ecstatic if she ever achieved half that. She'd never considered how ironic it was that they were called Mist Women when none of them could control the Mists. If there was a reason for it, she didn't know it.

It always came back to control though.

'You give me too much credit,' Yua said. 'I didn't choose this.'

'But that will be for Shizue to help with,' Willow said. 'Ichiro must have been pleased to see you. He asked for you as soon as he woke up.'

Yua swallowed the lump in her throat. 'Thank you for everything you're doing for him.'

'Don't feel guilty. It's human to make mistakes before we achieve mastery, is it not?'

Something about Willow's soothing voice washed some of her guilt away, but not all.

'Mistakes aren't supposed to injure people,' Yua said.

'Aren't they? How else do we learn if not because of consequence? I expect Aza understands this well.'

'I do.' Aza shrugged when Yua looked at her. 'I didn't get my scars from being lazy.'

Yua frowned. 'What scars?'

'The ones I cover with my clothes. You'd know if you'd seen me naked during the day, they are hard to miss in sunlight.'

Yua's stomach flipped, and she blushed. This wasn't a conversation she wanted to have in front of Willow.

'Have you seen Kei yet?' Willow asked.

Yua was grateful for the change of topic; the Seven must have sensed her unease.

'No, I…' Yua cleared her throat. 'I was about to go now.'

'She'll be glad to see you,' Willow said. 'When I checked in on her this morning, she told me that she doesn't blame you.' Yua found that hard to believe. 'She is down the corridor to your left. The room at the very end is hers.'

Yua thanked her and walked down the corridor. Her feet got heavier the closer she got. Her steps rang hollow in her ears and seemed to echo off the walls until she stood before the door. The handle was teasing her. She didn't think she could open it.

'We can come back if you're not ready,' Aza said.

Yua shook her head. 'I might not get another chance.'

'What do you—'

Yua pushed the handle down and entered.

She had imagined Kei's face being unnaturally pale, her cheeks sunken and hollow, her eyes matt and dying. She hadn't been more wrong. Kei was sitting up with a book and a cup of tea, and broke into a wide smile when Yua entered.

'Yua! I'm so relieved you're alright. Come here.'

Once again, Yua didn't know how to feel, and she was tired of it. She willed more confidence into her step and walked up to Kei. Her throat tightened, and her eyes stung.

'I'm sorry.'

'Nonsense. Let me see you.' Kei reached for her and shoved Yua's sleeves up her arms. 'No cuts. No bruises. You're really unhurt?'

'Yes, but…' Except for a little paleness, Kei looked so much better than Yua had feared. Most of her colour had returned, but Yua worried her darkness had forever left a mark on Kei's light. 'But you're not.'

Kei let go of Yua's arm and sank into her pillow, which she

had propped up against the back of the bed. 'Don't, *chiha*. You weren't yourself. My daughter would never have done this of her own free will.'

'It won't happen again.' Yua swallowed. There was one more thing she wanted to say, but she wasn't sure how. 'I promise. I...'

Kei took her hand. 'You don't need to say anything. Last night must have been terrifying for you. Just know that I don't blame you. I have every faith in you that you will master your power, and I promise to help you however I can.' Yua had never seen so much regret on Kei's face. She didn't like it. 'I'm sorry I haven't done more. We really thought we were doing the right thing, but... It's hard to ignore the evidence of our mistake now.'

A strangled sob escaped her. She'd never thought she would hear Kei apologise like this, and she'd offered her help. Yua wasn't sure how much it would mean after today, but right now, it meant the world to her.

Yua squeezed Kei's hand. 'You didn't know. Mist magic was new to you too.'

'That's no excuse.' Kei cupped Yua's face, and Yua leaned into it. 'I should have protected you better.'

'You...' Yua took a deep breath. 'You did everything you could, *meha*.'

Kei froze. Her surprise lasted only a second.

'I'm glad to hear you say that, *chiha*.'

Yua didn't know if Kei meant Yua's acceptance or that she had called her *mother*. Their relationship had only ever been hiding and secrets. She wished she'd been braver before she had doomed herself.

Chapter Thirty

When Yua entered the Seven's chamber, it was everything she'd expected. The room was mostly bare except for eight cushions near the large windows lining the back wall. The Seven and Kei sat on the floor during all important meetings to be closer to the earth and help them stay grounded when they made their decisions. Another cushion waited for Yua before them—she, too, was expected to stay grounded for the meeting. The windows were open to let in fresh air, which would clear their heads and carry away all prejudice. Fires burned in small braziers in the four corners to allow every attendant to argue with passion. Two small fountains flanked the door to signify the flow of the gift as well as to present a threshold between the novices and the Seven. Once they entered this room, their other worries had to wait outside. Yua didn't know if they had enchanted the threshold itself, but she felt heavier as soon as she stepped inside, as if the importance of this room weighed on her even before she'd started speaking.

The Seven had taken their seats. Their smiles were gone, and a heavy finality lay around them. Even Kei was there. Yoko sat to her left, and even though Shizue would usually sit on Kei's right, Willow had taken that seat today… in case Kei's condition worsened during the trial, Yua guessed.

All eight met her eyes, and the weight of their power threatened to crush her. They held her fate in her hands. If they chose to kill her here and now… Would she really be able to run away with Aza?

Kei gestured to the ninth cushion. 'Ohira Yua, please take a seat.' Kei sounded grim, like there was nothing more she could do. Whatever they had decided, Yua would have to accept it.

She sat and steeled herself.

'You place us in a difficult position,' Yoko said. 'We have discussed how to proceed and Shizue has filled us in as much as she could, but we wanted to give you the chance to speak for yourself before we come to a final decision.'

The colour drained from her face. Her defence that she had drunk Aza's blood without killing her no longer seemed like a strong argument.

She let her hand fall to the floor and hoped the ground beneath the foundations would lend her some strength.

'What would you have me say, Honourable Seven?'

She had read of trials which were a mere formality, which happened even though the decision had been made. They were humouring her, but why? She'd often seen Newai play with a mouse he'd caught. Sometimes, he'd let it run away only to pounce on it again. Was that all this was? An illusion of choice?

'We would have you explain what happened,' Yoko said. 'Shizue has told us her opinion, but she wasn't there herself. We need to have every detail so our verdict is just.'

Yua scoffed. 'You know what happened. I almost killed Kei and Ichiro. What more is there to say?'

'We need to understand how this power works within you if we're to assess it correctly,' Yoko said. 'Did you make the conscious decision to attack either victim?'

How could she sum up something so complicated in one word when she didn't understand it herself?

'Yes and no.'

'Please explain,' Kei said.

'I decided to drink from Aza—that's how it started. She saw I was struggling and offered me her blood because she thought it would help. It was my decision to take her up on it. I didn't choose to lose control after that.'

'From what Shizue has told us, you drank from her the night before as well. Did you lose control both times?'

She swallowed. What was the point? If they wanted to torment her, they'd failed—she was annoyed more than anything. 'No. The more I drank the stronger I felt. I stopped before I hurt her.'

She was even more annoyed that her one argument had come out all wrong.

'You said Aza offered you her blood,' Lena said. She specialised in politics and empathy, if Yua remembered correctly. 'Was she fully aware of the dangers?'

'I think so.' Yua frowned. 'But that doesn't excuse what I did. Why are you trying to divert the blame from me? I could have killed Ichiro and Kei. This is my fault.'

'We're not trying to excuse your actions, Yua,' Kei said. 'We only want to understand what happened. Did you mean to take this much from Ichiro or to attack me?'

'No. Never. The last thing I wanted was to hurt either of you.'

'As someone you've attacked, I'm in a unique position over the Seven. Can you describe how the first time you drank Aza's blood was different?'

She sighed. 'I didn't know what would happen, but as I said, Aza offered because I was struggling. It was difficult at first, but it got easier.' Right up until her Shadow had overwhelmed her.

'So, your control has improved from what it was, say, a year ago or two months ago?' Kei asked.

Yua grimaced. 'Not enough.'

'I have tested her myself,' Shizue said. 'She handled herself better than I expected. She resisted my blood, and while she didn't resist again when Aza offered hers, I can't ignore the improvement to her health when I saw her the next morning. My test would have exhausted another novice for days, if not weeks. With Aza's blood, Yua recovered overnight.'

Yua balled her hands into fists and scrunched her shirt; she hadn't realised she'd been gripping it. 'Why are you doing this? I almost killed two people!'

'We are almost done,' Yoko said. 'Do you think you'd be able to control yourself again?'

'Haven't you been listening?'

If her crimes didn't get her exiled, perhaps her insolence would. She didn't want to leave the coven if she didn't have to, but she didn't like that the Seven had an ulterior motive she didn't understand either.

'I don't know,' Yua said. 'For you, what I did to Kei and Ichiro is an isolated incident. For me, it's there all the time, and it's hard to keep it down most of that time. I can hear your blood now, for O-Yu's sake, all of you. I can smell it and I want it. This Mist demon, as Shizue calls it, is strong.' She wanted to call them idiots but bit her tongue; she'd take exile over death if there was a choice. 'So, no, I don't know if I can control it. Every time I smell fresh blood, it's a challenge not to lose my mind, which would be much easier than fighting it. I didn't want to hurt Kei and Ichiro. I don't want to hurt anyone. Stop trying to simplify it when it's complicated.'

Yoko exchanged a glance with Kei before she faced Yua again. 'We appreciate your honesty. Are you open to having your gift removed if we researched the possibility?'

She almost said *yes*, but then what would that get her? More time locked away, more time as a test subject, more time hiding. She was done with all of that.

'No. I hate what this has done to the people I love, but having it feels right, whatever that means. What I've done isn't right, but the way I felt after Aza's blood is. I'll accept whatever sentence you decide, but I won't part with my Shadow. I'm not me when I lose control, but that's momentary. Take it from me and I'll never be myself again.'

Kei closed her eyes and took a deep breath. 'You understand your sentence will be removal of your power, exile, or execution?'

Yua's heart soared at hearing the pain in Kei's voice. Her *meha* did care.

But it didn't change her choice. 'Then I guess exile or death it is.'

It hurt, but it felt right. She was at peace with either. If it kept her friends and family safe, she had no counter argument.

Kei's eyes reddened, but her voice was strong when she spoke. 'Shizue will take you back to your chambers. You will wait there while we deliberate.'

Chapter Thirty-One

Yua and Aza lay on the bed together and held each other. If this was her last day alive, she was glad she got to spend it with Aza.

Aza stretched next to her.

'I haven't even asked you how you feel,' Yua said. 'After I… After last night. We… did things.' She cleared her throat. 'I thought I had killed you.'

Aza snuggled into Yua's shoulder. 'Please, Yua, I don't die from a bit of blood loss. You'll have to try harder than that.'

Yua gulped. 'No thank you.'

Aza laughed. She really was fine. Alive. Even happy.

Yua was beyond grateful that she hadn't truly lost control until her Shadow had begun to hunt Ichiro.

Aza's smile turned into a grin. 'How are *you* feeling?'

Yua hesitated. 'I'm scared.'

'Did you mean what you said about feeling more like yourself?' Aza asked.

'Yes. I won't give up.' She bit her lip. 'Unless… Well, it depends on their decision, doesn't it?'

Aza rolled onto her side and sat up a little, supporting herself on her elbow. 'I agree with what you said. You look healthier. Like you've been sick this whole time and my blood cured you.'

That was exactly how she felt—weak and frail her whole life, but now strong and agile. Awake after sleeping for too long.

And inside her veins, her Shadow was quiet.

Despite the attack, she was more determined than ever to make it work. She had controlled it—once in the clearing and again when Aza had offered her blood—and she really did feel better for it. Her Shadow was a part of her. Who knew what she could do if she really embraced it?

Yua bit her lip. 'I have a plan, but I don't know if the Seven will accept it.'

All Mist Women loved knowledge. There was a chance, albeit a small one.

Aza sat up straight. 'What is it?'

She took a deep breath. 'I want to embrace it. My Shadow and I are one person. I want to see what happens when we work together instead of against each other.'

She wished she'd thought of it before Shizue had walked her back, but maybe it wasn't too late to add one last argument.

Aza smiled. 'I think that's a great plan. I'm sure the Seven will agree. If anything, I think Kei will be proud.'

Yua's smile fell. 'Maybe. But if they don't… I have a favour to ask. It's fine if you don't want to, I understand.'

Aza's smile disappeared too. 'What is it?'

'If they don't agree… if they'd rather kill me… Run away with me.'

Aza's eyes sparkled. 'Like we're eloping?'

Yua's cheeks burned, and her heart raced. 'Like we're two fugitives on the run.'

Aza grinned. 'That's still romantic.'

'Really? Running away from the law is your idea of romance?'

'Under the right circumstances.'

Yua searched for an answer in Aza's eyes and feared it at the same time. Could she leave on her own? Where would she go?

'So?' she asked. 'What do you say?'

Aza took her hand. 'Of course. I'll speak in your defence if they let me, but if the Seven vote against you, I'll run to the end of the world with you.'

Yua's heart leaped. Their reasons for running weren't ideal, but it was still the sweetest thing anyone had ever said to her.

'Thank you.'

She jumped when the knock came on her door. Shizue had returned.

It was time.

Chapter Thirty-Two

Shizue didn't say a word as she led Yua back to the Seven. Yua felt oddly displaced, like she was watching herself from a greater height. She didn't feel like herself, hadn't truly comprehended that tomorrow might not be hers. Her mind hadn't caught up to what her body already knew—this was her final march as the Yua she was today. Tomorrow, she would either be exiled, run away with Aza, or she would be dead or worse—if the Seven had decided to draw the darkness out of her, she would no longer be herself. She was more at peace with the first two options. They felt less damning somehow.

'We have a few questions for Aza first,' Shizue said. 'Wait out here.'

Yua frowned. 'You're leaving me alone?'

'We have reinforced the wards around the entire coven. You can try, but you won't get out, and I think you're very aware that trying to run now wouldn't help you.'

Yua gulped. Did Shizue know what she had asked Aza?

Shizue entered with Aza, and Yua sagged against the wall opposite the door. While running away with Aza was a nice idea, Shizue was right. The Seven would never let her run. Aza could use every trick she knew as a Sand Blade to hide their tracks, but the Seven would find her. There was nowhere they could run. Shizue might have bluffed about the reinforced wards, but it didn't matter.

You could leave on your own. I'll show you how.

Yua shook her head. She wouldn't leave without Aza. It was childish, but she didn't want to be alone. She'd had thirteen years of it.

Too soon, the door opened again.

'Are you ready?' Shizue asked.

'Does it matter?'

Shizue hesitated, then waved her inside. Yua had expected stepping inside to be difficult, but it was easy. It was too late for regrets or *if only*s.

Shizue joined the others, and Yua took her spot on the cushion. Aza gave her an encouraging nod.

Two more cushions had been placed next to Aza. Yua frowned. Who else was coming?

Yoko cleared her throat. 'We're allowing Aza to attend under the condition that her presence won't disrupt this meeting.'

Some of the Seven looked unsure, but others wore their usual calm masks. Yua wished she could have hidden her true emotions as well—they could at least have the decency to fake being upset at her impending exile or death. Their worries would be over once she was gone, but it wasn't like her fate was a gift to them. They'd voted on this—three for death, three for exile, and one undecided or whatever they'd chosen. O-Yu take them. She'd never hated them more than she did in that moment.

'Are we ready to begin?' Kei asked, looking... what was that? Pride? She was trying to hide it, but Yua saw it behind her controlled features.

Suddenly nervous, she swallowed. 'Yes, Honourable Seven.'

She hadn't wanted to be so formal and respectful, but Kei's expression had thrown her off. Maybe Kei had accepted that Yua had chosen her fate and stood up for herself despite the consequences. Was she proud to see Yua go down with her head held high? Yua wanted to believe that Kei would look more upset than this. Something was going on, and Yua couldn't fathom what.

'The Seven and I have debated your sentence, and we have come to a decision,' Kei said.

Yua breathed deeply to calm her racing heart, but it didn't work.

'Due to unforeseen circumstances, we believe we have found a more agreeable solution than the three presented previously. Aza, would you do us the favour of asking our visitors to join us? You should find them waiting outside the door.'

Yua turned around, but Aza looked just as confused. No one else had been outside when Yua had waited for Aza to give her brief statement.

'Yes, *kyastra*.' Aza opened the door…

And screamed.

Yua shot to her feet, but Aza was fine. She was hugging a woman who looked like she could have been Aza's twin. The same sun-kissed skin, the same dark hair, the same grin.

Aza was laughing with tears in her eyes and the biggest smile Yua had ever seen. 'My sister is here.'

Desma, if Yua remembered correctly. Aza's dagger was named after her.

She knew the second woman only from stories; although, she was surprised to see Queen Rachael of Rifarne in leather travelling gear rather than a dress. She didn't even wear a crown—but then, that fit the stories she'd heard better than a frilly frock and pompous gold would have done.

'Yua, that's my sister,' Aza said with tears running down her face.

Desma grinned at her. She was so much like Aza that Yua would have known them for sisters even without an introduction.

'It's nice to meet you.' Her eyes flicked to the queen; it felt odd to greet Desma first. Yua bowed. 'It's an honour to meet you, Queen R—'

The queen sighed. 'Please, just call me Rachael. I was hoping to get away from this royal title nonsense for a bit. I've got enough of that back home.'

Yua nodded, too dumbstruck to speak. She had heard that Queen Rachael wasn't a typical monarch because she'd grown up on the streets, but seeing it in person was another thing.

'Please, take a seat,' Kei said.

Yua blushed. She'd forgotten all about the trial.

They sat, and Aza scooted closer to Desma.

None of this made sense. What did the Rifarnee queen have to do with this? Unless… Was she to be exiled to Rifarne? Yua's heart missed a beat as she dared to hope. There were worse things. Much worse.

'Thank you for seeing us,' Rachael said.

Kei smiled. 'Not at all. We're glad you've finally come to your senses.'

Rachael shrugged. 'I had a Mist Woman. She's hard to replace.'

'It's been two years, has it not?' Yoko asked.

'I've coped just fine without one.'

'Then why the change of heart?' Yoko and Rachael talked like they were old friends. Yua couldn't decide if that was because they'd met before or if Mist Women generally treated everyone else as inferior, including queens.

'My husband insists I work too hard.'

'My queen is too humble,' Desma said. Rachael sneered. 'She wants to have more time for Cephy.'

Rachael's hand flitted to her belly.

Kei's eyes softened. 'How far along are you?'

'Three months,' Rachael said. 'Honestly, Cale is coping better with my pregnancy than I am.'

'A Mist Woman will be able to help,' Yoko said. 'Have you decided?'

Rachael nodded, but Yua grew more confused by the minute. Had Rachael decided what? If she wasn't exiled to Rifarne, what did any of this have to do with her?

'I have,' Rachael said. 'With your permission, I'd like to invite Willow to my court.'

Yua's heart dropped. Willow was leaving? They hadn't talked much, but she liked Willow. She seemed more human than the others.

'A queen should never ask for permission,' Kei said, but there was no real lesson in her voice. 'I'm surprised Kaida didn't teach you this. Or have you forgotten after two years?'

Rachael scoffed. 'Please, I know what Mist Women are like. Besides, this is Midoka. My word means nothing here, and to be frank with you, I'm too tired for a power struggle; my feet are killing me and I'm hungry all the time but can't keep much down. Could we hurry this up, please? I'd like to get home.'

Willow laughed. 'I accept and look forward to being your

adviser. It will be good to return.'

'You may leave when you're ready,' Kei said. 'Now, with that matter settled, we have a proposition for you, Yua.'

Her heart almost jumped out of her chest. She'd been prepared for the worst, but so far, this hadn't gone at all like she'd expected. She couldn't begin to guess where Kei was going with this.

'I accept whatever judgement you have for me.'

'Excellent,' Kei said. 'With Willow leaving, the Seat of Seven is one member short. We invite you to join us.'

'Sorry, what?'

This was so far away from what she'd expected, she wondered if she was dreaming. This wasn't a punishment, or was it? What was she missing?

Kei smiled. 'You have shown you're willing to take full responsibility for your actions, are honest, and understand the danger your gift represents. Most importantly, you've shown a keen willingness to learn and better understand yourself and your gift. As Mist Women, we encourage the careful study of new or unknown types of the gift, and we believe your unique abilities deserve representation.'

'But that's—I thought you were going to kill me.'

Kei's smile disappeared. 'It was an option at first, but we quickly decided that your gift was too unique to be simply thrown away. We could learn much about the Mists through you, or at least be prepared should anyone else emerge with your talents.'

Yua balled her hands into fists. 'I'm not your experiment.'

'Of course not,' Yoko said. 'Kei merely means that she and Shizue would keep an eye on you for a time until they are satisfied that you can control yourself. From what you and Shizue have told us, your ability has greatly improved in a short period of time. We are confident that you won't need supervision for long, and we know you'll understand that it's a safety measure on behalf of everyone else.'

This was happening too fast. She hadn't even thought of herself as a Mist Woman despite Willow's argument that she was more so than any other. But to become one of the Seven? It was an honour she'd done nothing to deserve. There was a punishment in there somewhere, and it made her nervous that she couldn't see it yet.

More than anything, Kei's words echoed in her mind. Did they really expect someone else like her to emerge? How likely was that? But if there was…They wouldn't need to hate themselves or make the mistakes she had, because they'd have a Seven looking out for them. Shizue meant well, but Yua doubted she cared in the same way. She couldn't. Unlike Yua, she hadn't lived it.

'You would be free to do any research you wish,' Kei said. 'As Yoko said, we would observe you for a time, but this is true for any new Seven. Our position comes with great responsibility and power. Initial supervision is a normal step.'

Yua looked around the others to see them all nod. The Seven wouldn't be watching her because she was dangerous but because it was routine procedure. She'd be like everyone else— or like every other member on the Seat of Seven, anyway.

'We understand if you need time to think,' Yoko said. 'It's a big decision.'

Yua nodded. 'Yes. I need a moment.'

'Feel free to use the garden,' Kei said. 'We will give you space and wait here.'

Yua stumbled to her feet and hurried outside.

The garden was meant to be a place of peace and inner calm, but it wasn't enough to quiet her internal battle. Just the thought that she might become a Seven was madness. The Seven were all exceptionally talented with their gifts. Yua had a Mist demon inside her. She had been ready to die, go into exile, if possible, but this…

She wanted to live, but she wasn't sure if being one of the Seven wasn't just another prison.

What she had right now was far from perfect. Death would have been an end. Exile would have meant more struggle, but also hope. Joining the Seven was so far removed from either option she struggled to wrap her head around it.

Yua was under no illusions that this was a reward for her skills. She didn't care what Yoko had said, the Seven—or Six, once Willow had left for Rifarne—wanted to study her, learn more about the Mists from her. Mist Women craved knowledge more than anything else, and Yua was their only chance at this kind of knowledge. She wouldn't be free for that reason alone, but worse, should the unthinkable happen and Midoka went to war, she would have an obligation to serve. Midoka hadn't been at war in a very long time, and it was beyond unlikely that it would happen now, but if it did…

Could she fight in a war?

Did she really have a choice? As things stood, the Seven would never let her go into the world. She was too dangerous, and their coven couldn't be held responsible for the slaughter she might cause. They enjoyed a lot of respect from all corners of the world and their standing was especially high in Midoka, but everything had a line. The Seven and Kei couldn't risk crossing it.

Yua either accepted or she died. It was as simple and as ridiculous as that.

I want to live.

I want to live.

I want to live.

She repeated it in her head until the overriding thought *I want to be free* sounded louder.

If she died now... It would be over. Her future, her opportunities—no matter how small—would be gone. If she joined the Seven, she would be watched and under too many obligations, but if she learned how to truly control her Shadow, use it as she now knew she could... Perhaps then she'd have a chance at freedom. Maybe, one day, she could live in peace and be happy.

And maybe, being a Seven wouldn't be so bad.

But she couldn't shake the weight of the responsibilities she wouldn't be able to escape. *What if? What if?* rang in her mind until it was hard not to picture herself on a battlefield, bloody and broken beyond recognition... or bloody from other people's lives and grinning like a monster.

Her Shadow grinned in response.

Could she accept those odds? She wanted to be happy, and she wasn't convinced that becoming one of the Seven was the answer. But she didn't want to die either.

Yua swallowed and re-joined the others.

'Have you made a decision?' Kei asked. So much hope in her

voice. So much pride.

'I have.'

Yua was still a little lightheaded, but the knowledge, secrets, and what she could do for others like her should there ever be others were too tempting to turn down. She had the chance to do something useful with her life. Really, it was no choice at all.

'I accept.'

Her ears were ringing. Her body was numb. This would take a long time to sink in.

Kei's mask fell away, and a proud smile lit her eyes. After Yua had drunk her blood, Kei had looked more her age than Yua had ever seen, but now she looked at least ten years younger. The things a little joy could do… Yua's heart danced. Something she'd said had done this. She vowed to herself that it was only the beginning.

'Then there's only the matter of your speciality,' Yoko said. 'Every Mist Woman has one, but we don't know what to call your… condition, for lack of a better word.'

Yua smiled. 'There is no matter.' This felt right. This was what she was, what she could be, without shame or hiding. 'I'm a Blood Wisp.'

Kei stood and the others followed. 'Then we welcome you amongst us.' Yua held out her hand for a formal handshake, but Kei pulled her into her arms. 'I couldn't be prouder, *chiha*.'

Her eyes burnt. She could do with a moment to think, but she had the feeling it would take her a good few years to wrap her head around the last hour. Her heart, her whole being, felt light.

She was one of the Seven. She was the Blood Wisp.

She was herself.

Chapter Thirty-Three

Yua sat on her roof overlooking Maishi Hou, Newai curled up and purring in her lap. The lights below imitated the stars above, each with their own magic. Under the light of the full moon, she felt empowered. Somewhere inside her, her Shadow demanded blood, but Yua shoved it down. It was easy right now because it hadn't been that long since she'd drunk from Aza, but what about tomorrow? The day after that? Her Shadow would have to get used to waiting. She'd make sure she was worthy of her new title.

Aza stuck her head out of the window. 'Hey.' She climbed onto the roof. 'Big day today, huh?'

Yua smiled, not taking her eyes off the lights around her. 'I don't quite know what happened.'

'It's a beautiful night.' Aza sighed. 'I need to talk to you.'

Her stomach tightened. She'd never seen Aza nervous before. 'What's wrong?'

'Rachael offered me to go with them.'

Yua's heart dropped. 'What did you say?'

Aza shrugged. 'Nothing yet. I don't know. My sister is in Rifarne, but you are here. What are we, Yua?'

'I don't know.'

She doubted Aza wanted a steady relationship. Not when Aza knew what she had in Rifarne. How could Aza know what

Midoka had for her when Yua didn't know? When Yua couldn't promise her anything?

'Maybe, in time, we could grow into something,' Yua said. 'But we might not.'

She wanted Aza to stay more than anything, but she couldn't stand the thought of Aza staying just so Yua could drink her blood every now and again. It was wrong. Aza had a sister in Rifarne—a sister she'd missed for years. Yua couldn't compete with that. Not until she'd had time to clear her head and make sense of everything that had happened today.

And if that meant losing Aza, so be it.

'You should go with Rachael.'

Aza turned away and stared into the night. 'What will you do?'

What indeed? She couldn't imagine she'd have a queue of volunteers, but she'd need blood eventually.

'I don't know.'

Aza smiled at her, but it didn't reach her eyes. 'The future is fun, huh? So much uncertainty.'

Yua's smile was more honest. 'I think that's what I like about it. I thought I would die today. At the very least, I was sure I'd be exiled. But now?' Her lips curled a little more. 'Now I can be anything I want to be.' Uncertainty and freedom weren't so different. She liked and wanted a bit of both.

'So I heard, Blood Wisp.' Aza's smile grew. Her eyes twinkled a little. 'It suits you.'

'When are you leaving?' If this was their last night on this roof together, Yua didn't want to fill it with regrets.

'Tomorrow. Rachael and Desma are waiting for me to tell them what I'll do, then they'll head home. Willow will follow tomorrow, and I'll go with her.'

Yua had never travelled through a focus point before, but maybe she would now Aza was leaving. Maybe that was the answer—go to Rifarne whenever she was thirsty. It seemed like too much hassle for that. The focus points would get her there in an instant, but she wouldn't put Rifarne at risk. Its queen was pregnant. The White Palace wouldn't be a good place for a hungry Blood Wisp.

'Unless…'

Yua straightened. 'Unless?'

'I could stay for now,' Aza said. 'You know, just until you can control yourself better. Then I can come here once a week or however long you can go without blood.'

They could slowly increase her tolerance. Her Shadow squirmed at the idea, which told her it was the right direction…

But it didn't feel right for a more personal reason.

'You shouldn't stay just so I can violate you. That's wrong on so many levels.'

Aza laughed. 'You're not violating me. It was nice once you got the hang of it. Last time was bliss until I passed out.'

'But I can't—'

'Or are you saying you want me to leave?'

'No. Please, I… I'd like you to stay. Just until I can control myself better.'

Aza sat closer. 'Just until then. Deal.'

In the meantime, she'd figure out where she wanted this awkward love with Aza to go. Maybe the awkwardness would fade and turn into something beautiful, or maybe it would fade. Either way, time would have the answer.

Not that she'd have time to nurture a relationship. Shizue and Kei expected her to train every waking moment, and she was excited to see what she could do. She felt stronger and faster as night fell, and she couldn't wait to stretch her ability to its limits.

This was who she was meant to be, and it felt good.

Thank you so much for reading *Blood Wisp*. Your support means the world to me (cliché as that sounds), and I'm very grateful that you've taken the time to read my book! I hope you enjoyed it and are looking forward to the sequels right now.

If you have two minutes, I'd love a review. This helps readers find their next favourite book, so your review or even just a rating makes a big difference.

Thank you.

Like freebies?

Join my mailing list and receive my novella *Shadow in Ar'Sanciond* and the short story *Pashros Kai Zo* (which isn't available anywhere else!) for free. You'll also get ARCs and hear about upcoming releases, early cover reveals, exclusive giveaways, excerpts, and all other announcements. Join at sarinalanger.com

If you'd like to hang out with me in an informal setting and get early peeks at new covers and maps, join my Facebook Reader Group 'Sarina's Sparrows':
facebook.com/groups/sarinassparrows

Let's Connect
sarinalanger.com
twitter.com/sarina_langer
goodreads.com/sarinalangerwriter
patreon.com/sarinalanger

Acknowledgments

You may have heard creators mention that producing their newest work was like drawing blood from a stone? *Blood Wisp* was like that.

This is my 7th book, and it was also my most challenging one. When *Blood Wisp* started, it was a novella—the whole trilogy was meant to be novellas—so the process of turning those three novellas into this first book right here has been immense and exhausting. I wanted to give up several times, but it's thanks to these wonderful people that I pushed on:

My editor Briana Morgan, who has believed in this book from the start and who was ecstatic to hear that it would indeed be a trilogy.

My first set of critique partners (back when this was a novella) Beverley Lee, Dana Fraedrich, Faith Rivens, Villimey Mist, Megan Gordon, and Moonika.

My second set of critique partners (after I rewrote everything and lost a lot of nerves) Beverley Lee, Dana Fraedrich, Faith Rivens, and Villimey Mist.

My beta readers Tris Moore, DovahTobi, and Julie Appleton.

My cartographer Glynn Seal for once again creating the most beautiful map from my honestly terrible sketches.

My formatter and cover designer, Becky and James Wright from PlatformHouse Publishing, for tidying up the interior, making it look swoon-worthy, and creating this edition's stunning cover.

This book wouldn't be what it is now without your incredible feedback and hard work.

Special thanks go to my Facebook reader group and my Patreon supporters for getting excited whenever I shared early teasers, ARCs, the covers, and all kinds of progress updates! You've seen this book in nearly every stage. I'm grateful that you were there with me.

More special thanks go to my partner and my daughter/cat for being patient with me, supporting me, and providing cuddles whenever I wanted to throw this book in the bin.

Thank you to everyone who rates and reviews books on Amazon, your blogs, Goodreads, BookBub, your social media pages, and wherever else you might be that I'm not even aware of. Your reviews make a massive difference, and authors all over the world are very grateful to you.

And finally, thank you so much to you, my reader, for having chosen *Blood Wisp* as your next book. I hope you enjoyed the journey, and if you choose to continue this trilogy, I hope you'll love the sequels too. Happy reading, Sparrow!

About the Author

Sarina is an epic/dark fantasy author and freelance editor from the south of England, where she lives with her partner and her daughter (read: her cat).

She is as obsessed with books and stationery now as she was as a child, when she drowned her box of colour pencils in water so they wouldn't die and scribbled her first stories on corridor walls.

('A first sign of things to come', according to her mother. 'Normal toddler behaviour', according to Sarina.)

In her free time, she has a weakness for books, pretty words, and plays video games.

She believes that the best books are those where every ray of light casts a shadow.